FAINT HEARTED

BOOK TWO

CURSED FAE SERIES

CURSED FAE BOOK TWO

Faint Hearted

USA TODAY BESTSELLING AUTHORS
LEIA STONE & JULIE HALL

To our readers.

Books by Julie Hall

JULIEHALLAUTHOR.COM/BOOKS

CREATURES OF CHAOS SERIES

Creatures of Chaos

FALLEN LEGACIES SERIES

Stealing Embers

Forging Darkness

Unleashing Fire

Supernova

LIFE AFTER SERIES

Huntress

Warfare

Dominion

Logan

SHADOW ANGEL SERIES

Shadow Angel Book One

Shadow Angel Book Two

Shadow Angel Book Three

Julie's books have won or were finalists in over 20 awards.

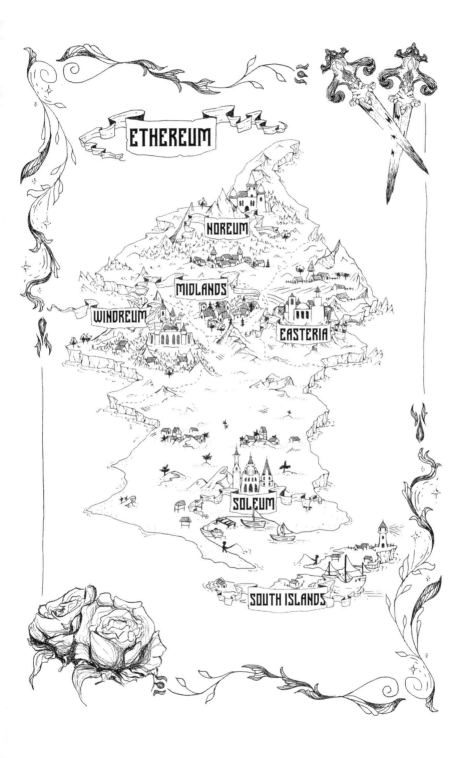

Chapter One

"**Y**ou expect to kill an Ethereum lord with swordsmanship like that?" Queen Liliana roared. "Grip the hilt tighter!"

I grasped it as she instructed, but was sure to growl at her in response.

"Good. Get mad. We only have two weeks to prepare you for the portal opening on the fall equinox, and anger is better than weakness."

"I'm not weak," I snapped, facing her and the half dozen tutors she'd forced me to work with every day.

Queen Liliana was very passionate about training me to take over from Dawn. She didn't speak much about the loss of her daughter, but I knew what it meant when the summer champion had not returned in time. She was gone, in her final resting place among the stars.

We'd never not had a summer champion return before, and it was now my task to bring back the heart of an

Ethereum lord. Lest my own lands be ravaged by the curse that currently befell Summer Court.

"Prove it." Queen Liliana snatched a blade from the instructor and lunged for me.

I gasped, leaping out of the way, but she pivoted and charged. She came down with a blow that was so hard, the block I made with my own sword barely held.

"You're crazy," I spat.

She had a wild gleam in her eye. "Yes. I'm crazy about saving our people. If you don't come back with that heart, we will all be filtering into Winter and asking for refuge."

Her words shook me and she came down with another blow that I blocked.

"I won't let that happen," I told her as we lunged, dodged, and slashed at each other.

Clack, clack, clack, the metal of my blade clinked with hers and I was ashamed to admit that I knew she was going easy on me. My parents never let me take more than two weeks of fencing as a child. The second my . . . condition appeared, they made me stop all physical sports and training. My gifts lay elsewhere, they said.

Queen Liliana cried out, slashing down on my sword so hard that it was ripped from my hand and fell to the ground. Her beautiful golden hair had been torn free of its bun and now lay in messy curls around her shoulders.

"What will you do now, Aribella?" She cocked her head to the side and stalked towards me. My heartbeat increased, thumping against my chest as I walked backward. "I know

2

your little secret," she taunted, and the color drained from my face.

She knew? Dizziness washed over me and I began my breathing exercises to calm the frantic racing in my chest.

"Show me how you can manipulate my mood and take my sword," she said, and relief rushed through me.

Oh, *that* secret. It wasn't a heavily guarded one, but my gift was quite unique and it made people uncomfortable, so I didn't share with many that I had it.

"Your highness, I could never use it on you in that way," I told her and then my back hit the wall.

She pressed the tip of the blade right to my throat, causing my eyes to fly wide.

She was truly insane.

Even the tutors that were present gasped.

"Rip this sword from my hands or I'm shoving it in your throat," she declared.

My mouth popped open in shock.

"Three . . . two . . ." she counted and then I pushed the emotion of frantic desperation into her.

Suddenly, Queen Liliana fell into tears, screaming and crying. She looked around the room in anguish, distracted, as if she'd lost something. I took that chance to slip away from her blade and pluck it from her hands.

Seeing her weep openly, grasping her chest as if her very heart hurt, killed me. So did the fearful looks that the tutors were giving me. Once people learned of my gift, they never treated me the same again.

I pulled the emotion back, like peeling a blanket off of her, and the queen's face went from desolate sobbing into a full-fledged grin. "Oh, my darling, you've been hiding that all this time?"

I felt badly for Dawn then, how her childhood must have been being raised by this woman who only seemed proud when you showed her how well you would kill or disarm someone.

"I am sorry," I told her honestly.

She wiped the tears off her cheeks, grinning. "It felt so real. If I hadn't known you had the power, I'd have thought it was me. Don't ever apologize for such things. This is how you will save us all. Let's work more with this power since your swordsmanship is hopeless."

I scoffed. She just called me hopeless like it was nothing and yet, I still wanted to please her. I looked up to her, in a way. She didn't treat me like a delicate, breakable flower. Like my parents did.

"Okay," I said hesitantly.

Falana, our household secretary, entered the training room holding her clipboard and cleared her throat. She wore her bright red hair in its signature bun and waited until I stepped over to her before she began speaking in low tones. "We have an issue at the southern border that King Leonard wants you to look into. You will be gone a few hours."

I peered back at Queen Liliana, who dismissed me with her hand. "We will pick up cartography mapping after dinner."

4

I groaned. As much as I loved books and learning of all kinds, the preparation I was currently undergoing was relentless. I awoke to weight training, then after breakfast I had Ethereum history, then potions, then lunch, and after that it was four more classes before bed. I was exhausted every night and my friends had all but given up on expecting me to hang out.

Following Falana, I stepped out into the hallway and grabbed a clean towel from one of the maids. Wiping my face, I smoothed my palms over my slacks. "What issue are we talking about?" I asked Falana now that we were alone.

The Courts in Faerie were historically matriarchal, but my mother, Queen Beatrice, was never interested in the day-to-day ruling. Everyone knew that my father, even though he was only a consort, was the true ruler of the Fall Court. I was still training to take over from him and I couldn't shirk those duties, no matter how important training to go to Ethereum was.

The past couple of months had tested every ounce of my stamina, but I was happy to report that I'd had no episodes. Maybe I could have lived my whole life like this. My mother had wrapped me up in metaphorical eggshells my entire life and now that I was living a "normal" existence, I kind of liked it.

"Well, it's unclear, my lady. A farmer has sent word of a well going bad," she said, peering down the hall to make sure we were not being overheard.

I stopped walking. "The Fall princess is traveling to the

southern border and eating dinner on the road to check out a dry well?"

I wasn't normally snobbish, but this was beneath me. Was Father mad at me? Why else would he send me on this errand?

Falana stepped closer, lowering her voice. "The farmer says the water he pulls up is blacker than a raven's feather. Your father wants it confirmed by you personally. You're the only one he trusts."

I gasped. Black water. The curse. *No.* We had two more weeks. Had it already started in Fall?

My heart ramped up its beating and dizziness washed over me as I stumbled backward a little.

"My lady!" Falana reached out and grasped my arm, but it was too late. Blackness danced at the edge of my vision and then I lost consciousness.

I came to in the back of a carriage. Falana was fanning me with her sandalwood fan, my favorite scent wafting over me. As a child I almost welcomed the fainting episodes because Falana was always there to bring me out of it. The scent of sandalwood became my favorite as I associated it with healing.

"How long was I out?" I asked, sitting up slowly.

I'd clearly thought too soon about not having had an episode, and I immediately felt shame that I'd just experienced one. I'd been beginning to think I was healed or had grown too strong for them to affect me like this. It was so disappointing to find out that I'd been wrong.

"About ten minutes," Falana said. "I had Donte discreetly put you in the carriage. We just left the palace gates. I didn't want to waste time, and I hoped you would wake quickly."

I smiled. "Thank you."

I eyed the fan, wondering if she knew how much I loved it and cherished her mothering all these years. My family didn't believe in nannies raising children, like the other rulers. My mother had been the one to put me to bed, wake me up, and kiss my boo-boos. But Falana was like a nanny in a way. My mother couldn't handle seeing me in distress, so Falana always stepped in during my episodes.

"Did anyone see?" I asked her.

"No, my lady."

We were quiet the rest of the ride to the southern border, where the farms lay along our land. I opened the curtain and gazed at the beautiful orange and yellow trees, smiling when a gust of wind would come and knock the leaves off and then drag them down the road. Then magically, more leaves would grow back in their place within seconds.

Eternal fall.

It was the best season in my humble opinion, but every princess thought that about their court. Changing leaves, crisp cool air, pumpkin hand pies, nutmeg cream, cinnamon scones, and fires crackling in fireplaces. Nothing beat fall.

7

When we finally reached the farm in question, my stomach growled in protest for dinner. Falana had packed some muffins and dried meat, but I'd have to eat it on the way back because the farmer was running for the carriage with wide eyes.

I cleared my throat, ready to calm the situation and put on a strong face for my people. Half a dozen guards flanked our carriage, but I'd trained them to look relaxed and not hostile. I didn't want my people thinking I was protecting myself from them.

Falana left the carriage first, opening the door for me, and I stepped out next.

"Princess Aribella," the farmer cried out, dipping into a low bow. "I'm so glad you came. You must see, it's the curse, I'm sure of it. I heard what happened in the Summer Court and now it's coming for us. We must tell everyone—"

I pushed the emotion of calmness into him and he stopped rambling, taking a deep breath.

"Let's check out the water together and make a plan, shall we?" I asked him with a smile.

"Yes, princess," he agreed, his posture much more relaxed.

The last thing we needed was a panic on our hands. If all of Fall Court got wind of this, there would be a full-blown exodus into Spring, and we couldn't have that.

The farmer walked me over to the well, around which his wife and three young children, all under five years old, were sitting, two of them eating apples. As I approached, they stood, wiping their hands and standing straight. The little ones curtsied so low their hair almost touched the ground, and I smiled at them.

"Hello," I called to them, but they all moved to hide behind their mother, suddenly overcome by shyness.

The farmer's wife looked worried but was holding it together for the children. She curtsied to me. "Nice to meet you, my lady. I'll take them inside for bath time." She widened her eyes meaningfully, as if she didn't want me to say anything about the black water or the curse in front of them.

I nodded and they left.

Once they were out of sight, the farmer began to crank the well handle, raising the bucket. "I had my wife sit guard just in case," he said.

I slowly pulled the calmness away from him. I never liked to leave an emotion with people for too long. I didn't want it to feel fake or unnatural.

As my powers receded from him, he looked a little panicked, so I quickly tried to assure him. "If the curse is here, that's okay. We have a plan for that. My father and I aren't going to let anything happen to our people."

He nodded, seeming to relax a bit, and then the bucket came up.

It was filled to the brim with black water.

I frowned. "Anything that could have caused this? Oil? Someone tampering with the well?"

He shook his head. "Smells like water. It was clear yesterday and the well shaft looks untouched."

I leaned forward and smelled the bucket. It smelled like nothing, not putrid or oily. I tried to cover the shudder that ran through me. This made it real.

The curse was here, in the Fall Court, and I was leaving in fourteen days to carve out the heart of an Ethereum lord, lest all the people I cared about died.

Chapter Two

"**A**gain!" Queen Liliana shouted.

Another week had passed since the black well incident and we'd thrown all of our efforts into my training. A bead of sweat rolled down my neck, soaking into the collar of the cotton shirt I wore under the tight leather battle corset. I wasn't even wielding a physical weapon, but that didn't mean that my tutors were not armed.

The training today had been grueling. Queen Liliana had forced me over and over again to use my powers and unarm my opponents, sometimes facing me off against two or three adversaries at a time.

I was sure I was littered with bruises from the number of hits I'd taken this afternoon. Had the swordsmen been using real weapons during this training session and not blunted ones, I'd have had several serious, if not life-threatening, injuries. But as important as I knew this training was, I struggled to keep my mind on the task at hand.

How could I when the curse threatened to take over our lands?

With only a week left before the fall equinox, the effects of the curse had already started to appear. More and more of our water sources had been polluted by black water. The land had stopped regenerating in places, so when the leaves that fell off the trees or crops were picked, rather than magically replenishing, the vegetation withered and died. And there were reports from our western border of wildfires being caused by raining embers.

Every day more and more Fall fae arrived at the palace, seeking refuge. Tired, scared, and sometimes injured, they looked to my parents and me for answers and assurances we didn't have and couldn't give.

We were already overextended because of the refugees from the Summer Court. Even before the Fall fae had started to arrive, tents ringed the palace and the surrounding areas. Our physicians had been working almost around the clock to help the Summer fae injured by the curse. Our food stores were practically depleted. And now my own people were begging for help and we had nothing left to give. How had we come to this?

"Master Tor. You and your apprentice come at Princess Aribella from opposite sides," Queen Liliana said, snapping me out of my wandering thoughts for the millionth time this afternoon.

When I glanced over at her, it was obvious by the

pinched look on her face that Queen Liliana knew I was distracted and didn't approve. I'm sure she understood the stress I was under, but as a ruler herself, she expected me to be able to compartmentalize, just like she did.

And if I'd learned anything about Queen Liliana over the last several weeks, it was that she never left room for failure.

It wasn't that Queen Liliana was cruel, per se, but no part of her was soft. I could only imagine what it was like for Princess Dawn to have grown up with a mother who was so single-mindedly focused.

I didn't believe Dawn had been unloved. Whenever she was brought up, a flash of true sorrow darkened Queen Liliana's eyes. She loved her daughter, that much was clear. But still, the pressure the Summer princess must have lived with day in and day out had to have been intense, and so my heart went out to the fallen Summer champion.

"Aribella, be ready this time. You're waiting too long to take down your first opponent, giving your other attacker the opportunity to overwhelm you. You need to be fast and decisive. Don't give your enemy time to reach you. Bring them to their knees before they know what has hit them."

I nodded and kept my mouth shut against the excuses that wanted to spring free. It wasn't as easy as she was making it sound. Using my powers on multiple people simultaneously was taxing and left me physically exhausted. Which was dangerous for my condition. But she didn't know that.

My magic was rooted in the Fall Court, specifically the changeability of our season. Our weather could one day be as balmy as a summer night, and the next a dusting of snow would coat the early morning grass. In some ways our season was volatile, but I embraced and loved the unpredictability of our Court. Unlike the Summer and Winter Courts, where every day was pretty much the same, the Fall Court went through transitions. There was nothing stagnant about the Fall Court, and that made life exciting.

My magic was similar in nature, but rather than shifting weather patterns, I could shift emotions and feelings. With a push of my magic, I could calm a rage-filled fae, or settle an anxious heart. But on the flip side, I could also fill a fae up with so much hopelessness and despair that they couldn't function beyond falling to their knees and wailing.

Although I would never do that. I loved my people and only used my powers to protect and nurture, never to harm. In truth, I'd never explored the limits of my magic and had no desire to do so, but that was exactly what Queen Liliana was demanding of me.

My power was like a muscle I hardly ever used. In many ways it was weak and atrophied. It would take time to grow in magical strength. Time I didn't have. But I'd seen improvement over the last several days that we'd focused on using my magic as a weapon.

We'd been at this for hours already today though, so I wasn't sure how much more I could take before my body gave out on me. But even so, I dug into a wellspring of strength inside me I hadn't known existed until recently and lashed out as soon as the pair attacked.

First, I pushed hopelessness on to Drake, Master Tor's

apprentice. He was a young man, brown-haired and only a few years older than me, but he had the stamina of a work-horse. Even after hours of sparring, he hardly looked winded. The moment my magic pushed into him, he faltered, his blunted sword dropping from his hand immediately.

Satisfaction filled me, but rather than revel in my success, I pressed a wave of grief toward Master Tor. I hoped to over-whelm him as I had Drake, but even though tears started to drip from the aged fae's eyes, he didn't lose his grip on his sword or halt his attack. Instead, he came at me with his weapon raised, and I was forced to drop to the ground and roll out of the way to avoid his blow.

I felt the swish of the blunted practice sword as it narrowly missed my head.

Mustering my last bits of energy, I pushed more sadness into Master Tor as I popped to my feet and backpedaled, but my repeated assaults that day must have dampened its effects because he didn't let up. Not even through his tears and the obvious sorrow I hammered him with.

He took another swing at me and I dodged out of the way.

Panicked from not being able to stop his attack, I pressed anger on the master, which was a fatal mistake.

Anger only fueled his violence, and he came at me so fast that the tip of his weapon slid across my leather corset as I twisted away. Had the material been anything other than hardened leather, I had no doubt, blunted blade or not, it would have left a mark on my flesh.

I was shaken, and I tried to pull back the anger I'd set

upon him and pour more of the sadness, but his attacks were coming too quickly for me to focus on my powers.

Beyond exhausted, what little energy I had left went toward dodging and weaving his blade. He wasn't softening any of his strikes, which meant that if one of his attacks landed, I'd be seriously injured.

"Stop," I yelled, throwing my hand up to signal an end to the sparring session, but filled with enraged grief, the sword master wouldn't back down.

This was the downside of my magic. I had to be careful what I filled people with because their reaction to specific emotions could be unpredictable. I could change how they felt, but I couldn't control what they did with those feelings.

Sometimes, like now, it backfired on me.

Shouts rang out around us and I had a vague notion that other fae were running toward us, but my attention was acutely focused on the man now trying to take off my head.

I'd never been so glad for practice swords in all my life.

"Stand down, Tor," Queen Liliana screamed, but it was no use.

I dipped low to avoid another one of his slashes, but when I looked up, the blade was arching back toward my head on his downswing. It may have been blunted and therefore incapable of taking off my head, but it still could break my neck from the force of the impact.

I knew I wouldn't be able to twist away fast enough, so in desperation I did something I never had before and flung out my power with no planned emotion, just a wild burst of raw magic with zero direction.

The magic left me in a rush and shot out in all directions. I didn't even have the time to aim at Master Tor. Instead, the burst hit every single fae in the room, draining me immediately.

My heart hammered in my chest, quivering against my breastbone.

Weakness pulled at my limbs as my legs shook and I dropped to the ground in a heap, completely depleted. Master Tor's sword clattered to the floor next to me and I breathed a sigh of relief, yet I didn't have enough energy to look and see where he was.

All around me wails of misery rose into the air, and I realized with growing horror what I'd done. I'd pushed a feeling of debilitating despair into all the fae in the room.

Yes, it had stopped Master Tor's attack, but if I didn't pull back my magic, the fae around me might fall into despondency and hurt themselves.

I tried to push myself to a sitting position, but it was useless. My arms felt so weak they shook with the effort.

My heart pounded like a war drum as sweat dripped down my brow. My muscles were as weak as a newborn's, and my vision blinked in and out as flashes of blackness began to take over.

Lying on the ground, I gathered what little reserves I had and slowly pulled my power back into myself.

I wasn't going to be able to hold on to consciousness for much longer; that much was a certainty. My heart was frantically quivering in my chest. But just before everything went black, I sucked the last drop of despair from the fae I'd unknowingly attacked. Then I was taken into darkness.

When I opened my eyes, my mother stood over me, wringing her hands. I wasn't in the training gym anymore, instead I was lying in my own bed with no memory of how I got there. The concerned look in my mother's eyes told me everything I needed to know.

I'd had another episode. And it was bad.

Twice within one week. I wasn't getting better like I thought. If anything, I was getting worse.

"How long have I been out?" I asked, which was usually the first question out of my mouth whenever I came around after a fainting spell.

A pleat appeared between my mother's brows. "Eighteen hours. Falana took care of you, and when she saw you stirring, she called for me."

I sat up so quickly I got a little dizzy again, but I ignored it.

"Eighteen hours?" I gasped. I'd never been out for so long before.

Throwing off my bedsheets, I slid out of bed. I'd been changed into nightclothes while I was unconscious. I might have been embarrassed by that, but it wouldn't have been the first time my maids had had to do the task.

Going to my armoire, I threw it open and started searching for clothes. I'd been training with Master Tor and

Queen Liliana in the late afternoon, so if eighteen hours had passed since then, it was already well into the next day. I only had days before the portal would open and I was to leave for Ethereum. I couldn't afford to lose any more training time than I already had.

"Dear, what are you doing?" my mother asked as she watched me flit around the room, looking for shoes to go with the pants I already had clenched in my arms. "You should get back in bed. You need all the rest you can get."

"Rest?" I let out a humorless laugh. "There's no time for rest, I have to get back to Queen—"

"She left," my mother said, cutting me off.

I froze, turning my head to look at her. My mother was chewing her bottom lip. That was never a good sign. She thought it was a horrible habit unbecoming of royalty, and only did it when she was exceptionally anxious.

"Left? Left where?" I asked.

She sighed and pity filled her gaze. "When she saw what happened, your father and I were forced to explain your condition."

No. Not that.

"Mother, you didn't."

Whenever someone found out about my weak heart, I was always treated differently after. We'd managed to keep my ailment secret most of my life. Only my parents, the royal physician, and a few trusted members of our staff knew. We never wanted our people to think that they would someday be led by an invalid.

Up until now my people didn't need a warrior, they

needed a leader. I was strong in mind and spirit, just not so much in body. That's really what counted, that I would be a good leader like my father. But I knew with nauseating clarity that Queen Liliana wouldn't see it that way, which was why I wasn't surprised by my mother's next words.

"She's left, along with the tutors and trainers. They've gone to the Winter Court to prepare the next princess."

Even though I wasn't shocked, the words were still a knife to my chest.

Queen Liliana didn't think I could do this, so she'd already moved on to Princess Isolde, training her to be the champion she didn't believe I could be.

I stood frozen, soaking it all in and trying not to cry, trying to stay strong and find the confidence in myself that no one else seemed to have in me.

"Maybe this is for the best," my mother started as she stepped closer to me. "I never wanted you to go to Ethereum. You're many wonderful things, Aribella, but not an assassin. Your place is here, safe in the palace with your father and me. Let the next princess travel to—"

"Mother, this isn't something I have a choice in," I snapped.

Dropping the clothes I had collected, I pointed out toward the window. Even now I could see two groups of Fall fae making their way toward the palace. They were too far away to make out details, but I imagine they'd arrive looking like the others had. Threadbare clothes dripping with black, oily water, carrying only the meager belongings they were able to save.

Frightened. Hungry. Looking to us to help them.

"The curse isn't coming anymore, it's here," I said to my mother. "Fall fae from all over our court are beginning to suffer. The portal won't open in the Winter Court until the winter solstice over three months from now. Our court won't be able to hold on that long. Look at what happened to the Summer Court. If I don't go to Ethereum when our portal opens and bring back that heart, our whole court will fall. I can't let that happen. I won't. My people, *our* people need me, and I don't intend to let them down."

She pressed her lips together, but her bottom lip started to tremble and her eyes filled with tears.

"I can't do it," she started to wail. "I can't let my only daughter go and sacrifice herself. Let the whole of Faerie suffer, I don't care." Falling into me, she started to sob.

Part of me softened toward her. I was fortunate to have a mother who loved me so much she'd be willing to do anything, sacrifice anything, to keep me safe. But the other part of me resented her. She was always so worried about me hurting myself that she was often suffocating.

I understood that my mother didn't have any real interest in ruling. She was happy to just decorate, take care of me, and throw parties. I never judged her for that; she always seemed to have weak nerves and ruling a kingdom was not something she seemed cut out for. But I was not my mother.

"Don't say that, Mother," I said, trying to soothe her. "I'm a born princess of Faerie, just like you were before me. Our duty first and foremost is to this Court and Faerie. My life isn't worth any more than any of our subjects'. You taught me that."

My words just made her wail louder. The sound grated on me, but I forced myself to rub a hand on her back as she continued to cry into my shoulder.

"You're not cut out for this, daughter."

I tried not to bristle at that. I knew my mother didn't mean to put me down. She was in a fragile place right now, terrified her fears since my birth were going to come true and that she would lose me. That one day I would never wake from one of my episodes or that I would die on this quest to bring back the black heart of an Ethereum lord.

And the truth be told, her fears weren't unsubstantiated. What I was setting out to do was dangerous. The first champion had trained her whole life for this fight and still failed.

But I wasn't going into this naively. I was acutely aware of my disadvantages, but I believed what I lacked in physical strength could be made up for in wit, intellect, and a heavy dose of my magical ability.

"It's okay if you don't believe in me because I believe in myself," I started gently to soften the bite of my next words. "But know this, Mother. In less than a week's time, I *will* go to Ethereum. And the moment I land in front of the black-hearted lord, I will carve that organ from his chest." I growled the last part.

My mother stopped crying. Pulling back, she blinked up at me, seemingly stunned that I was holding my ground.

Had I been so accommodating throughout my life that standing on my own two feet surprised her? It made me sad to think that I'd spent so many years holding myself back. Trying to appease a mother who was more content to see me tucked away safely than facing life head on.

But no more. It was time. I was going to spread my wings and jump. Whether I fell or flew would be up to me, but either way, I was going to do this.

Faint hearted or not. For Faerie, and also for myself.

"I *will* get the black heart and bring it back to the Fall Court or die trying. That is my vow, and nothing you, or anyone else in Faerie, say or do will stop me."

Chapter Three

I left my room and my weeping mother to get some air and went to the one place I knew would make me feel better.

The library.

The books had always taken me to far-off places, away from my hovering mother, my weak heart, and all of the responsibility. Whether I read a romantic tale about a long-lost prince reclaiming his throne and seeking a wife, or I was reading about biology and the organs encased in the body, reading soothed me.

I turned the corner and yelped when I ran into Master Duncan.

"Sorry." He reached out to steady me by grasping my shoulders. "How are you feeling?" He frowned.

There it was. The inevitable look of pity that came once someone knew of my condition.

"Fine," I said. "Shouldn't you be on your way to the Winter Court?" I tried not to sound hurt, but failed.

He shrugged. "I told Queen Lilliana that I would be right behind her. I wanted to stay back a bit and see how you were."

That was very sweet. My heart softened towards the tutor, whom I had barely gotten a chance to know.

"I'm . . . ready to do my duty and give this my all." I tipped my chin high.

He grinned. "So you're still going?"

I scoffed. "Why wouldn't I? These are my people we're talking about."

He clicked his tongue. "Your mother made a very compelling case for this weak heart you've had since birth. She claims going through the portal will kill you before you even have a chance to fight."

I growled. "Mother."

No wonder Queen Liliana had left.

"She loves you very much. Parents will do anything to protect their children."

"Well, I want to protect my people," I told him.

"Good. I was hoping you would say that. I think I can delay one or two more days before the Queen wonders where I am and sends a search party."

I stood straighter at that. "You're going to help me?" Hope bloomed in my chest and he gave me a warm smile and nodded.

"Dawn was a fearsome warrior. She could wrestle a man twice her size, blind you with a blast of light, cut you in half with a sunbeam, and she knew over fifty poisons that would end your life."

My eyes widened. "She sounds like the perfect champion."

He shook his head, reaching up to rub his chin. "I've gone over and over the scenario in my head. If Dawn had landed in front of an Ethereum lord, she'd have come back with the heart in a matter of minutes. I'm sure of it. She was one of the most powerful champions we ever had record of when it came to magical ability."

Chills raced up my arms. "What do you think happened then?"

He sighed. "Dawn's mind wandered often: it was her one weakness. I think she went through that portal and landed elsewhere in the realm and succumbed to the many dangers of Ethereum."

I blew air out through my teeth, shaking my head. "Poor Dawn."

He grasped my shoulders, and I peered up into his gaze. "We can learn from Dawn's mistake. You have a sharp mind, you are focused. We should have started training you to go through the portal weeks ago, but Queen Liliana was focused on your combat training, so it got pushed off. But if we start now, you can master the meditations needed to pass through the portal and successfully land at the feet of an Ethereum lord."

I felt determination rise up inside of me. "Let's do it."

"Now imagine the river you are sitting next to has red water." Master Duncan's soothing voice infiltrated my mind and the vision I'd been holding of sitting next to a bubbling, clear-blue brook was changed. The water was now red.

I nodded to indicate that I'd done as he asked.

"Good, now in that water are hundreds of fish all fighting to swim upstream."

Immediately the fish entered my mind's eye, and I saw them flip and flop, thrashing against one another and fighting for purchase to get up the creek.

I nodded again.

"You can open your eyes now, Aribella," Master Duncan said.

I snapped my eyes open to see him beaming at me. I'd grown fond of our little sessions. They were calming and I was good at meditating, able to easily imagine what he described and nothing else. We'd been doing this for two straight days and I'd gotten good quickly.

"Incredible," he said. "After years of training Dawn, I forgot what it was like to have a focused student." That last part was said with a smile, and so I knew he was being playful.

"Dawn couldn't have been that bad," I told him.

He laughed. "She would fall asleep. Or play with the hem of her skirt, or one time she whistled a tune. So you see, no one is perfect. We all have our strengths and weaknesses."

I also barked out in laughter then, before the smile was wiped from my face.

"Do you miss her?"

He nodded. "She never knew her father, so we all sort of helped raise her. I loved her." His voice broke, and he cleared his throat and stood. "Well, I think you're ready and I can't possibly delay another moment or the Queen will send messengers back to inquire after my whereabouts."

I stood as well and walked him to the door of the supply room where we had secretly been meeting. I didn't want my mother catching wind of what I was planning. I'd really come to respect Master Duncan. I was sad to see our time come to an end but knew it was inevitable.

Master Duncan held out a hand, and I shook it. "Thank you for everything," I said.

He squeezed hard, affection shining from his gaze. "I think everyone underestimates you, Aribella. *That* is a weapon you can use. I think you'll do fine. And please know that I'll be rooting for you."

I smiled genuinely. It was a kind thing to say. I was honored to have his support, but nervousness still sat in the pit of my stomach like a hunk of lead.

Could I really do this?

"Well, make sure to get the Winter princess ready just in case," I told him.

He chuckled darkly. "Just come home alive. Faerie cannot handle another loss."

He was right. There wasn't even a funeral for Dawn. They had accepted her fate, but if I didn't return either, it would be chaos. Two of four court princesses dead . . . it was inconceivable.

It was in this wild moment that I thought about the line

of succession and how I didn't have any children yet and had no cousins or aunts. My mother had been too emotionally weak to have more than one child—I'd heard her tell my father that once. But if I died, then the entire Fall Court royal line went with me. My mother's monthly bleeding had stopped last year. I was it.

Dizziness washed over me and I swayed.

Master Duncan frowned, reaching out to hold me upright. "You okay?"

I nodded. "Just a lot of pressure." I laughed nervously.

He gave me a serious look. "Remember. Don't give them a chance to speak. They weave lies that will have you confusing your left from right. Land before the lord and take his heart. Come home. That's it."

I straightened my back, taking a cleansing breath. "I will."

The next evening, the night before the portal was to open, my father sent Falana to call me to dinner. I put on one of my nicer dresses and met him and my mother in the small family dining room that we ate in when it was just the three of us.

"Hello," I greeted my parents as I entered the room.

My mother sat next to my father, gripping his hand so tightly that her knuckles were white. My father's face was an unreadable mask.

Something was up.

"Please sit down," he said calmly.

I swallowed hard. "What's wrong?" I asked as I took a seat.

"Don't stress her," my mother said to my father, looking at me pitifully as if she expected me to faint at any moment.

I wanted to roll my eyes, but I knew it was just because she loved me so fiercely.

"Stress me about what?" I asked in the calmest voice I could muster.

"Your mother and I have spoken. We forbid you to enter that portal—"

"Father!" I stood so fast that my chair knocked over.

His eyes flew wide. I'd never yelled at him. I loved him. He was my favorite, though I knew it was awful to admit. He never treated me like a flower petal that would crush at the slightest touch.

"You will not enter that portal, Aribella. You will come with us to the Spring Court where Queen Gloria has graciously accepted to house us and our people, while Winter takes Summer refugees. Come winter solstice, Isolde will travel to Ethereum and bring back the heart, freeing us from the curse, and then we will return to the Fall Court and clean up what is left of it. It's not ideal, but it's for the best."

My face felt hot. I was so angry it felt as if steam would come out of my nose.

"You don't think I can do it?" There was fury and hurt in my voice.

My father pulled his hand from my mother's clutches and stood. Rounding the table to stand in front of me, he placed a hand on either of my shoulders and looked me right in the eye.

It was like looking in a mirror. His rich brown eyes stared back at me, reminding me so much of my own.

"Whether you can or not, it's not worth the risk. You are our only heir, my precious daughter, and I would do anything to keep you alive. You will understand one day when you have children."

"Because you will be alive to have children," my mother reminded us both.

I knew then that I'd have to do the one thing I promised my father I would never do. Use my magic on him.

"We leave in the morning. So let's enjoy our dinner and get some rest." He sat down and I moved to my chair, picking it up from where I'd knocked it over and then fell into it as if it were a dark hole trying to swallow me up. A hole I willingly wanted to drown in right now.

"Yes, Father," I told him.

Tomorrow I was going to have to use my powers on my own parents and run away. When I said that nothing would get in the way of me saving my people, I meant it. The history books would not write that Princess Aribella of the Fall Court was too weak or scared to go to Ethereum.

Chapter Four

I barely slept. I felt sick about what I knew I was going to have to do. My mother often suffered from bouts of anxiety and so, with her consent, I had used my power to calm her. But I'd never used my magic on my father because he'd explicitly asked me not to.

"All set?" my father asked as I approached the carriage with a giant fake smile plastered on my face.

I simply nodded so he would get into the carriage and then my mother went in after him.

Our people had already begun the miles-long caravan toward the Spring Court and we were the last, bringing up the rear so no citizen was left behind. It was noble if you looked past the fact that we were all total cowards, fleeing danger. I didn't blame my people. They should go to safety elsewhere, but my mother, father, and I should stay with the land until the very last moment.

When I saw that Falana had jumped into the carriage

ahead of ours, I leaned my head into the carriage and prepared to push the most complex magic I'd ever done over my mother and father. It would have to be multilayered.

"Father, Mother," I spoke softly. "I won't be going. I need to stay back and help this little girl I found."

Their faces melted with concern, but I pushed contentment into them and the concern washed away.

"What girl?" my mother asked, confused.

"A little orphan who needs me. I'll take her to Spring Court by horseback and we will be a half-day behind you."

I pushed the feeling of calmness throughout both of them, and then a little confusion because I didn't want them digging for all the details. It was better to make up a semi-believable story and then just nudge them to accept it.

"Isn't that nice of me? Responsible? And loving?" I pushed emotions with each word.

My father's eyes glazed over as he nodded first, then my mother. "Be safe," he said almost dreamily, and guilt wormed its way through me. I hated that I had to do this.

I was pushing gratitude and pride and so many emotions into them, I wasn't even sure how to tease them apart now.

"Okay, I love you." I tried not to let my voice catch. This would be the last time I would see either of them for a while. Or maybe ever.

"Love you, darling. You will make such a great mother one day." My mother squeezed my hand and my face fell.

I knew she was just saying that because of my story about taking care of the orphan, but it stung. I wasn't sure I would ever be a mother. I wasn't sure I would survive the next forty-eight hours.

"And a compassionate future queen," my father added.

I hugged them both and then slipped away, back into the palace before anyone else needed to be emotionally manipulated.

That's what it was. Suggestive magic was a kind term for what I did. Mind control or brainwashing was more accurate.

I'd never tested the limits of my magic, to how far I could physically be from a person before pulling the emotions back, but we were about to find out. Because I had about twelve more hours before this portal opened. The danger with such a long period of time is that my parents were susceptible to anything anyone told them. Someone could advise my father to cut out my mother's heart, and he might think it was a fabulous idea.

The thought made me sick.

I just had to make it to tonight, then I would pull my magic back and the emotions I forced on them would disappear.

Assuming I could.

My parents would probably realize what I'd done and head back here, but by then I'd be gone.

The day passed quickly and night fell on me, along with a bundle of nerves. I'd packed my bag with maps that Master

Duncan had given me and a few Ethereum coins. I wore the leather-corseted outfit I'd trained in and I'd broken the glass case holding the red carnelian faestone-encrusted dagger that I would need to carve out the heart of the Ethereum lord and return home again. After sharpening the dull blade, I stashed it in a sheath at my waist and made my way to the throne room.

My steps echoed as I strode toward the raised dais at the end of the cavernous stone chamber. If Queen Liliana hadn't found out about my weak heart, there would have been a grand ceremony to see me off.

Queen Liliana, my parents, the masters I trained with over the last couple of months, as well as my friends and courtiers from the Fall Court would have all been in attendance. But instead, I was sneaking away in the middle of the night like a criminal.

There were no well-wishers to see me off and offer me support. No final hugs or tears of pride from my parents. It was only me and perhaps a few mice who had ventured out into the open now that the palace was empty.

The palace had never been so quiet, and it was eerie to know that I was the only fae remaining here. In all of our history, there had never been a time when the Fall Court had been abandoned. I understood my father's decision to evacuate our people. They were the beating heart of the Fall Court, and it was our duty to protect them. But complete abandonment of our lands felt wrong. Like we were giving up.

I would never give up.

As I walked up the steps to the dais, only the moonlight streaming through the windows lit my way. I reached the thrones, skimming my fingers over the top of my mother's and father's gilded seats. They were the same height, signifying that they both ruled over the Fall Court equally, even though everyone knew it was my father who kept things running.

My father was a just and fair ruler and if I made it back —no, *when* I made it back—I intended to be just like him.

Passing the thrones, I went to the back wall. The door to the mirror room was cleverly hidden within the wall, blending seamlessly into the mortar between stones. It was almost impossible to find if you hadn't been shown where it was. Many of the residents of the palace didn't even know it existed. And why would they? A Fall princess had never served as champion before.

I ran my fingers along the stones, feeling for the break at the door's edge. It took a little bit of time to find it in the low light, but eventually I worked out where it was and pressed in the stone that would cause the hidden door to pop open.

The door groaned as it slowly moved, as if protesting being woken after such a long rest.

When I entered the windowless room, the air was stale and filled with dust. The space was empty except for a full-length mirror propped up against the wall.

I was relieved to see that the portal hadn't opened yet, and the mirror looked perfectly normal. Its ornate frame was probably impressive at one time, but now was caked with so much dust that its luster and details were hidden.

Using my sleeve, I cleared some of the dust from the mirror's surface, and when I stepped back, I was immediately underwhelmed. All I saw when I stared into the mirror was myself. A petite girl with fair skin and a mane of braided red locks hanging over her shoulder.

I hated to admit it, but she didn't look fearsome or mighty, both things I believed a warrior should be. She looked breakable, like a delicate piece of porcelain that was beautiful to look at, but rarely used because of its fragility. And in her eyes, in *my* eyes, I saw the most un-champion-like emotion of all.

Fear.

At that moment, I wished I could work my own magic on myself. I'd infuse my body to the brim with courage, wiping away the uncertainty shining from my eyes.

I wanted to step through the portal, knowing I could complete my mission, rather than fearing I'd fail like the champion before me and be forever cut off from the people and land I loved, or worse. I knew I only had thirty days to find an Ethereum lord and carve out his heart before the portal home would close and trap me there forever.

Before my eyes, the glass in the mirror started to ripple. I caught my breath and took an involuntary step back as metallic swirls appeared within the frame.

It was exactly how Master Duncan had explained it would be.

It was time.

Now, even if my parents figured out what I had done, they couldn't stop me and so I took a deep breath and pulled for the emotions and feelings I had left with them: content-ment, amiableness, gratitude, and pride. I sighed in relief when I felt them snap back into me like a rope breaking over a long distance.

I didn't want my father being taken advantage of while I was gone, and I had no idea how long my powers lasted when used in this way.

Next, I closed my eyes and envisioned the black heart of an Ethereum lord, pumping not only black blood but its evil magic throughout its host as well.

Holding the image in my mind just as Master Duncan taught me, I opened my eyes and walked forward. Fear threatened to overtake me, but I pushed back against it. I was determined to enter Ethereum with open eyes and my head held high.

Right before stepping into the portal, I paused and pulled my faestone dagger from its sheath, clutching it tightly in my fist.

Master Duncan's command flitted through my mind. *Strike before the villain has a chance to even utter a word.*

With the image of the black heart still firmly in my mind's eye, I took a final step forward and into the mirror.

Chapter Five

W alking into the portal was not as simple as I thought it would be. No sooner had I passed through the mirror when I felt a sharp tug at my middle. Then with a jerk, I was yanked forward.

I didn't have time to get used to the sensation before I found myself standing on a candlelit table and looking down into the shocked, gray-blue eyes of an Ethereum lord.

I had purposefully chosen to go through the portal late at night, expecting the Ethereum lord to be fast asleep, or at the very worst, well into a pint if he was a drinker. But instead I was standing atop his dinner table, my foot planted on his plate. What looked like mashed potatoes squished out on either side of my boot.

Who eats a meal this late at night?

Maybe it wasn't late here, but there was no time to dwell on that.

I quickly pulled my wits about me. It didn't matter why he was eating so late. All that mattered was that if I didn't act now, I'd lose the only advantage I had against the beast of a man in front of me: surprise.

Dropping low, I slashed out with my dagger, aiming for the dark lord's heart. I was swift with my movements, but the lord was faster and shoved away from the table, stumbling to his feet.

Disappointment hit me like a slap in the face when I saw that I had torn his shirt but missed his flesh.

We both froze for an instant, sizing each other up. It was only for a few heartbeats, but it was long enough for me to catalogue the lord's features.

He was a large man, easily a foot taller than me and almost twice as wide. His black hair was shorn close on the sides, and the middle was braided back to the crown of his head and then up into a messy knot, showcasing his long, pointed ears. His gray-blue eyes were almost piercing enough to detract from the vein of scars that cut through one eyebrow and down to his cheek.

Despite the circumstances, I felt a twinge of attraction and immediately chastised myself. He was undeniably handsome, and the scar that should have been grotesque or scary somehow only added to his allure.

Taken aback by my body's reaction, I gave the lord precious time I shouldn't have, affording him a moment to look down at his chest and see the rip I'd made. Immediately, he became enraged.

"You dare attack me?" he yelled, and then with an animalistic growl, he rushed me.

I slid off the table with speed I wasn't aware I was capable of, twisting out of the giant lord's grasp. Rather than running away from him like he probably expected, I adjusted my grip on the dagger and spun back toward him, swiping out again.

This time, I managed to make a shallow cut at the base of his throat before he reared away. But the nick didn't faze him and he dodged my next strike, grabbing hold of my wrist with an iron grip.

The blade was only inches from his chest, right over my intended target. I tried to push the dagger forward and into his heart, but the lord was just too strong. I could see a few drops of black blood coming from the wound I'd made on his neck, and it was the motivation I needed to know I was in front of the right person.

His eyes dropped to my dagger and flared as if he recognized it. When his gaze bounced back to me, the hatred in their depths burned so strongly I almost felt singed.

"It's you," he practically spat before twisting my arm so that I was forced to let go of the dagger as he took it into his own fist, and my stomach sank.

I brought my knee up to hit him between the legs, but he shifted out of the way. The distraction gave me the opportunity to twist out of his grasp and put a few feet of space between us.

My wrist throbbed where he'd held me. I wouldn't be surprised if he'd broken it. But the pain hardly registered as I stared at the beastly fae who stomped toward me with murder in his eyes.

Use your magic, Queen Liliana's words from training rang in my head. *It is your greatest weapon.*

I had no excuse for not using my magic yet. It was a disastrous mistake that very well might cost me my life.

Stupid. Stupid. Stupid.

I had trained all that time that it should have been the first thing I did, yet I'd been too preoccupied with the physical fight. I should have been ready considering all the preparation Queen Liliana had put me through, yet when the moment of truth came, I'd choked.

I was disappointed in myself, but there was no time to wallow.

Before the dark-haired lord had a chance to use my own dagger against me, I summoned my power and pushed fear into him, blanketing him entirely in the strong emotion.

I expected him to drop to the floor immediately, a blubbering mess of hysterics with wide eyes, tears, and clamoring for an exit. Any other fae I unleashed this much fear on certainly would have been incapacitated immediately, but not this Ethereum lord. The only indication that he felt the effects of my magic was in the widening of his eyes and the slight tremor that now wracked his body. But he was still able to take another step forward, forcing me to take one back.

My own fear rose in my chest as I staggered away. After a few steps, my back bumped into the stone wall behind me, halting my retreat.

Almost out of options, I dug deep and threw more at my adversary, just as Queen Liliana taught me. To show him no mercy, for he would show me none as well.

In a split second, I piled hopelessness and panic on top of the fear.

The lord's steps faltered, eyes going wider, but his grip on the faestone dagger didn't waver. His gaze clouded over and he shook his head like he was trying to fling off the imposed emotions, but he couldn't.

"What are you doing to me, little witch?" he bellowed, his voice full of the distress his body refused to show.

Shadows began to move along the walls, and a wave of fresh fear rolled over me. With his free hand, he reached up and gripped the side of his head, and then his eyes slid closed.

Now was my chance.

With his eyes closed, I darted around him and toward the table. I grabbed the serrated steak knife, intending to slit his throat with the blade, but when I twisted back toward the lord, it was just in time to see dark shadows shoot out of his palms.

The dark, snake-like ropes flew through the air and wrapped around my body, forcing my arms to my sides, immobilizing me.

I gasped, trying to flee then, reasoning that if I escaped I could come back and attack him another time, but more rope-like shadows attached to my legs, causing me to crash to the ground.

My shoulder took the brunt of the impact, but then my

head snapped to the side, hitting the stone floor with a sickening thud.

My heartbeat skipped, causing blackness to invade my vision.

No. Not now. If I pass out now, I'm dead.

The reality of the situation fell on me like a cascade of stones.

I'd already failed.

I was without the faestone dagger and incapacitated in every way. My magic didn't have enough of an effect on the Ethereum lord to overcome his brutish strength.

Rather than bringing home the black heart of an Ethereum lord, I would die in a foreign world, which was exactly what everyone expected of me.

Grief and sadness swamped me, hurrying along the effects of my weak heart, and my vision went hazy as my breathing shallowed.

Through the haze, I watched as the lord stomped toward me, his footfalls rattling in my brain.

He nudged me onto my back with nothing more than the toe of his boot. When I looked up into his blue-gray eyes, I saw my powers still affecting him, and yet he was functioning normally.

How powerful was this fae that he could stand up against my magic?

After he killed me, my magic would most likely eventually fade, just like they would if I went unconscious, but it would take time. At least I'd die with the satisfaction that the

Ethereum lord would mentally suffer, even if just for a little while, because of me.

It wasn't much, but it was something.

As the lord watched me, the binds he cast around me tightened, stealing what was left of my breath. My vision continued to darken as my heartbeats ratcheted faster, and it wasn't long before I fell into familiar blackness.

Chapter Six

I came to with a pounding headache and my first thought was that I somehow wasn't dead. My eyelids snapped open, and I whimpered when I noticed the floor-to-ceiling steel bars that caged me in.

I was in a cell.

Terror ripped through me as I sat up and took stock of my surroundings. The back wall and two side walls were stone, and the front was fully barred in with a small slot for what I hoped was for sending food and water through.

It was almost completely dark inside the cell. The only light that illuminated the space was a tiny sliver of sunlight that filtered in from a small strip of a window high above my head at the back wall.

There was a bedpan in the corner and the entire place smelled of damp urine. I would have almost preferred death to this. No bed, no clothing, not even a pillow.

A man screamed somewhere down the hall and the hair

on my arms stood straight up. I noticed a pair of shackles on the far wall, bolted to the stone, and sighed in relief that I wasn't currently in them. A small kindness.

"Hello, little witch," a familiar voice growled.

I spun, ready to throw every emotion and feeling I had at the monster, but the bastard flicked his hand out and a thick band of shadows wrapped around my throat, cutting off my oxygen supply.

"Before you do anything rash," he said. "I want you to know that I have given your little dagger to my blacksmith, who assures me it can be melted down and made into a door stopper, rendering it harmless."

My heart sank at that and I grasped frantically at the black band around my throat, desperate for oxygen.

"If I don't check in with him every hour on the hour, he starts melting, and your way home and to save your people, goes with that dagger."

My eyes flew wide. *How did he know that?*

He released the black band, and I coughed, gagging and sputtering for precious air.

"You're not the first, little witch, to try to kill me," was all he said, and then he walked away.

Dawn? Was he talking about Dawn?

"Wait!" I screamed hoarsely. But it was no use; he was gone.

Had he been the fae who ended Dawn's life? He must have been. Who else but a powerful Ethereum lord could have stopped Dawn from completing her mission?

I knew firsthand just how unstoppable of a force he was

and my heart went out to the fallen Summer princess. I hoped whatever had happened to her, she went quickly and hadn't been forced to endure this vile dungeon like I was.

My heart hammered in my chest, and I had to take multiple deep breaths to calm it down. Passing out in here would be the worst thing I could do. Fae knows what kind of people came in and out of this cell. I didn't want to be unconscious and helpless for hours.

My hands shook as the temperature dropped and night fell outside. Slowly, my tiny cell grew darker and darker until I couldn't even see my hands in front of my face.

The moonlight outside didn't reach me, and I was beginning to wonder if this was some kind of magic. Was it some blanket of shadows to make it so dark, you began to wonder if you existed at all?

"Hello?" I said, just to make sure I was still in fact here.

I could feel my legs, but I couldn't see them. I held my hand inches from my face and saw nothing but darkness.

Panic began to well up inside me as my fellow prisoners all began to scream, cry out, or wail. I had no idea there were so many people in the dungeon with me until this moment. Dozens of voices carried through the space.

"I'm okay. I'm real. I'm safe," I began to mutter to myself, feeling insanity press in on me.

This darkness was supernatural in nature, and there was only one fae whom I knew of that could manipulate shadows like this.

The Ethereum lord was doing this to torment us all.

It made me feel better about my attempts to kill him. I

had always been told that the Ethereum lords were evil, but this was the proof I needed.

Something slithered across my ankle, cold and smooth like a snake, and I screamed bloody murder, backing up until my back hit the right side of the wall.

"It's not real!" a muffled voice shouted next to me.

My heartbeat spiked, my breath came out in fast, short bursts, and I knew I would pass out again if I didn't relax.

"What?" I managed while trying to keep it together.

Feeling around with my fingers, I noticed a little drain grate at the bottom of the wall between mine and whoever was next to me.

"The snakes aren't real. They are shadows, a trick from Lord Stryker to bend us toward insanity," the voice said. It was a male voice, a young one I'd guess, only sixteen or seventeen.

Something slithered across my ankle again and I burst into sobs, screaming as I reached around me for anything solid I could protect myself with. A bedpan would do.

"Lady, I've been here for two weeks. They aren't real. Grab it next time. It dissipates."

My stomach felt like it was in my throat. Was he insane? Grab a snake?

There it was again, that slithering.

Figuring I had nothing to lose and that if the snake was venomous, I'd rather die sooner than later. I grasped it in my fingers, recoiling when I felt something solid in my hands, but almost a second later it melted into shadows.

I sighed in relief, panting as I realized the fae next door was right.

"Once you stop fearing them, the snakes stop," he said through the grate. "It's like his magic knows."

My breath settled, and I finally felt like I could speak. "Thank you," I told him. "What's your name? I'm Aribella." I needed to keep talking, or I'd think about this darkness and go insane.

"I'm Eli," he said.

I took a few more deep breaths, grateful to have someone to talk to between the terrified screams of the other prisoners. "You said the lord's name is Stryker? I'm not from here."

"Yes, Lord Stryker is the most brutal of the four brothers," he said darkly.

Brothers. Interesting. I knew there were four lords at any given time, but I didn't know these current lords were brothers. How lovely that I happened to land before the most mentally unhinged of all of them.

"Why are you here?" I asked Eli, desperate to keep him talking and the panic at bay.

His voice shook a little. "Lord Stryker thinks I am part of some underground smuggling ring. I'm not, but my cousin is, and I was in the wrong place at the wrong time." I wondered if it was the complete darkness getting to him or the topic.

"Smuggling?" There were a lot of things you could smuggle. Drugs. People. We had a nut in faerie that made you high when you ground it up and drank it in a tea. It was outlawed, but people still sold it behind the scenes.

"Gold. Gems. Lord Stryker owns all of the mines in the Eastern Kingdom. All the riches are delivered to his vaults here in Easteria. He's the richest lord alive."

Ahh, that made sense. Rich men were always a bit unhinged.

"Right Easteria." I played dumb. I mean, I'd seen it on the map Master Duncan had given me, but I didn't know about the gem and gold mines.

The guy whimpered then, and I knew something scary must have happened.

"Hey, I'm going to make you feel better, okay? It's part of my magic," I told him and then pushed the feeling of peace over him. There was no reason we both needed to be terrified of this place.

"How?" he breathed and sighed in contentment. "That's incredible."

I smiled; glad he was feeling better. "I've always been able to. So tell me more about Lord Stryker?"

Now that the man was in a calm and peaceful state, he opened up like a book. "He took over Easteria very young, after his older brother died in a freak accident. I don't remember much about the Eastern lord before him. I was young myself then, and the Warrick family is wide reaching. They have more cousins and uncles and brothers and nephews than you can imagine."

I frowned. "How old are you?"

"Fifteen."

My stomach sank. Lord Stryker was torturing a fifteen-year-old.

"So he got drunk with power and money and now he's a sadistic maniac?" I mused.

"Not exactly. My mother said he used to be kind in the beginning. But then people started asking for loans, favors, lying to him to get money, or begging him to save their farm only to find out they had a gambling addiction. My mother says money brings problems."

His mother was wise. "So that's when he built a magical dungeon of darkness that feeds off of his prisoners' fears?"

I could hear the boy smiling. "No." He chuckled. "It was after the love of his life tried to kill him in his sleep. She used a poisoned blade, which is how he got those scars."

My heart shuttered in my chest and I sat up straighter. "What?"

"Yeah . . . that's when the curfew started, and the interrogations, and then this place was built." His voice had darkened.

I was speechless. His lover tried to kill him? "Why did she—"

"I just told you, Aribella. He's the richest man in Ethereum. You must come from money if you can't understand why that matters here."

I cleared my throat. "My family is well off. Merchants," I lied.

"Well, mine aren't. Where I come from, we only have a day's worth of food in the cupboard and we gotta thinking about where we can get coin for the next day," he said.

I nodded, even though he couldn't see me. "But to steal it from someone doesn't sound like the right way."

I could almost imagine him bobbing his head in agreement. "It's not. That's why I said no when my cousin asked. But I understand why others do it. The chance to have that kind of money would change my life."

I frowned, feeling bad for the kid. "Well, what job did you do? Before this."

"I worked in the gold mines. I've held unimaginable wealth in my hands, only to have to give it away at the end of the day." He sounded wistful.

I sighed. It was a sad tale, but I didn't agree with stealing because someone had more than you. We were both quiet for a moment and I felt the heaviness pull at my eyelids.

"Aribella?" he asked, his voice thick with sleep.

"Hmm?" I wondered aloud, laying down myself and attempting to get comfortable, despite the circumstances.

"Can you keep your power over me until I fall asleep? This is the best I've felt in weeks."

It was the least I could do. He'd kept me sane in a terrifying moment and now that I didn't fear the snakes, they'd left me. Just like he said.

When I heard a soft snoring coming from the grate beside me, I pulled the peace back into myself, not wanting to leave him with it overnight in case he needed to be alert or afraid of something.

Fear was a good emotion in some cases. It kept us safe from harm and told us when to run from danger. If I kept him blanketed in peace, it could harm him eventually. He might not fight back if attacked.

Hugging my knees to my chest, I tried to calm my nerves. Lying in the dark on hardened stone, I thought it would be impossible to relax but eventually sleep took me.

I awoke to the sound of scraping metal. My eyelids sprang open, and I looked up at Lord Stryker, hovering above me.

"Enjoy the night?" he asked with a handsome smirk.

There were two guards behind him, both with swords held aloft. I might be able to subdue all three of them, but I couldn't go anywhere without my dagger. I would need it to get back to Faerie. A portal back to my kingdom wouldn't open until I used it to carve out a heart from an Ethereum lord's chest. If his blacksmith melted it down, I was a dead woman, along with my people. Besides, I wasn't even sure I could subdue the big fae before me. His power was like none I'd ever encountered before.

I sat up, glaring at him, and his smile grew.

"You're trying to find a way out of this. A way to kill me and still get your dagger."

I clenched my jaw. Did he read minds?

His eyes raked up and down my body, and then he scowled at me. "*Don't* use your power over me."

I frowned. "What are you talking about?"

Color crept up his cheeks and he cleared his throat. "Nothing. Get up, we need to speak."

I stood, brushing off my dress, and eyed the bedpan. "I have to pee, so unless you want to help me pull down my pants, I suggest you get out."

His eyes sharpened. "Little witch, the last thing I ever wish to do is help you out of your garments."

I growled when he didn't move. "Fancy a show then?"

I started to unlace my pants to call his bluff when he turned, stepping out of the cell and shutting the iron door as he and his guards gave me their backs. "Tell me when you're done."

"This is foul," I grumbled as I hovered over the pan.

I felt my cheeks heat in mortification and anger. I couldn't believe I was actually doing this. A princess of Faerie, relieving herself in front of three men. My parents would be horrified.

"If I pee on my feet, I'll make you kiss a horse," I threatened.

"Then you can kiss your dagger goodbye," he shot back.

When I was done, I stepped away from the bedpan and fought the urge to gag. "Just kill me if you're going to kill me. This is beneath my station."

He opened the door again and shot me with a glare. "The next ten minutes will determine how long you live. I'm glad we are on the same page about that."

Fear spiked through me and I swallowed hard. The two guards rushed in and hooked a hand under each of my armpits and pressed a blade to my throat.

"Walk," Lord Stryker growled.

I did, all the while my mind spun. How could I convince him to let me live and not in his dungeon, but in the castle?

Maybe I could get him to trust me and then double-cross him later. Master Duncan had given me about a ten-minute rundown of what to do in case I was captured and seduction was one of the options I'd laughed off. With how inexperienced I was, it wasn't something I thought I could pull off. But now, without access to a weapon and knowing that Lord Stryker was strong enough to withstand my power, it was a reality. Could I . . . without using my power . . . seduce him into giving me my dagger back?

It felt cruel, especially knowing his past lover had all but done the same, but I seemed to be out of options.

I followed the giant lord to a room at the end of a hallway that was lined with prison cells. I was scared to look into the open door for fear of what I might find, but was forced to when we reached the threshold. In the center of the room was a chair, and beside it was a tray full of different tools.

Torture tools.

I reared backward but the men held me in place and forced me into the chair and then strapped me to it.

"You would torture a lady?" I scowled at the lord, who picked up a pair of scissors caked with dried blood and began to sharpen the blades on a stone.

He looked around the room. "I see no ladies here. Just a murderous witch who hails from a long line of murderous witches."

I wanted to argue, but he was right. I was here to kill him.

"You stole our magic. Cursed our lands. Our people are dying because of you and the vile curse your ancestors put over us," I spat.

He rolled his eyes. "Is that what they tell you? Because if so, you've been grossly misinformed."

Shock ripped through me. Whatever could that mean?

No.

No, he was lying. That's why Master Duncan said not to let them get a word out. The Ethereum lords were liars.

"I think you can still function without your pinkies. What do you think?" He held up the scissors and I felt the blood rush from my face.

My heart pounded and sweat beaded on my skin. Dizziness washed over me and blackness danced at the edges of my vision.

Not again. Not right now.

I breathed in and out deeply through my nose, trying to fight off the fainting spell, but when he stepped closer and held the scissors up to my pinky finger, my heart rate tripled and then everything went black.

$$Chapter\ Seven$$

I gasped as I came to and immediately peered down at my hand. I sagged in relief when I saw that I did in fact still have all of my fingers.

"You fainted." Lord Stryker's deep gravelly voice came from behind me and I jolted, but then yelped when I realized I was still strapped to the chair.

"How long was I out?"

Lord Stryker watched me keenly. "Hours. I had my lunch. I thought you were dead, but alas, no such luck. Does this happen often?" He seemed curious, as if I were some science experiment.

Was there a point in lying here? In a world where I didn't know a single soul. Perhaps revealing my greatest weakness to my enemy would be a mistake; I knew Queen Liliana and my mother would tell me it was, but I hoped that knowing about my ailment might actually soften him toward me.

"Yes."

He frowned. "Interesting."

He walked over and picked up the scissors again and I balled my hands to fists. "There is no need for torture, Lord Stryker. I will tell you whatever you need to know."

He raised one eyebrow as if he didn't believe me and I arched one in return as if to say *try me*.

Setting down the scissors, he crossed his arms over his chest and peered down his straight nose at me. His pose was probably meant to be intimidating, but I was too relieved he'd put the shears down to be properly threatened by his imposing figure. Besides, I think I was somewhat getting used to his size and scowls. And his scar, which may have been menacing to others, didn't faze me at all. If anything, it added interest to his face, which was vexing to me.

"Explain your magic," he ordered, and I held back a sigh. Of course he had to start there.

"I can influence emotions and feelings," I said. Choosing my words carefully, I went for the simplest explanation for my magic, hoping that he would accept that at face value and move on.

"So mind control," he said, his frown turning into a full scowl.

I winced. I'd often referred to my magic as mind control to myself, but I hated that implication. I did not strip away a fae's free will. At least, not completely. I couldn't tell them to jump and they would do it.

"No," I said, shaking my head and shooting him a glare. "I don't control minds."

The look he gave me said that he thought I was lying.

"Yes, my magic has a persuasive element," I admitted. "I can alter how someone feels, or at least their perception of how they feel, making them angry or calm, more agreeable and the like. But if I could control minds, do you really think I would be strapped to this chair and at your mercy?"

He tilted his head a fraction, considering my words. After a long pause, he gave a small nod. "Then explain to me how this magic of yours works. And I want *details*. Does it work on all fae? Can you use it against more than one at a time? Do you have control over how long it lasts?"

After his last question, a spark of anger flashed in his eyes and I had to school my features to keep from smiling. He probably struggled with the emotions I pushed on him for hours after I'd passed out. The thought of that gave me no small amount of pleasure.

"I've never met anyone my magic doesn't work on," I said. "However, recent developments have shown that some can hold up against my influence better than others."

I gave Lord Stryker a pointed look. I was still a little baffled about how he'd been able to function with so much of my magic piled on him. That had never happened before.

If he was pleased with his ability to best me, he didn't show it. His face remained hard and unchangeable. Like one carved from cold stone.

"Go on," he said.

I didn't want to reveal so many of my secrets, but what other choice did I have? My own secrets weren't worth my life, or my fingers.

Under duress and repeated prodding from Lord Stryker, I spilled *all* of them.

Yes, I could push my powers on multiple people at once. No, I didn't know how many. Yes, I had control over the intensity of the feelings I forced on fae. No, I couldn't direct anyone to do something specific, but if I pushed enough of the right emotion on someone, then they could be persuaded in a direction. Yes, I could pull my magic back at will, and if I passed out before doing so, the magic would linger but eventually fade.

The questions went on and on, and the better part of an hour had passed before Lord Stryker's interrogation finally ended. He knew everything about my power now.

I bit my bottom lip in annoyance and frustration and the lord's gaze dipped down to my mouth before immediately popping back up.

Interesting.

Maybe my seduction plan had some merit after all? But his next words caused those ideas to flee from my mind completely.

"So you are a manipulator then." It was a statement, not a question. He snorted a humorless half-laugh. "I wouldn't have expected anything less from a deceitful Faerie witch."

I kept my mouth shut as heat rose to my cheeks.

I wanted to disagree, but he was right. Not about being deceitful, but my magic was about manipulation, and it was something I'd always felt a degree of shame about. It was a large reason I was always so careful about using it, at least up until recently. Over the last couple of weeks, I'd used my magic more than I had in the previous nineteen years of my life combined.

"I've answered all your questions. Now, it's my turn," I said.

He chuckled, but the sound held no humor. "You are not in a position to make demands. I don't answer to Faerie filth."

The insult would have stung if I cared at all about what he thought of me.

"What did you do to Princess Dawn?" I demanded anyway.

His upper lip peeled back from his teeth and he growled, "Not nearly as much as I would have liked."

Horrible images of Dawn being tortured flew through my mind. The man was truly a monstrous beast.

"You killed her, didn't you? Tell me where her body is." If I made it back to Faerie, I wanted to be able to tell her mother what had become of her and that her daughter was laid to rest properly. Dawn deserved that much.

"Killed her?" Lord Stryker's dark eyebrows shot up. "Well, I suppose it would be a comfort to you to think that."

"A comfort?" I said, disgusted. "How could it ever be a comfort to know that one of our princesses had been brutally murdered?"

"Because the truth is far more disturbing than whatever nonsense you've convinced yourself happened to the would-be assassin."

"What are you saying?" I asked, confused. Was he trying to tell me that Dawn wasn't actually dead, or just that he hadn't been the one to kill her? It was clear that he'd crossed paths with her. He said he hadn't done as much to her as he'd have liked. Could she still be here in his dungeon, alive, but unable to complete her mission, like I was?

A kernel of hope sparked in my chest.

If she was here, perhaps I could rescue her. Then, after I figured out a way to get my dagger back and kill this villain, we could both return to Faerie.

"Where is she? What happened to Princess Dawn?" I growled.

A smug smile lifted the corners of Lord Stryker's lush mouth, softening his face. Something pulled tight low in my gut and I hated myself a little for my body's reaction.

"Oh, I will tell you what happened to your Faerie princess," Lord Stryker said, "Not because you demand it from me, but because I want to see your face when you learn the truth."

My brows bunched in confusion.

"Your Princess Dawn is not dead," he said, and my heart leaped for joy. "But she is no longer *Princess* Dawn, but rather *Lady* Dawn."

"Lady Dawn?" I still wasn't following.

"Yes. *Lady* Dawn of the Northern Kingdom, to be exact. She is living in luxury, married to my brother, the Ethereum Northern lord, and ruling by his side. She has abandoned your world."

My whole body went still with shock. I was struck speechless.

"No." I shook my head. "You lie. There's *no way*

Princess Dawn would have betrayed her Court and all of Faerie like that."

But the haughty look on his face made me nervous. It didn't look like he was lying.

"She can and she did," he said confidently.

"But, why? How?" My heart began to pick up speed.

"Likely she realized the superiority of our world and somehow tricked my foolish brother into believing she cared for him. Love," he said with a sneer, "is nothing more than a fool's illusion. Someday my brother will realize that. Hopefully, it's before he finds a faestone dagger embedded in his back."

My mind whirled. It didn't make sense. Dawn had been trained as our champion since birth. Even if she did have affection for one of the Ethereum lords—which was almost impossible to fathom: I was experiencing firsthand how evil they were—she wouldn't just abandon Faerie to perish under the weight of the curse. If it was in fact true that she'd married one of them, there had to be an explanation. Although at the moment I couldn't think of anything that would make abandoning her quest, her duty to our people, acceptable.

"I just don't believe you," I muttered. I couldn't. Not without proof.

"Enough of this," he said, waving a hand in the air as if to dismiss the whole thing, not caring if I was convinced or not. "As entertaining as our time together has been, I have other matters to attend to today."

He thought this was entertaining? He truly was warped.

Stepping away from me, he went to his tray of torture devices and picked up a needle dagger. My heartbeat started to flutter.

"What are you doing?" I assumed that at the end of this questioning, at worst, he'd put me back in my cell, but apparently he had other plans. "I answered your questions," I protested, squirming against the straps that held me in place.

"And for that, I'm grateful and will make it a quick death. But I think even you can understand how I can't let an enemy with such strong magic live. Especially an enemy whose one goal is to take my heart."

The breath stalled in my lungs. He was really going to kill me. And why wouldn't he? It would be stupid to keep me alive.

Lord Stryker took a step toward me, adjusting the dagger in his hand so it was positioned over my heart.

"No, no wait," I yelled in desperation. "I can help you."

He narrowed his gray-blue eyes at me and goose bumps broke out on my skin.

"You can help me by dying," he said. "And then when the next princess shows up, she can help me in the same way."

I gasped. That was something else he'd gotten out of me during his interrogation. That if I failed in my mission, another princess of Faerie would come to Ethereum with the same goals.

I'd thought I was garnering goodwill with him at the time, but now I realized I might have just signed their death warrants along with my own.

"No, I mean, I can be of use to you *alive*. I can use my magic for you instead of against you."

I was bargaining with a monster, but I had no other choice. If I died now, it would be another three months until the next champion arrived in Ethereum. My land would be withered by then, and Lord Stryker would be ready for her. I had to do whatever I could to buy myself time to figure out how to escape, retrieve my dagger, and kill this monster.

Out of desperation, I pushed some of my magic into him. Just a touch of calmness mixed with acceptance to get him to believe me, that I could be an asset to him, but he realized what I was doing immediately and only got more agitated.

"*Stop* using your witchcraft on me," he yelled and held the pointed knife to my throat, pressing it in slightly so that a single drop of blood escaped.

I hissed, leaning back as far as the restraints would allow, and pulled back my magic immediately. My heart was beating faster than a hummingbird's wings, but I saw in his eyes that his anger dampened when my magic retreated. The blade hovered over my skin, yet didn't bite into my flesh.

"I can help you discern who deserves to be in your dungeon and who doesn't," I said, trying to calm my heart. I had no doubt that if I fainted now, he wouldn't bother waiting until I woke to make good on his threat.

He scowled. "Everyone in my dungeon deserves to be here."

I started to shake my head, but stopped myself because I didn't want to accidentally touch the blade. "That's not true. The boy beside my cell, he's innocent. He's not a smuggler "

The lord laughed darkly. "A likely story. Every one of the prisoners here claims innocence. You're as naive as you look."

"It's true. I used my magic on him already to discern the truth." That was a bald-faced lie. I hadn't done anything to Eli to know if he was telling the truth, but I believed in my heart he was. Enough to stake my own life on it. "And if he's blameless," I continued, "how many more are trapped in this abyss as well? Do you care so little about your subjects you are content to torture the innocent?"

I saw indecision flash over his features, and it gave me hope. Appealing to his mercy was a risky move because I wasn't sure he had any. There was a very good chance this lord didn't care who was or wasn't innocent. He might just relish causing pain. But I felt a glimmer of hope when he hesitated.

"And I can find out who deserves to be here in his place," I added, trying to appeal to his need for justice.

He narrowed his gaze. His striking gray-blue eyes assessed me. "How did you discern the truth? You didn't mention that as part of your powers before."

"My magic is multifaceted," I said, thinking quickly. "I

can relax someone enough that they will spill all their secrets. They won't even think of lying."

At least I hoped I could. It wasn't specifically something I'd tried before, but in theory it would work.

Something flashed in Lord Stryker's eyes and if I didn't know better, I'd say it was fear, but it was quickly wiped away. He stepped away from me, removing the blade from beneath my chin. I let out a sigh of relief, but it might have been premature.

"Prove it to me," he said with a gleam of calculation in his gaze.

"How?" I asked.

He crossed his arms over his chest and shrugged. "Figure it out. But don't even think of using your magic on me again, or I'll run you through without a thought. If you want to stay alive, at least for another day, prove to me you can be useful in this way."

He called out to his guards, and the two that had strapped me to the chair entered the room, along with another I didn't recognize. They looked to their lord for instruction, but Lord Stryker just stared at me, waiting for me to prove my worth.

I assessed the three guards, trying to tamp down my panic and come up with a plan. I choose the guard in the middle for no other reason than he looked a little shifty to me, as though he might have secrets.

Centering myself the best I could, I pushed my powers onto him, starting with calming and then moving on to contentment. Then I started to layer on more feelings and emotions. Security. Comfort. Vulnerability. The feelings of being validated, of being supported. Anything I could think of that would make a fae feel both safe enough to reveal their secrets, and inclined to do so. The fae's eyes started to appear glassy after only a few moments, and then his posture slackened.

Manipulating my magic like I never had before, I did my best to weave emotions together to make this fae believe he was in a safe environment. So that nothing he said was of any consequence, and he'd feel encouraged to talk.

The fae's eyes went to half-mast and he swayed a little, almost as if he were drunk. I hoped I hadn't pushed him too far. I'd never done this before, and if I failed, I would surely die.

"What is your name?" I asked him.

He stumbled a little and one of the other guards had to help him remain standing. The two looked at Lord Stryker in panic, but he only nodded, as if telling them to let this play out. Perhaps I'd laid my magic on too thick. I pulled some of my power back, worried I'd overwhelmed him.

My heart was in my throat until he answered, slurring the syllables, but finally telling us his name was Garrett.

I could tell by the look on Lord Stryker's face that it was correct, but he wasn't impressed. He shrugged. "Getting a fae to admit to their name is hardly the same as pulling a hidden truth from someone." He tested the sharpness of the tip of his dagger with the pad of his finger, his eyes never leaving mine. A clear threat.

I swallowed, wetting my dry throat. "Garrett," I said,

hoping against all hope that these weren't the last words I would ever utter. "What do you think of your lord?"

I was betting that Garrett, or any of the guards working for Lord Stryker, had hidden animosity for their cold master.

Garrett's gaze didn't even shift to the Ethereum lord before he answered. "My lord is a strict ruler, but fair."

Oh no, this wasn't going to prove anything.

"But he has so many riches that he could be sharing with the rest of us," he went on without any prompting.

Okay, now we were getting somewhere. Surely Lord Stryker would agree that his guard wouldn't normally speak so freely around him.

But Garrett wasn't done. "That's why I like to help myself to a little bit of his treasure every now and then when he asks me to watch over it. He has so much, I'm sure he won't miss the amount I swipe from time to time. Besides, my wife has expensive tastes."

I caught my breath and the two guards standing beside him began to back away slowly, as if they knew this wasn't going to end well, and they didn't want to be associated with him in any way.

This was incriminating evidence for sure, proving I could convince someone to tell the truth, but I hadn't wanted the guard to actually get into trouble. Stealing from your lord was a serious offence, and the stormy look on Lord Stryker's face said that this guard's deeds wouldn't go unpunished.

I felt sick to my stomach and was just about to pull my

power back, stopping Garrett from admitting anything else, when he damned himself further.

"But the heist my brother and I are planning next month will mean that I can live like a lord for the rest of my life. After we sack the royal treasury, we'll go live in the Midlands. Lord Stryker will never find us. The fae there hate him and will protect us."

I yanked my magic back and immediately the guard straightened, snapping to attention. He looked at his lord and dread filled eyes, then his gaze swiveled to me and filled with hatred.

"What have you done?" he screamed. Pulling his sword, he started toward me.

I was practically defenseless, still trapped in this blasted chair, so I gathered my magic to lash out and protect myself in the only way I could.

Before I had a chance to push extreme panic on him, black shadows shot from Lord Stryker's palms and wrapped around Garrett's neck and face, smothering him completely.

The guard fell to the ground in a heap, his features obscured by the lord's dark shadows.

I didn't know what Lord Stryker was doing to him, but the guard's screams echoed throughout the small room. If my hands had been free, I would have covered my ears to block out his tortured wails.

Suddenly, the screams stopped and the shadows cleared. The fae lay face down on the ground, unmoving. I couldn't tell whether he was alive or dead.

"Take him," Lord Stryker ordered, and the other guards

snapped from their shock and hefted the fae between them, dragging him from the room.

"Is he . . . dead?" I asked, my voice shaking with horror. What had I done?

Lord Stryker's head turned toward me. His stormy eyes speared me, somehow looking colder than they ever had before.

"Well done," he said, his deep voice monotone, emotionless. "You earned yourself another day among the living."

Chapter Eight

That night was no less horrifying. The darkness, the screams, the slithering. And to make matters worse, they'd moved Eli because he was no longer next to me. Then come morning, I was given my first meal since I'd gotten here. A stale piece of bread in cold broth. It was disgusting but I lapped it up like a starving dog.

Lord Stryker came by a little after my "meal" and brought me into his torture room again. As we passed the hallway, I became nervous to see a long line of guards queued up and leading into the room. There must have been a hundred of them.

"Umm, what's going on?" I asked Lord Stryker.

He led me into the room and closed the door so that we were alone. He loomed over me, watching me with an inexplicable gaze.

"If you want to live another day, you will use your truth magic on all of my guards and ferret out the disloyal."

I sputtered, nearly choking on my own spit. "You want me to use my magic on *all* of them out there?"

Lord Stryker nodded and then pulled a dagger from the sheath at his thigh. "Or we can arrange for you to take a nice dirt nap."

Dirt nap? I got the joke after a few seconds of thinking about it.

I growled. "Ha ha, funny. First of all, using my power that much will weaken me. I'm no good to you unconscious. Keep ten of them and send the rest away to come back tomorrow." I flicked my wrist with the command and he raised an eyebrow. "Second of all, I need *real* food." I grabbed my tiny waist. "I don't have much in the way of reserves, and using my magic takes strength."

His gaze slowly raked over me, and my body heated at the gesture.

"And thirdly. If this is going to be a long-term arrangement, I would appreciate a bed and bath." I placed one hand on my hip and tipped my chin high.

He burst into laughter, a deep and rumbling sound, and I knew I'd asked for too much too soon. My stomach growled, knowing it would not be eating honey-glazed pork or chocolate cake anytime soon. Oh, how I missed my palace chef.

"That was cute. Sit down," he ordered, all evidence of his mirth gone.

He thinks I'm cute. Maybe I could work with that.

"One more thing." I dared to push my luck.

He just glared in response.

"Is my dagger still safe with your blacksmith?" I tipped my chin. If he did anything to that blade, I was as good as dead, and so were my people.

Stryker rolled his eyes. "The weapon you intended to carve out my heart with is perfectly well, I assure you."

I sighed in relief and got to work.

In the end, I questioned sixteen of his male and female guards before I fainted. One of whom was harboring a minor secret that he'd smuggled truffles out of the kitchen for his daughter's twelfth birthday because they were her favorite.

As the dizziness washed over me and the blackness danced at the edge of my vision, I almost welcomed the void.

When I came to, I reached above my head and stretched, the sunlight warming my face as I yawned. I dug my head into the soft pillow, wanting just ten more minutes before meeting Father and Mother for breakfast.

"Little witch." Lord Stryker's gravelly voice reached me, and my eyelids snapped open.

I was in a bed. An amazingly soft bed with luscious, white satin sheets. I moved to sit up when something tugged at my ankles. I lifted the bedding and glanced down at my leg only to find metal biting into the soft flesh. I was chained to a four-poster bed. And not only that. Someone had changed me into a thin white robe.

Shock ripped through me, but I tried not to let it show.

"I didn't take you for a man who likes to tie his women up before bedding them."

I could barely believe the crass words had left my mouth, but if I was going to play the seduction role, I needed to play it hard.

Lord Stryker looked horrified at the thought of bedding me. "You smell like a pigpen. Bedding you is the last thing on my mind. I'm not completely unhappy to see you are alive, though. You proved useful, and I have more people for you to question."

Alive? That was a little dramatic, wasn't it? Of course I was alive.

A woman in a white apron with small horns protruding from her forehead came over to press her fingers to my wrist. "Her heart is finally steady, my lord. I think she's going to make it."

Make it? I sat up quickly, scooching down so my leg didn't pull on the shackle. I tried not to stare at the unseelie fae. I'd read about them, of course, seen sketches of what they might look like, but never had I gazed upon one in real life. It was less jarring than I thought it would be.

"How long was I out?" I asked, peering down at myself again. It looked like someone had attempted to give me a sponge bath and there was a tube hanging out of my arm and going to a clear bag that hung on a post. I'd seen them in the medical ward back in Faerie for severely dehydrated patients, but I'd never had need of one.

"Three days," the woman, who I assumed was some type of nurse, said.

Three days?

Fear flushed through me. That was the longest ever.

The nurse called out to someone who stood at the door. "She needs food. Start with mush and work up to solids."

Mush. My stomach groaned in discomfort. It felt hollowed out and like it would swallow me up at any moment.

"No. Mush isn't necessary. I'll take a steak, roasted potatoes, chocolate cake, honey chicken, and vegetable soup please." I smiled sweetly. "Oh, and some soft bread with butter would be wonderful."

The nurse raised her eyebrows and she looked at Lord Stryker, who appeared to be trying to conceal a smile. "She gets the mush. We will see if she can earn the steak," he ordered.

I genuinely wanted to weep then. I hadn't realized how much I loved real food until this very moment.

"And please, for the love of my sanity, bathe her and let me know when she can use her magic again," he told the nurse.

"Yes, my lord." She bowed and he left the room.

The woman peered down at me and clicked her tongue. "I've been doing this awhile. Never heard a heartbeat that faint on someone who survived."

Her words frightened me to my core. I knew my heart was weak, of course I knew, but my mother babied me so much my entire life I had never really experienced anything like this. Three days? I had never thought it might kill me . . . until now.

After taking the tube and needle out of my arm, she unlatched the cuff around the bed post only to quickly reattach it to her own leg. So instead of being bound to a bed post I was bound to a nurse.

I eyed her. She wasn't tall, but she had some girth. I was weak, but after I regained some of my strength, I thought I could take her.

She must have read the calculating gleam in my eye because she sneered at me. "I feel it wise to tell you that my magic is powerful. If you try to subdue me, I will boil your blood from the inside out."

My eyes widened and I nodded. Scratch that, I would not be trying anything with her.

After a blissfully hot bath where I scrubbed my hair and skin so raw with scented soap that I was quite pink, she gave me a housemaid's dress to wear. It was navy blue cotton, simple and clean, so I wasn't complaining.

When the mushy oatmeal came, I scarfed it in under a minute.

"What's your name?" I asked her, practically licking the bowl clean. I was back to being tied to the bed.

"Shantel," she said as she felt for my pulse like the doctors did back home.

"I'm fine now," I told her. "Once I wake up, I'm fine until the next overexertion."

She pursed her lips but nodded. Shantel didn't like me, but she seemed serious about her job of keeping me alive.

I begged for another bowl of mush and she had it delivered. "Don't eat too fast or you will throw up," she cautioned.

I inhaled the bowl and asked for a third, but a huge belch had me retracting the request. I put my hand over my mouth after, my eyes wide. Somewhere along the way, I'd forgotten I was the crowned princess of the Fall Court. It's amazing what an empty belly and a few days in a dungeon had done to me.

"Apologies," I said. "I forgot myself."

Shantel just waved me off, ignoring my unrefined behavior. "Rest. Tomorrow we will see how you feel so you can complete this project for Lord Stryker."

Project. Is that what we were calling it when I interrogated fae to see if Lord Stryker needed to kill them?

I was tired, though. "Hey, did you hear about the Northern lord marrying someone named Dawn?" I asked her.

Her gaze clouded over and she looked at the doorway as if to make sure we were not being overheard. "We don't speak about that abomination," she said and got up and left the room.

Abomination? Wow. They must really have done it. Dawn married an Ethereum lord.

I lay there in shock for a full hour before I drifted off to sleep.

The next several days were a monotony of questioning Lord Stryker's guards, castle staff, and anyone else close to him. I was beginning to see this man's paranoia when he sent me his very own tailor. What, did he think he was stealing fabric from him?

But his suspicions proved fruitful. It began to become sad—the amount of people I caught that had stolen from him or planned to was surprisingly large. I even stopped an assassination attempt on his life.

After a full day of interrogation, Stryker moved bent down to unlock my leg cuff so I could be returned to my bedroom, but I grasped his hand to still him.

He looked up at me, a wayward strand of hair falling across one eye.

Although I still referred to him by his formal title out loud, at some point over the last couple of days, I'd shifted from thinking of him as *Lord* Stryker, to more often than not just Stryker. It wasn't a development I wanted to think too deeply about. We'd spent so much time together a familiarity had developed.

"I'm sorry that you can't trust anyone in your life," I said honestly.

Today was the first day that my heart had softened to his cause. I didn't condone what he did, but today I understood it. The man was so rich that a quarter of his household staff was either stealing from him or thinking about it.

His breath hitched, and his eyes fell to my lips.

"I told you not to use your power on me," he growled.

I grinned. "I wasn't."

He released my hand and a slight flush crept up his cheeks.

"I have interrogated every person you have asked me to, at the risk of my health, for days on end. I want to ask two things from you in return. If I may." I humbled myself.

He stood, leaving me locked to the chair. "And what might those be?"

"I would like you to bring the prisoner named Eli up to me so that I may prove his innocence and he can be released."

His gaze darkened. "What do you care about some kid from the mines?"

I matched his glare. "I care about innocence and justice. I am a princess where I come from. I have a duty to my people, as you have a duty to yours."

He bristled at the accusation that he might not be doing his duty very well.

"And the second thing?" he asked.

I straightened in my chair. "Tonight, for dinner, I want a twelve-ounce medium-rare steak with garlic potatoes. I'm sick of the mush, and I've earned it." I'd eaten mashed potatoes, broth, creamed rice, oats, and anything else you could think of that made a slop noise when you threw it in a bowl. I was done with that.

The corner of his lips quirked into a smile.

"Jennings," he snapped, and the door opened to reveal his most loyal guard. My interrogation had gotten the man a promotion. He loved Lord Stryker and would never think of stealing from him, and wanted to kill anyone who dared speak against him.

"Yes, my lord." Jennings stood erect, waiting for a command.

"Go fetch the miner boy. Eli," he said and relief washed through me. He was giving me what I wanted. Well, half of it.

He peered down at me then. "I'll tell you what. If Eli is innocent, like you say, you get your steak dinner."

I gulped. "And if he's not?"

"Then I'll make you carry out his sentence."

My stomach clenched.

"And what is his sentence?" I asked.

Nervousness rushed through me as Stryker held my gaze. He wasn't smiling, but the gleam in his eye told me he was taking pleasure in making me squirm. "Death."

The uneasiness in my belly exploded into full-blown panic.

"What's that look for, little witch?" Stryker asked with a hint of a smile. "You've been so adamant that the young boy is innocent, that he was falsely accused. Surely there's no need to worry."

I swallowed my fear, not wanting Lord Stryker to see the truth, that I hadn't actually used my magic on Eli, so I didn't know if he was in fact innocent. Although it felt like he already knew.

I put my shoulders back and lifted my chin, putting on my princess front and forcing all emotion from my face.

"And when you learn he's innocent?" I said, challenging him.

Something sparked in Stryker's gaze, and if I didn't know better, I'd say it was respect. "If the boy is in fact innocent, like you claim, he'll be released and given rations to bring back to his family for the amount of time he's been in my dungeon."

I blinked back at him. I'd hoped for the release, but hadn't expected Lord Stryker to go above and beyond, atoning for a false imprisonment.

He must have seen the shock on my face because his mouth flattened into a scowl. "I'm not a monster," he snapped, and I kept my mouth shut because I still wasn't fully convinced that was true. "If the boy is blameless, that means I've deprived his family of an extra set of hands to help feed them all this time. They are owed their due."

"That's very . . . *just* of you," I said, reining in my emotions once again. They had a nasty habit of getting out of my control when I was around the growly fae. Something I found very annoying.

"I pay my debts," he reiterated, getting agitated, but before he could say more, the cell door creaked open and a guard hauled in a young unseelie fae that I assumed was Eli.

With his rounded face and lanky figure, he looked even younger than I'd imagined. On the cusp of being a young man, but not quite there yet.

I'd met many different types of unseelie over the last several days, but I'd never seen someone like him before. His skin was gray with hardened patches over his cheekbones, the ridge of his brow, and along both forearms. It almost looked as if he was partially made of stone. Two small horns peeked out from his mess of black curls. And rather than nails on the ends of each finger, he had small talons that came to a point.

The boy's wide eyes swiveled back and forth over the room, taking in Stryker first before swinging over to where I was tethered to the torture chair at my ankle. At least I wasn't strapped down fully like I had been the first day, but it was still obvious I was as much Stryker's prisoner as he was.

When his gaze collided with mine, I saw that his eyes were filled with terror. My heart instantly went out to him.

"The prisoner you requested, my lord," the guard said and pushed the boy further into the room.

"M-m'lord," Eli said and tried to bow deeply, but he was shaking so badly that he stumbled a step. The guard roughly yanked him up by the scruff of his neck, and Eli winced.

"Stop," I yelled, pulling at my ankle restraint as I positioned myself to leap up if needed. "Don't touch him."

Fear flashed over the guard's face, showing he had some sense after all, and he instantly removed his hand from Eli and took a half step back.

That's right. I might be shackled to this infernal chair, but that didn't mean I wasn't dangerous.

"Aribella?" the boy tentatively asked, his gaze searching. He must have recognized my voice.

I nodded, forcing a smile to help put him at ease. "Yes, Eli. It's me."

He breathed a sigh of relief. "I didn't know what happened to you," he said. "I was moved into a different cell. I was worried that Lord Stryker might have—" His head snapped toward Stryker, who he'd likely momentarily forgotten was there, and he shrunk into himself.

Stryker took a step forward and fear filled Eli's eyes again.

I made a noise of protest and shot Stryker a look of admonishment. Couldn't he see the fae was terrified enough?

Catching my glare, Stryker rolled his eyes, but didn't move any closer to Eli. Instead, he gestured toward him as if to say, *get on with it already.*

"It's going to be all right," I assured the young fae. "I've told Lord Stryker that you are innocent. You're here right now so we can prove it, and then you'll be released to return to your family."

Eli peered back at me, his face part-hopeful and the other part still stuck in fright. "Prove it? How?"

Oh no. If Eli kept talking, he might reveal I hadn't used my magic on him to get him to tell me the truth. I couldn't let that secret get out. Stryker would be furious.

"Remember how I used my magic on you back in the cell?" I asked, knowing he was going to nod, which he did because I'd used my magic to calm him. "Well, I'm just going to do that again. I'll make you feel relaxed, and all you have to do is tell Lord Stryker what you told me before. The truth about the smuggling and how you had nothing to do with it. And I promise everything will be okay. Can I use my magic on you again?"

I hadn't asked any of the other fae I used my magic on if they were okay with it, but none of the others had been a terrified young boy who'd had to endure weeks of torture in Lord Stryker's horror-filled dungeon. The boy had been through enough. The least I could do was show him this kindness.

Eli nodded, his curls falling onto his forehead as he kept a wary eye on Lord Stryker.

Taking a deep breath, I tried to calm my heart. I felt it flutter, an early warning sign that an episode was coming on. I'd already exerted myself today, so I probably shouldn't be using much more of my magic, but I wasn't going to let Eli suffer just because I was worn out. I could do this.

Closing my eyes, I took some relaxing breaths, willing my heart to slow. When I felt the beats even out, I pushed my magic on Eli like I'd been doing for days on others. I'd done this so often now that it wasn't hard anymore to layer on the emotions and feelings I needed to in order to put a fae in a truthful state of mind.

After only a few seconds, Eli's body started to relax, then his eyelids drooped. I peered at Stryker to make sure he saw that Eli was in a suggestible state of mind. He nodded to me.

"Eli, are you part of an underground smuggling ring that is stealing gold and gems from Lord Stryker?" I asked, getting straight to the point.

Eli shook his head. "No. My family could use the coin, but I would never take something that wasn't mine."

Anxiety I hadn't even realized I'd been holding on to exited my body, leaving me feeling almost euphoric. I knew Eli was trustworthy.

I shot Stryker a triumphant look. I was about to pull back my magic, but he held a hand up and told me to wait. Stryker took a step toward Eli, but this time the unseelie barely noticed the lord moving closer.

"Do you know anything about the smuggling ring?" Stryker asked.

Eli nodded, and fear pierced my heart. I'd forgotten that he said his cousin asked him to be part of it. Stryker might still punish Eli for knowing something, even though he wasn't technically part of it. But even if Eli went free, he was about to damn one of his family members.

There was nothing I could do about that now, though. If I pulled back my magic, Stryker would just force me to use it against Eli again.

"My cousin, Caleb, asked me to join, but I told him no. I didn't want any part of it."

I released a relieved sigh. At least Eli was clearing his own name. There's no way Stryker could accuse him of being a traitor. Even under the influence of my magic, it was clear he was a loyal citizen who wanted to do the right thing.

"When will the thieves strike next?" Stryker asked, taking another step forward so now he was practically in Eli's face.

"I don't know," Eli answered calmly.

"Who is helping them get away with it?"

"I don't know," Eli answered again, his voice monotone.

"Well, what do you know?" Stryker ground out. A muscle in his jaw popped because it was clenched so tightly.

After spending so much time with him over the last several days, I'd picked up on some of his tells. The clenched jaw was definitely one of them. He was furious, and that didn't bode well for Eli or his cousin.

"About what?" Eli asked.

A vein throbbed in Stryker's temple and I worried he was only seconds away from lashing out at Eli. I didn't think the young fae was being purposefully evasive, just that Stryker wasn't asking the right questions. With my magic keeping Eli enthralled, he was simply answering them as honestly as possible, not picking up on what Stryker was really looking for. Details on the smuggling ring.

"Eli," I said, jumping in to try to defuse Stryker's anger. "Could you tell us the names of any of the other smuggling conspirators?"

Eli shrugged. "I'm not sure of any of them other than my cousin."

"If you had to guess," I said, prompting him to keep going. I hoped that if he gave Stryker enough good intel, he would still honor his promise and let Eli go.

Eli lifted a hand and started scratching his head, completely unaware of how tenuous his position was right now. "Well, my cousin fell in with a rough group a few months back. If I had to guess, I'd say it was the lot of them who were running everything."

"Do you know any of their names?" I asked, and Eli rattled off a few, which made me breathe a little easier, and the vein in Stryker's brow stopped throbbing.

"And when your cousin approached you, did he say specifically what they were going to smuggle?" I asked.

Eli nodded. "Yes. He said they were going after the rubies. Said that they had a contact in the mine that would let them in at night to steal some of the gems."

I glanced over at Stryker. "Is there more than one ruby mine?"

Stryker shook his head. "Rubies are only mined in one location in the Jewel Spring Mountains."

The Jewel Spring Mountains sounded only vaguely familiar. I wish I'd spent more time studying the maps of Ethereum.

"Have you had any reports of any gems going missing?" I asked Stryker.

Stryker crossed his arms over his chest. "Not rubies, but plenty of others. They seem to hit only one mine at a time, stripping me of that gem and moving to the next."

"Which means you might still be able to stop the heist," I told him, feeling invested now.

"Perhaps," Stryker said. "But even if they do manage to steal from me, I'll make them illegal to trade with and they'll never be able to sell them on the open market."

"That won't matter," Eli said, surprising us both. "They don't sell the goods here in the Eastern Kingdom. They take them to the Southern Kingdom to hock them, selling them on the black market there. That's how they've gotten away with it for so long."

I was nervous about how much Eli actually did know about all of this, but when I looked back at Stryker, his anger seemed to have vanished. Instead, he had a thoughtful look on his face.

"Do you have any more questions, Lord Stryker?" I asked, forcing my tone to stay light so I didn't make things worse by angering him.

"We're finished here," he said. My body sagged in relief as I pulled back the emotions and feelings I'd pressed upon Eli, but then tightened back up when he addressed his guard, "Get someone to take her back to her room and tell Shantel to pack a week's worth of clothing and supplies for her."

"A week's worth of clothing. Why?" I asked, feeling my heartbeat start to elevate.

"Because tomorrow we're leaving for the Jewel Spring Mountains," Stryker said.

I didn't know how I felt about leaving the castle. It made me nervous, but perhaps it would be the perfect opportunity to escape. The only problem was that I needed to find my dagger. I couldn't complete my mission without it.

"And my dagger?" I asked.

Stryker shot me a look that made the hairs on the back of my neck stand on end.

"Your dagger will remain safely here with my blacksmith where it cannot hurt me," he growled.

Okay, point taken.

Stryker started for the door.

"Wait," I called and he paused and looked over his shoulder at me. "What about Eli?" I asked. "Will you set him free like you promised?"

Stryker cast a quick glance at Eli, who was standing with his head hung low, staring at the floor. "The fae might technically be innocent, but he knows more than he let on and now he knows our plans. I can't allow him to go back just yet, but I will let him stay in my guest cottage until our investigation into Jewel Spring Mountains is over. Rations will also be sent to his family. I'm a fae of my word."

Relief rushed through me at that. He'd get out of this shadow dungeon, which was something.

Stryker strode toward the door and flung it open. He paused right before leaving the room and I braced myself, worried about what proclamation he might say next.

He looked at his guard. "And tell the kitchen staff to make a steak and send it up to her room for dinner," he barked. "Twelve ounces, medium rare, with garlic potatoes, hearty vegetables, a loaf of bread, and the cook's chocolate fudge cake."

My mouth started to water at the mention of the delicious food, but then Stryker's gaze swung to me and it went dry again. There was a hunger in his gaze that didn't look like it could be satiated with food. I didn't think he meant for me to read his face so easily, but I had. No one had ever looked at me like that before.

"She'll need to keep up her strength for where we are going," he said in way of an explanation and then left.

The door banged shut behind him, and I jolted at the

noise. I didn't know if I loved or hated the feelings Stryker just stirred in me. I only knew that they confused me. And that was dangerous, because no matter what, I was still determined to complete my mission. And that meant this could only end one way: with Lord Stryker's black heart in the palm of my hand.

Chapter Nine

I had nearly wept last night when the meal had been brought to my room. I ate every bite, I licked every crumb of chocolate cake from my fork, and afterwards I was so full I felt sick. Lord Stryker had shown me a kindness by giving me the meal, in fact more than I'd asked for, but I couldn't forget the monster that he was or what his ancestors had done to my people.

They stole our magic, cursed our land, and fled to this world in hiding.

A small bag of extra clothes was packed, and Shantel led me down the stairs to a carriage that waited out front with a royal entourage of fifteen heavily armed guards on horseback. I recognized every single face. I had interrogated each one of them and they'd gazed at me in fear.

"They call you the truth witch," Shantel told me with a slight smile, as if the name amused her.

Truth witch. That didn't sound very nice.

I ignored her and watched as she gave my bag to the porter and gestured to the front door of the carriage.

This was the first time my ankle had been unshackled, and the freedom felt amazing.

With a wave goodbye, I opened the carriage door and stepped inside, then swallowed a gasp when I saw Lord Stryker sitting on one of the bench seats.

"Oh, hello," I said, trying to cover my surprise as I shifted to sit across from him.

There was plenty of room for the both of us in the carriage, but it still felt like his essence filled every inch of the space, leaving none for me.

I settled in my seat and then my gaze flicked down to his ankle.

I groaned when I noticed the shackle ringing his ankle with a length of chain and an opened shackle attached to it. He smiled and picked up the other end, reaching beneath my skirt to grasp my left ankle.

"Excuse you." I pushed my skirt down and tried to yank my leg out of his grasp, but he held on.

Stryker rolled his eyes. "Don't flatter yourself, little witch. Desire is the last thing I feel towards you. You'd have to put me under one of your spells to get me to touch you like that."

His words hurt, like a knife through the heart and I couldn't help but frown. I shouldn't care what this monster thought of me, but hearing an attractive man say that he wouldn't ever desire to touch you never felt good.

He looked up into my gaze, saw the hurt on my face, and swallowed hard.

"You realize I have feelings, right?" I growled.

"Witches don't feel anything," he growled back, clicking the cuff into place and banging on the ceiling with his fist.

With a jerk, the carriage took off and Stryker nearly fell on top of me, before throwing himself back into the seat.

I was fuming mad at him. He thought I was a witch without feelings? How dare he insult me in such a way.

I glared at him for a solid hour, thinking murderous thoughts, thinking of things I would say to him and how many different ways I would win an argument. Thinking of how I would use my magic against him if I wasn't so terrified he'd turn my faestone dagger into a puddle of molten metal if I did.

The entire time he whittled, paying me no mind. A little knife was perched deftly in his giant paw of a hand and he scraped against a wooden block delicately, but I couldn't tell what he was carving yet.

"I'm not a witch!" I shouted after an hour passed and Stryker jumped, nearly piercing his own palm with the carving knife. "*You* are the one with the dark magic who comes from a long line of Ethereum lords that stole the magic of Faerie. *You* are the reason my people are at the risk of dying and losing their home. *You*, Lord Stryker, are a monster." My chest was heaving by the time I'd said my piece, but I felt better.

Stryker peered at me with venom in his gaze. He slowly set the knife and wood block down and leaned forward, getting into my personal space and breathing over my face. A fresh cinnamon scent washed over me, causing unexpected heat to bloom in my lower gut. My heart fluttered in my chest and my palms began to sweat.

"I will only say this once," he warned, his gaze flicking to my lips for half a second and then back up again. "Whatever you think you know about me and the past Ethereum lords is a lie. You have probably been lied to your entire life. *You* are the one who comes from a long line of assassins that have come to our peaceful home and killed our uncles, cousins, fathers, and children for centuries. *You*, Aribella, are the monster."

I reeled as if I'd been slapped, the back of my head hitting the window. "No. That's not true." I shook my head to illustrate my point. "*Your* ancestors put a curse on our lands. Every hundred years it ravages Faerie and without the heart of an Ethereum lord, it won't stop. Our water turns black, our crops fail, it's trying to kill us."

He raised one eyebrow. "Have you ever taken a moment to think why you need *our* hearts to stop a curse on *your* land? It sounds like you are stealing our magic, not the other way around."

His words shocked me into silence.

Why did we need the heart of an Ethereum lord? Because it contained the magic of Faerie that had been stolen, and we were just getting it back? That's what I'd been told, but . . .

I shook my head, reaching up to rub my temples. Lies,

these were lies. That's why we were coached to never let them speak.

Stryker watched me with curiosity. Was there even a little compassion in there, too?

But I wasn't done arguing. "For the record, I do not hail from a long line of assassins like Dawn does. The Summer princess always travels to Ethereum and returns with the heart. I'm from the Fall Court. None of my ancestors have ever traveled to this realm, and I've never killed a fae in my entire life."

"Yeah, I can tell," he said mockingly.

I reached out to smack his chest, but he caught my hand midair, his big thumb pressing into the middle of my palm. We locked eyes and it felt like all of the oxygen had been sucked from the space. I could hardly breathe, pinned by his gaze.

His eyes narrowed. "Are you using your power?"

Hurt washed over me, and I yanked my hand back. "I assure you that your feelings are entirely your own."

But his wall was back up, and he was watching me through a veil of suspicion.

I shook my head. "Do you trust anyone?"

He laughed dryly. "No. Least of all a witch that can manipulate my feelings."

I sighed and leaned my head against the cushioned side of the carriage.

"This is going to be a long ride."

After riding for what felt like forever, we stopped for the night. The guards made camp in a beautiful green meadow just off the main road. A fire and multiple tents were set up. Lord Stryker hooked his elbow into mine and all but dragged me to the largest tent, our ankles still shackled together. When we got inside, he unlatched the shackle from his ankle first, then mine, and tied me to the post supporting the middle of the tent. Off to the side were two large cots, both with light blankets as the weather was agreeable.

"Umm, are those two cots for you and me?" I asked nervously. They were awfully close together.

Stryker walked over to the large desk in the middle of the room and glared at me. "Yes, I don't trust anyone else to keep an eye on you."

"I'm not a big runner," I announced, but he ignored me. "So you can take this off." I shook my foot to rattle the chain.

Stryker just ignored me, and I growled in frustration.

A messenger came in holding a few letters, and Lord Stryker waved to him, leaning back in his desk chair. "Tell me."

The messenger nodded. "The farmers send their thanks for the compensation of their lost crop due to fungus contamination."

Stryker waved it off. "Yes, yes, they are welcome. Next?"

The messenger burned the letter in a metal bin of glowing coals near the open door. Moving to the next, he shifted a little uncomfortably.

"The moment you left the castle in Easteria, there was a

robbery attempt by three civilians. They were subdued and nothing was taken. They are in the dungeon awaiting your return."

Stryker just sighed, looking over at me as if to say, *see, I can't trust anyone.*

But I was still stuck on the fact that he'd compensated his local farmers for a crop loss. He didn't need to do that.

Stryker waved his hand again and the messenger put that letter into the fire too, pulling the final one up to read.

"It's from your brother, Lord Roan. Again," the messenger said and Lord Stryker froze, body going stiff.

I sat up straighter, sure that he wouldn't allow the private message to be read in front of me, but Stryker nodded, indicating that the messenger go on.

"His people are still sick. It's getting worse. They are overwhelmed and out of supplies. There is a list of what he desperately needs. He's . . ." His gaze flicked to me. "Asking for any information on where the next princess of Faerie might be. It looks like this went out to all of your brothers."

My heart knocked against my chest. They were looking for me? What sickness was over his people?

Stryker sharpened his gaze. "Tell him nothing of Aribella."

The messenger nodded. "Of course, my lord. And the sickness?"

Stryker stared at his hands as if they might make the decision for him. "Send the supplies he needs anonymously, in unmarked boxes."

The messenger dipped his chin in agreement, pulling out

the list of supplies and tucking it into his pocket. Then he burned the letter before leaving the tent.

I frowned. Why would Stryker not want credit for helping his own brother?

"What sickness?" I asked, unable to help myself.

Stryker was looking over some papers and signing things on his desk. "Some plague that your predecessor caused. It's my understanding that it began on their wedding night. I don't really care."

My brows bunched together in the center of my forehead. "Dawn?" A plague began affecting the people of the north on the night Dawn married? Was it just a coincidence, or something more?

Stryker glanced over at me. "I assume she used her little witch magic to influence my brother to fall in love with her and marry him. The plague is probably her spell backfiring."

"Dawn doesn't have magic to influence like mine: it's unique. She manipulates sunlight and she's incredible at it, but she certainly can't control your feelings *or* start plagues." I was desperate to stick up for my fellow princess of Faerie.

He said nothing and I was tired of talking, so I leaned back against the support pole and dreamed up ways to escape. All of which ended with me just roaming the realm alone forever, without the faestone dagger, as my people back in Faerie died.

I thought of fleeing and trying to find Dawn but, as unbelievable as it was, it sounded like her loyalty to our people was dead and her devotion now lay with her new husband. I was on my own in this. I needed to gain Lord

Stryker's trust and get the dagger back, and I could only come up with one way to do that.

Despite his protests, I saw the spark in the Ethereum lord's eyes whenever he looked at me. And he repeatedly accused me of using my magic on him when I hadn't. There was something there, I was sure of it.

Forgive me, Mother.

Operation seduce the meanest fae alive was now in full effect.

After grumbling about how hungry I was for the fourteenth time, I was finally untied and Stryker brought me outside to eat. Probably just to shut me up, but I was okay with that to get a small amount of relief from these chains. We all ate by the fire and then turned in to our tents for the night. The cotton dress that I was wearing wouldn't be terribly uncomfortable to sleep in, but since I was now shamelessly going forward with "operation seduce Lord Stryker" I turned to him as we stepped into our tent.

Gathering my courage, I gave him my back. "Can you unlace me?"

"What?" His voice dropped an octave.

I peered over my shoulder at him, doing my best to give him my imitation of a sultry glance. "You have deprived me of a dressing attendant and I can't sleep in this giant, heavy thing."

I felt a little silly, but then I watched his Adam's apple

bob right before he strode over and began to yank at the laces quickly.

"Careful there, big boy, you're going to tear it," I scolded him.

His fingers stilled, and he began to gently unlace the thicker corset portion of my dress, revealing the thin, white cotton chemise I would sleep in. I couldn't see him, but I could hear his breathing and it had definitely gotten heavier.

Once he was done, I let the heavy dress fall to the floor and stepped out of it. Turning, I faced him and even though I had intended to ignite his interest, I was still surprised to see him staring at me with hunger in his gaze.

With slightly shaky hands, I grasped my chemise at the knee and pulled it up to reveal my bare legs. "Shackle me, captor," I told him, and he gave me a slow grin that caused those legs to go weak.

What was I doing? Trying to seduce him and lose myself in the process?

Stryker bent on one knee and grasped my ankle with his bare fingers, enclosing the cold metal cuff there, dragging his fingers across my calf as he fastened it.

I nearly moaned at the touch and had to shake myself to snap out of it. He'd accused me of witchcraft time and time again, yet it felt like he'd just put a spell over me.

I shouldn't be having these feelings for a monster. An Ethereum lord.

After securing the other end of my shackle to his own ankle, Stryker rose to his full height and looked down at me. A heavy energy swirled in the air between us, making me lightheaded. Or was that just my faulty heart pumping too quickly?

Then I felt the cold bite of metal into my wrists. When I looked down, I saw that he'd bound my hands together too.

Really? "Is that necessary?"

"I said that I didn't trust anyone else to keep an eye on you, but I never said anything about trusting *you*. I don't take chances while I sleep anymore." With that he dragged me over to the cot and connected a chain to my bound wrists, securing it to the frame of the cot.

I swallowed a sigh. It would be uncomfortable to sleep with my hands connected and one foot shackled to him, but I would make do.

All my dreams of actually escaping while on this assignment started to look slim.

With my gaze still fastened on Stryker, I pulled back the covers on the cot and slid in between the crisp sheet and light blanket. The awareness that we'd be tethered to each other in sleep created an intimacy that I was sure he hadn't intended.

I swallowed, wetting my suddenly dry throat and then ran my tongue over my lips. Lord Stryker's gaze flared and I held my breath in both anticipation and dread, sure he was going to do something. But after several seconds, he turned his back, shucking off his coat as he readied himself for bed.

With my heart still beating erratically, I couldn't discern if I felt relief or disappointment that he'd turned away from me.

After laying his coat over the foot of his cot, Stryker doused the only lantern in the tent, plunging us into relative darkness. It took my eyes only a few moments to adjust and then I picked up the outline of his body as he yanked his shirt over his head to sleep bare chested.

I sucked in an involuntary gasp and Stryker froze, glancing over his shoulder at me. I wanted to turn away, to pretend that I was already sleeping, but I couldn't make myself do it. My fingers itched to reach out and graze over his muscular back, and I had to ball my fist to keep from doing anything.

Would his skin be as warm and smooth as I imagined?

Stryker's gray-blue eyes seemed to flash in the low light, like a predator's gaze. Goose bumps broke out on my arms and the fine hairs on the back of my neck prickled. My body knew when I was in danger, even if my mind was leading me in another direction completely.

Stryker removed his boots, secured the other end of the shackle to his ankle, and then slid under his own bedding. The chain pulled taut as he shifted positions, reminding me of how we were still physically connected, even if we weren't sleeping in the same bed.

Somewhere between leaving the Easteria castle and arriving here, there was a change going on inside me. I didn't know if it was because I'd seen Stryker be merciful towards his people and brother today by compensating for the lost crops and sending supplies. Or if the handsome lord and our close proximity were wearing down my defenses.

"Go to sleep, Aribella," Stryker ordered in a deliciously gruff voice before turning on his side and facing away from me.

I wanted to obey him and fall into blissful unawareness, but how could I sleep when my body had never felt so alive?

As I stared at the giant mountain that was Stryker's form, I finally understood how Dawn might have truly fallen in love with her own Ethereum lord.

Chapter Ten

If I'd thought the carriage ride the day before had been tense, I was wrong. Today was infinitely worse. Whatever moment we'd shared the night before seemed to widen the gulf between us rather than soften Stryker toward me like I'd hoped.

He'd hadn't spoken a word to me that morning when we'd woken, and barely looked in my direction. After yanking his shirt and coat back on, he'd shackled me back to the support pole in the tent and then left. I was just glad he'd removed the wrist cuffs first. A maid appeared a few minutes later to help me wash up and get into a new dress.

I didn't see Stryker again until I reentered the carriage to find him sitting on the bench seat with a tense jaw and his arms crossed over his chest. He hadn't so much as flicked his gaze toward me when I took a seat across from him, or since then, for that matter. I'd tried to engage him in conversation

more than once, but the most I'd gotten out of him were a couple of grunts. He'd been a veritable statue for hours.

I occupied myself by looking out the window. Stryker's land was breathtaking. On our way to the Jewel Spring Mountains, we passed fields of red tulips, buttery daffodils, and pink peonies. Their fragrance wafted through the open window of the carriage, creating a heavenly scent. The cherry blossom trees that lined a good portion of the road were dripping with so many white and pink blooms that it was a mystery how the fragile limbs weren't stooped all the way to the ground. The colorful lightness of the Eastern Kingdom contrasted so acutely with the demeanor of its lord; it was hard to reconcile that Stryker ruled over this land.

But even the beauty of his lands couldn't lift my spirits and I went over the night before in my head again and again, trying to figure out where I'd gone wrong. I replayed the evening before I struggled to devoid myself of emotions. I'd been attracted to the dark lord. It wouldn't do me any favors to lie to myself about it. But I would have bet my life, my very court, on the fact that he'd been affected as well. So why was he ignoring me now?

My plan to get my dagger back and use it to cut out Lord Stryker's heart relied on my ability to seduce the cold lord, but the sad truth was, I was no seductress. Surely someone skilled or trained in this way would know how to break through this barrier he'd put up between us, but as it was, I was clueless.

Will you even be able to kill him? My mind whispered

quietly to me, causing doubts to swirl and a rock to settle in my stomach.

I wasn't an assassin any more than I was a seductress. But it didn't matter what I was or wasn't, so I hardened myself and deadened my heart.

I had a job to do, and one way or another, when all was said and done, I would hold Stryker's heart in my hands, or die trying. Lives depended on it.

The carriage came to a sudden stop and I jolted forward, face planting into Stryker's broad chest. Embarrassed, I mumbled an apology as I tried to right myself, only to somehow get my hand tangled in the fabric of his coat and fall more fully into him. I was practically sitting on his lap now, and I felt my cheeks heat as I remembered how adamant he was in the carriage the day before about not wanting to touch me.

As I tried to clumsily extract myself, he set his hands on my biceps and gently, but firmly, moved me off him and back to my own seat. His hands lingered on me a moment longer than necessary, but then he cleared his throat and removed them. Now I was the one who couldn't bring myself to look at him.

"Are you hurt?" he asked, and I was surprised that he cared, let alone asked.

"No. I just wasn't prepared for the stop," I said by way of explanation.

When I finally looked up, it was to see him staring back at me for the first time that day. I thought I saw a touch of vulnerability on his face before he shuttered his features.

Breaking our stare, he leaned to the side and yelled out the window, asking the driver what had happened.

"I'm sorry, m'lord," the driver responded. "There are some beggars in the road. I'll get the whip and clear them out."

"No!" I shouted.

A whip. How barbaric.

Before I even realized what I was doing, I'd gotten up and reached for the carriage door to stop the driver. The problem was I'd forgotten I was shackled to Stryker and so I only made it to the first step before my leg pulled out from under me. My momentum kept my body moving forward and I shrieked as I tumbled headfirst out of the carriage.

I squeezed my eyes shut, putting out my hands, bracing myself for the pain of the fall, but rather than connecting with the packed dirt below, something wrapped around my middle and halted me mid-fall.

When I cracked my eyes open, it was to find I was hovering in the air, my body horizontal to the ground. It took me a moment to realize that Stryker's rope-like shadows were wrapped around my waist and chest, keeping me suspended in the air.

Craning my neck, I peered over my shoulder to see Stryker exit the carriage behind me. His hand lifted to control his shadows. With a flick of his wrist, my body shifted vertically, and as Stryker descended the steps, my feet also touched down on the ground beside him. I was about to thank him for saving me from the fall when the crack of a whip rent the air.

The beggars.

Before I could take off again, Stryker reached down and scooped me up with an arm under my knees and another behind my back as he tucked me into his chest. There was just enough slack between our shackles that he could carry me in his arms comfortably.

With purposeful steps, he strode forward, barking at his driver to stand down. Once we rounded the horses, Stryker set me back down and snatched the whip from the driver's hand.

The fae beggars were huddled together in the middle of the road with their heads together and backs facing us. They were green-skinned unseelie with delicate, transparent wings. They looked like a family: a father and mother with two small children, and with horror, I realized the driver had already struck one of them. The one I assumed was their father had a rip in the back of his shirt, right between his wings, which was turning red with welling blood.

The children were crying hysterically, and the man and woman apologized to them, trying to steer them off the road and out of danger. Without thinking of the repercussions, I sent my magic out, blanketing the whole family with calm, trying to make them feel safe and less frightened. The children stopped their hysterics almost immediately.

Stryker's accusatory gaze swung to me, but I refused to feel guilty for helping them. The poor fae were traumatized, so I just raised one eyebrow as if challenging Stryker to tell me not to use my magic.

"It's okay. We won't hurt you again," I said in a soothing voice as I stepped toward the family.

Stryker moved with me so I could comfort them better, but even with my calming magic on them, the family shrunk away from me, keeping their faces hidden.

I looked at Stryker with a troubled gaze. The fae that was whipped needed help. As a royal, I healed quickly, but not all fae did.

Thousands of times as a child, I wished that my royal healing would extend to my heart, but my heart was not an injury that could be healed. It was a defect I was born with. And these fae were vulnerable. Some could die from infection before a wound healed.

"Do we have a physician with us, or a healer?" I asked. The latter was rare, but some of the Ethereum lords were known to employ them, according to Master Duncan.

Stryker pressed his lips into a hard line. I couldn't read his expression, but then he turned his head and barked an order, calling for bandages and healing ointment. That must mean there wasn't a physician or healer with us, so it was up to me.

Bending over, Stryker opened the shackles at our ankles, separating us. He gave me a look that I interpreted to mean that he wasn't letting me out of his sight, but that was fine because I was just grateful to be able to move freely.

One of Stryker's men came running with the bundle of supplies he'd asked for. The family had moved off to the side of the road, and when Stryker and I approached, they tried to shuffle away from us.

"We're so sorry, m'lord," the father said with his face still turned away. His body shook, probably from the pain of his wound. "We didn't realize it was you. We came down from the Northern Kingdom to stay with family, but were robbed while we slept last night. We just wanted to ask for some coin to get to my brother who lives a few towns over. Please grant us mercy to leave you in peace."

When I looked at Stryker, his brow was knit. He seemed lost for words.

"You're not in trouble," I said, speaking for Stryker. "We're sorry for what happened with the driver." I pushed more of my calming magic on the family, trying to help them feel peaceful and safe. "We only want to help. Would you please let me dress your wound?"

I thought for a moment he would refuse, but the soothing emotions I was pouring on them must have finally started to work because the family broke apart and turned to us, each of the children clutching one of their parents.

I gasped when I got a look at them. Black veins webbed out from their eyes, weaving across their faces and disappearing under their clothes. The father was by far the worst, but the mother and both children showed signs of a similar ailment, whatever it was.

"The plague," one of Stryker's guards shouted behind me, and then I heard their feet running in the other direction. The plague? Like the one from the letter sent from Stryker's brother, Roan?

I tried to move closer to the family. These fae needed

help, but Stryker's arms wrapped around my stomach and he hauled me back into his chest.

"What are you doing?" I complained as I squirmed against him.

"Can't you see?" he snapped. "They're diseased. Contagious."

I glanced back at the family and they'd shuffled even farther away, cowering from us.

"You don't know that," I said to Stryker and then called out to the family. "What happened to you?"

The father and mother exchanged a glance.

"We're not contagious. We're cursed," the father said, once again speaking for his family. "All the unseelie in the Northern Kingdom have been struck with it. Those of us with stronger magic have been hit the hardest: some unseelie have been in a coma-like state for months. None of our healers have been able to help, and every day we grow weaker. It won't be long until I'm unable to provide for my family. My brother lives here in the Eastern Kingdom and offered to shelter us."

A curse? And just in the Northern Kingdom?

"Has this curse spread to anyone in the Eastern Kingdom since you crossed the border?" Stryker asked, his voice sharp with concern.

Fear flashed over the unseelie's face, but he shook his head. "No. It only affects unseelie who were within the boundaries of the Northern Kingdom when the curse hit on the night of Lord Zander's marriage to Lady Dawn. I swear it."

That reminded me of how the curse on Faerie started in the Summer Court and only passed through the realm one court at a time. Could the Northern Kingdom curse be somehow linked to the same curse on Faerie, or was it just a coincidence it had only struck one of the Ethereum kingdoms?

"And you say only the unseelie have been affected?" I asked.

He nodded.

I glanced over my shoulder at Stryker. "Let me go," I demanded. "I'm in no danger."

He looked down at me with tight features. "We don't know if what he says is true."

I could make him tell us the truth, but there was no time for that. Even now, I worried for the fae because his green skin had gone deathly pale. He was losing blood, and curse or no curse, he needed someone to tend to his back.

"Well, if he's lying, I'll just be one less problem you have to worry about," I snapped, and then ripped out of Stryker's grasp. I had no doubt he could stop me with only a flick of his magic, but he allowed me to cross to the family.

The father let me tend to his wound and I was relieved to see that even though it had bled a great deal; the cut wasn't as deep as I feared. After cleaning it the best I could, I slathered ointment on it and used the small strips of tape as stitches to pull the cut together. Then I covered it with clean bandages and gave the leftover supplies to his wife, who accepted them with profuse thanks.

I couldn't really do anything to help this family. I knew

nothing of this curse or how to stop it, but I hoped my kindness helped in some small way. I was about to turn to leave when Stryker appeared next to me, holding a bulging pack.

"Some clothes to replace your own, food, and coin," he said as he handed over the bag to the father. "I will also lend you one of my horses. Just set it free when you reach your brother's home and it will know how to find me."

He snapped his fingers, and one of his guards leaped off of his horse and handed Stryker the reins.

"Thank you, m'lord," the father said, his forehead practically touching the ground with how deeply he bowed. When he straightened, there were tears in his eyes.

Stryker nodded stoically and then laid a hand on my arm. "We should continue our journey so we can reach the inn by nightfall."

We'd done all we could for the family, so I nodded and after bidding them farewell, followed Stryker back to the carriage. I peered up and noticed that the driver had been replaced. I don't know what happened to the first one, but I hoped he was punished in some way. The man who had given up his horse for the family now rode next to the new coachman on the bench seat.

We settled back into the carriage, and Stryker rubbed his bottom lip as we started forward once again.

"Do you instruct your men to whip beggars often?" I couldn't help the growl that escaped me.

Stryker gave me a pointed look. "Last time a group of 'beggars' ambushed our carriage, I got this." He lifted his shirt to showcase a nasty puckered scar on his gloriously chiseled abdomen. "Sometimes beggars are raiders, but he never should have whipped an unarmed man with children."

I nodded, satisfied with that answer.

"Do you think the family can be cured somehow?" I asked.

"I don't know," he confessed. "If the illness is a result of a curse as they claim, I don't think there's much anyone can do for them."

His voice was even and his face expressionless, but I still felt as if seeing his brother's people for himself had deeply affected him. But perhaps that was just wishful thinking. How much empathy could a monster really have?

We fell into silence once again. I couldn't say exactly what occupied Stryker's thoughts, but my heart was heavy as my mind swirled with thoughts of curses and black hearts and the piercing gray-blue eyes of a particular Ethereum lord who I no longer knew if I could kill.

We reached the inn at nightfall. We were staying at the base of Jewel Spring Mountains in the small village of Blackrock below the ruby mine. The same ruby mine that Eli had said would be stripped of its riches.

Stryker wanted to interrogate people immediately to ferret out who was trustworthy, but the mine foreman was able to talk him out of it. The mines were closed for the day and ripping people from their beds would not be seen as reasonable.

After a warm meal, Stryker walked us upstairs to a room at the inn with only a single bed. I crossed my arms and gave him my most seductive glare even as my stomach tied in nervous knots.

"Stryker, if you want to share a bed, you can just say so. You don't need to invent excuses." I jingled the cuff on my leg that connected to him.

The left side of his mouth quirked as if he wanted to smile, but thought better of it. "Oh, have no fear. We won't be sleeping in the same bed."

I glanced around the room again, confused because there was definitely only one bed in the room.

When I turned back to him, he wasn't even trying not to smile anymore. Humor shone clearly in his eyes at some joke I wasn't privy to.

"There's only one bed," I said, stating the obvious.

He nodded. "I've asked that a bedroll be brought up for you. I'm sure you'll find the floor quite comfortable."

"The floor!"

The ground was worn hardwood that at least looked clean. I'd certainly slept on worse since arriving in Ethereum, but still. Phantom pains shot up my back just thinking about a full night on the hard surface, but maybe the bedroll would make it manageable.

Someone knocked on the door, and when Stryker opened it, the innkeeper was there. He handed Stryker a bedroll, a thin blanket, and the most pathetic-looking pillow I'd ever seen.

"Seriously?" I asked with a frown when the innkeeper

left and Stryker shut the door. I planted my hands on my hips and gave him my most haughty stare. "A true gentleman wouldn't allow a lady to sleep on the ground while he lay on a soft bed."

He looked over his shoulder at me and his gaze raked over me in such a blatant way that there was no disguising the hunger in his eyes. Immediately, heat bloomed low in my gut.

"I never claimed to be a gentleman," he said, his voice as rough as gravel.

The breath caught in my throat. I was wholly unprepared for the sensations igniting in my body and tried to take a step away from him, but the shackle prevented me from going too far.

Stryker bent over to spread the bedroll on the ground, breaking our stare, and I finally felt like I could breathe normally again.

I suddenly felt very glad we weren't sharing the small bed. The floor would be just fine.

Clearing my throat, I willed my body to calm down, praying he hadn't seen me blush in the low light.

After arranging the bedroll for me, Stryker straightened, looking weary. "I'm tired. Can we not argue and just go to sleep? We'll both have a long day tomorrow." As he said it, he pulled out the handcuffs and slipped the cool metal around my wrists.

I rolled my eyes, annoyance chasing away any longing still pumping through my veins. "Do you really think after today I would try to strangle you or something?"

He just stared at me, as if that's exactly what he thought. Great.

Stryker kicked off his boots, and I pulled my shoes off as well. He dropped his heavy coat and shirt to the floor and slipped into the tiny bed, the chain that tethered us tugging on my ankle.

Even lying in the bed alone, he hardly fit. His feet hung over the end and he was practically falling off the edge. I had to admit the both of us never would have fit unless I laid right on top of him.

Unwanted, a vision of myself sprawled across Stryker's chest rose to my mind. Our bodies pressed together and mouths were only inches apart.

The image was so vivid that it stole my breath with its intensity. It took a long moment to beat it and the sensations it caused away, which concerned me.

Seduction was shaping up to be a bad idea. I was too inexperienced to pull off something like this. I had no clue if it was even working on Stryker, but all this play acting only seemed to be confusing me more. Perhaps I needed to come up with a different plan?

Exhaustion pulled at me, and I decided to make that a problem for my future self. What I needed now was a good night's rest to get my mind back on track.

I'd worn a lighter dress today, one I could sleep in, so I laid down on the bedroll, grudgingly admitting to myself that it was surprisingly soft. The pillow was indeed abysmal, though.

With a deep sigh, I released all the tension I'd been

feeling and snuggled under the scratchy blanket. I rolled on my side and stared up at Stryker's profile as the moonlight filtered through the window and illuminated his face. He was already asleep, his breath slow and even.

He was a frightening man. He had shadow powers and kept people bound in a dark dungeon. But he also gave that family a horse today, and coin and clothing. He gave his brother aid when asked, but refused to take the credit for it.

He was a complicated fae, but I wasn't sure he was the evil monster Queen Liliana had told me to kill. To carve out his heart without ever letting him speak? It sounded cruel, but maybe that's just because I had let him speak and now I was under some spell. A spell that made him insanely attractive and morally gray.

It was a long time before I slept.

"My lord," A gruff voice woke me.

I screamed when I noticed a guard looming over the bedroll.

"What is it?" Stryker's voice called from the bed beside me, and everything came rushing back to me. I was at an inn. Sleeping on the floor next to Stryker.

The guard stepped back as Stryker sat up. I quickly scooted off my bedroll to get out of the way, and then Stryker got to his feet.

"One of the security guards we posted at the ruby mine

is dead. We sent someone to relieve him and found his throat had been slit."

The room was plunged into a supernatural darkness.

"Who did it?" Stryker growled.

The guard was now obscured by shadows, not even any moonlight illuminating him. "W-we don't know yet."

"Put on your shoes," Stryker said to me as he undid my hand and ankle cuffs. I did as I was told, too tired to argue.

After unshackling us, Stryker hooked his elbow into mine and yanked me towards the door. Within a few minutes, we had gotten on a horse; me hanging onto Stryker's waist, and then took off up the mountain with a dozen of his guards.

As we rode, wisps of shadows rolled along the trail beside us. Stryker's magic was terrifying and impressive all at once.

I clung to his waist as the horse we rode on galloped up the mountain on a well-worn path that had been covered with bricks. It was wide enough for a cart.

Within a half hour, we had reached the top and the sun was beginning to rise. I wanted to take a moment to admire the sight, but Stryker dismounted quickly and then grabbed my waist, yanking me forward and off the horse as well. The shadows amassed around us as we walked, undulating menacingly.

A guard rushed to meet us, sweating and red-faced. "I've woken the inventory clerk and he says half the rubies are gone."

The shadows that had been trailing us converged into

the shape of a four-legged beast that grew until it was almost twice Stryker's size. It clawed at the ground and snapped its teeth in anger and then tipped its head back and howled at the sky as Stryker balled his fists.

I began to back away, but Stryker glanced over at me and I froze.

Stryker's dark magic was even more powerful than I imagined, and for a moment I almost didn't recognize him. But upon seeing my face, his own softened and a look of what might be regret or shame flashed across his features. As quickly as the beast had materialized, he dissolved into wispy shadows and was gone.

Stryker turned back to his guard, his body still taut as a bow. "How long do we suspect they have been gone?" His voice could cut glass.

"Two to three hours, sir. Maybe even four," the lead guard said. "What do you want to do?"

Stryker took in a deep breath, as if trying to steady himself. "We ride to the south. To capture these thieves in the black market they are no doubt going to sell *my* jewels in."

Before anyone could speak, Stryker grasped me by the hips and I yelped as he tossed me onto the back of his horse. He came up behind me this time and tore down the mountain like a rabid animal.

I didn't say a word. The truth was, my heart hurt for the Ethereum lord. No wonder he didn't trust anyone. No wonder I'd become so valuable to him.

The truth witch.

Everyone was trying to take advantage of him, steal from him, plot against him, and why? Because he was rich? That wasn't fair.

Once we got to the inn, we were packed up and ready to go within thirty minutes. Stryker sent a messenger ahead to inform his brother, Adrien, the Ethereum Southern lord, that he would be coming to his lands and why.

I got the impression by the way he spoke to the messenger that he hadn't talked to his brother in a long time.

Once we were in the carriage, Stryker secured the shackles around our ankles once again. We rode in silence for the first few hours; the carriage bounced wildly as we tried to make good time.

"I don't blame you," I said suddenly, and Stryker startled a little, as if he'd forgotten I was there. He was staring out the window at the morning sun, lost in thought.

"For what?" There was a vulnerability in his voice, as if he were begging me not to go too deep.

"For who you are. Why you don't seem to trust easily, how tight your security is. I can't imagine living with someone always plotting against me in my sleep."

He raised one eyebrow. "Are you plotting against me in your sleep?"

I smiled. "Maybe at first, not anymore," I answered truthfully, and his face went slack as more of that vulnerability showed itself.

He sighed, staring wistfully off into the mountains and giving me a full view of the scarred lines on the side of his face. Lines that, according to Eli, were given to him by a lover who had betrayed him. In truth, when I looked at his face, I hardly noticed them anymore. I didn't see a scarred man. I only saw Stryker, a devastatingly handsome fae who was starting to inch his way into my heart.

My heartbeat fluttered. This was bad. So bad. How could I save my kingdom if I grew attached to the man I had to kill in order to save it?

The simple answer was that I couldn't. I couldn't kill him. Couldn't save my kingdom.

"I would give it all up to have a normal life," he said suddenly, and I sat up straighter at that. "The riches, the castle, the lordship." He flexed his hands. "Even the power."

My heart shattered in that moment. "Why don't you?"

He peered at me, shaking his head. "An Ethereum lord is chosen by the magic in our bloodline. It chose me when my predecessor passed. There was no question, no ceremony, no consent. I have black blood, therefore I am destined for this."

We sat in silence for a moment. Both of us trapped by the weight of our titles and responsibilities.

"I guess I could give you back your dagger and then you'd free me from this life, but the burden would only fall to one of my nephews."

A single tear slipped down my cheek. I tried to swipe it away quickly, but it was too late. He saw and cocked his head to the side in interest. When our gazes locked, I knew with a certainty that I wasn't looking into the eyes of a monster, of a dark evil being beyond reach or reason as I had been told, but simply those of a man.

We'd been lied to growing up. If everything he said was true, then we had.

"It's not much different from a Faerie princess. I have no say; I am royal by blood."

It was true, and yet I loved my people, my palace, my duties.

My people.

"My people are going to die," I said, because even though it had been at the back of my mind, it was at the forefront now. A few more tears slipped over onto my cheeks. "And there is nothing I can do." I tried to control my emotions, not wanting Stryker to see me like this.

He watched me like you would watch a cat playing with a ball. Curious as to what I would do next. "My brother and his witc—wife said something about finding another way to help her people," he said, and I perked up at that.

She did? Dawn was looking for another way? Of course she would if she'd fallen in love with the Ethereum Northern lord. She wouldn't have been able to kill him either. And she wouldn't just abandon our people. I should have known that.

"Or you can always seduce me into giving you the dagger and take my heart," he mused.

I stiffened, because he was too good at reading me. Then I shrugged. "Seemed like a good idea a few days ago. Now I'm sure I couldn't have done it."

He went still. "Seduce me?"

I gave him a small smile. "Carve out your heart. Even to

save my people, I can't take your life. I'm not a killer, Stryker. I'm just a bookworm with a weak heart."

The energy in the carriage felt charged. Stryker's chest heaved slightly and I could see the pulse in his neck throbbing.

I leaned closer to him, wanting to reach out and touch him, but thought better of it. "Maybe you can help me? Get word to Dawn and I can try to find another way to save my people." I would do anything for there to be another way to break the curse. A way that didn't involve killing a man I was getting more and more attached to every day. "I don't want to hurt you or anyone else, but I can't give up on them." There was a pleading in my eyes.

Stryker swallowed hard, shaking his head as if dislodging his own thoughts. "I need some air," he said.

Reaching down, he unlocked his shackle and then, before I could say another word, he leaped out of the moving carriage and onto a cloud of waiting shadows.

Chapter Eleven

S tryker left me shackled to one of the corner posts inside the carriage and rode beside us on a horse, sending me a clear message that he didn't want to have any more conversations like that. We didn't stop to rest or sleep in our tents, instead, we rode through the night and all the next day. Stryker and I slept in the carriage sitting up. Barely sleeping was more like it. What had been a leisurely ride to the Jewel Spring Mountains on the way over had become a race to the southern border now. We rode fast and hard and I often felt nauseated from the way the carriage shook.

It felt like we'd been on the road forever by the time we reached the southern border. The flowering dogwoods, redbud, and magnolia trees of the Eastern Kingdom turned into beautiful and lush palm trees. The sun was low in the sky.

After crossing the border, we rode deeper into the

Southern Kingdom for several more hours. It was late into the night and at some point I'd nodded off again, but I woke with a jolt when the carriage finally came to a stop and Stryker's voice rang out.

"Get a ways off the road and make camp, then wait for word from me," he ordered one of his men. I peeked out the window to find him mounted on his horse only a foot from the carriage.

"You," he said, calling another one of his guards. He lowered his voice when the guard moved closer. "Take five men and change out of your uniforms and into plain clothes. Go to the gambling halls, brothels, and taverns and try to dig up any information you can about the black market here. Ask about rubies for sale, but be discreet."

The guards nodded before taking off, and then Stryker looked down and caught me peering at him from within the carriage. The moment his gaze connected with mine, I felt my heartbeat flutter. I took in a slow breath, embarrassed it only took a single glance to get me so flustered and at the same time thankful there was no way he could know that my heartbeat just spiked. But even as I thought it, his gaze dropped to my neck where I imagined he could see my pulse jumping wildly in my vein.

"Where are we?" I asked.

Why does my voice sound so breathy?

Stryker frowned down at me, but it only made my heart beat faster. What was wrong with me? The air between us had changed since that raw conversation in the carriage. He hadn't shackled himself to me in a while, and he'd stopped calling me a witch somewhere along the way.

"Just outside the town of Beggar's Hole," he said, and I let out a half-laugh.

"Beggar's Hole? You're kidding." That can't actually be the name of the town.

His frown turned into a full-blown scowl. "I wish I were. This is a gambling village in the northern region of the Southern Kingdom. A cesspool of corruption and our best guess as to the location of the black market where my stolen riches are being sold.

"We don't want to ride into town in a group and tip off the thieves, so we're splitting up. Some of my men will stay back and wait for my orders. You'll be riding with me. I'll need you by my side if we have to interrogate anyone. We're going to pretend to be a married couple to keep suspicions low."

Married couple?

I should have balked at that, but instead it somehow felt . . . right. Like an exciting role to play. And I wasn't half as freaked out about that as I should have been. Maybe I wasn't fully awake yet?

"Oh, very well," I said, proud that I managed to keep my voice steady.

Stryker dismounted and then came to the carriage, swinging the door wide open. Without getting in, he reached forward and grasped my ankle.

It was a chaste touch, but a pulse of warmth shot up my leg from where his fingers wrapped around me. I didn't have to look in a mirror to know that my cheeks were heating, but luckily Stryker's focus was on my shackle and not my face.

Reaching into his pocket, he pulled out a key and then a moment later, the shackle fell off my leg. Even though the shackle hadn't been terribly uncomfortable, it still felt amazing to be free of it. I looked down at Stryker with a question in my eyes only to find his gaze fastened on my lips.

Noticing I was watching him, he quickly straightened and cleared his throat. If I didn't know better, I'd say he was embarrassed.

"I can't keep you shackled if I want people to believe we're married," he said in answer to my unspoken question.

I shrugged. "Some people have weird marriages." I tried for a joke and was rewarded with the corner of his lips curling, but the smile was washed away almost as soon as I'd seen it.

He pressed his lips together in a hard line then and gave me a curt nod. Once I descended from the carriage, he put his hands on my waist and gently helped me onto the saddle of his horse before swinging up behind me. He barked a couple more orders to his men, and then we were off.

We moved at a brisk pace, but nowhere near as fast as we had the last time I rode in front of him when we were racing back to the inn from the plundered ruby mines. Stryker's arms wrapped around me from behind as he held the reins, his chest a firm but warm wall against my back.

His cinnamon and sandalwood scent was everywhere and utterly intoxicating. I had to stop myself from turning my face and burying it in his chest to get a better hit of it.

Being this close to him was turning out to be some sort of exquisite torture I'd never experienced before. I couldn't help but wonder if he felt it, too.

It was too short of a ride before we reached Beggar's Hole. The moon had passed the midpoint of the night sky, yet the streets were filled with rowdy fae. Rowdy *drunken* fae.

As Stryker slowed our horse to a walk, I took in the establishments that lined the main street. They were all still lit up and brimming with life. The balconies on the three-story townhouse on our right were filled with scantily clad women, yelling to the men below. My ears started to heat from embarrassment when I heard some of the things they said, and I pointedly looked away. I felt Stryker's chest rumble with laughter behind me.

On the other side of the street, a fistfight had broken out in front of a gambling hall. Shouted accusations of cheating rang out as two men grappled with each other. Stryker had to jerk the horse over when they fell to the ground and rolled into the street, but the fae that passed them hardly offered more than a cursory glance before moving on.

Beggar's Hole was like a whole new world. One I wasn't sure I was ready for, but I felt secure with Stryker's strong presence at my back. Something that I definitely wouldn't have said a few weeks ago. It's amazing how much can change in only a few weeks.

Stryker turned our horse down a side street and stopped in front of a narrow, four-story townhouse wedged between two near-empty taverns. There was a sign above the door that read, "Rooms for Rent".

He dismounted and tied the horse's reins to the hitching post out front. I started to get off as well, but before I could do much more than swing my leg over the horse's neck, Stryker's hands were on my waist, gently helping me down. He took his time, letting my body slide against his and not stepping back until my feet touched the ground. Even though I hadn't exerted myself at all, I found I was breathless.

"We'll stay here for the night," he said, his voice gruff.

With a hand on my lower back, he led me into the townhouse. The clerk behind the counter was half-asleep and jolted when Stryker announced we needed a room. After collecting payment, he sleepily handed a key to Stryker, telling him the room was on the top floor at the end of the hall.

As we climbed the four flights of stairs to reach our room, I felt Stryker's gaze on my back like a physical caress. This wasn't the first time we'd shared a room together, but something about *this time* felt weightier, more meaningful than before. Maybe it was because I was unshackled, so I felt less like his prisoner, even though in actuality I very much still was. Maybe it was because we were posing as husband and wife.

My stomach tumbled when we reached the dimly lit room. It was sparse, with only a washbasin atop a simple dresser, and a wooden chair next to another single bed that was pushed in the corner.

The bed wasn't much bigger than the one at the last inn. I eyed it, wondering if I was going to have to sleep on the floor again. And then I thought, if given the choice between the floor and sharing a bed with Stryker, which one would I choose?

I peered over at Stryker to find him staring back at me and knew instantly what my answer would be.

Heat bloomed in my gut and I pressed a hand to my chest, feeling my heart beat frantically beneath my palm. A wave of dizziness washed over me and I stumbled a bit, grabbing the foot of the small bed for support.

Stryker stepped in front of me, his unguarded gaze tinged with concern. "What's wrong? Is it your heart?"

Seeing the worry shining in his eyes only made my weak heart beat faster. Thank the stars he wasn't a mind reader because if he knew the thoughts running through my head, I would surely die of embarrassment.

"I'm fine," I said, taking in slow, even breaths through my nose to calm myself.

Taking my arm, Stryker led me to the side of the bed and encouraged me to sit down. The blanket beneath my hand was scratchy, and I focused on that to distract my mind from other, more excitable thoughts.

When I finally felt as if I had myself under control, I glanced up into Stryker's gray-blue eyes. So often Stryker's face was shuttered toward me, but looking at him now was like reading an open book. It was all there, plain for me to see.

Longing. Sadness. Concern. Desire.

I wondered if he realized how much he was revealing to me.

"Is your heart okay?" he asked.

"The spells come and go. I'm fine now," I assured him, but I could tell he wasn't convinced.

He reached out and took my hand, startling me. He placed his fingers on my wrist and then his lips moved silently, taking count. It took several moments to realize he was tracking my heartbeat.

"I'm fine, really," I said, suddenly shy. I tried to pull my hand back, but he held firm. When he swiped his thumb over the tender flesh on my wrist, I couldn't help the small intake of breath.

How could such a chaste touch feel so criminally good?

One corner of Stryker's mouth hitched up in a smirk. Smiles were infrequent for the Ethereum lord, and smirks were even rarer. It made my stomach tumble all over again.

"Your heartbeat is picking up," he said. "Should I be concerned?" He was teasing me, but the air between us was too charged to banter back.

I licked my lips to find them already sensitive. Stryker's gaze dropped to my mouth and I swear shadows swirled in the dark corners of the room.

Stryker leaned forward and the breath stilled in my lungs. Lifting a hand, he brushed a strand of my thick hair behind my ear and then let his fingers trail along my jaw.

"So soft," he all but whispered.

We were on the edge of a cliff. I felt it. One step forward and we'd fall over together.

Stars. I never wanted anything more than to take that step.

My eyelids felt heavy, and I let them drop to half-mast. I slanted my head back in silent invitation and heard Stryker's breath catch.

He moved even closer, aligning our lips so they were only a hair's breadth apart. So close I could almost taste them, but rather than closing that minuscule space, he held still.

My eyes slid closed of their own accord and I started to tilt my head, too desperate to feel his mouth against mine to wait for him, when I heard an all too familiar click.

I reared back and my eyes snapped open when I felt the cold metal cuff circling my wrist rather than his warm fingers. I was disoriented for only a few seconds, and then a churning cauldron of anger boiled over inside, searing away the last vestiges of desire he'd awoken in me.

He'd shackled me to the bed and used seduction to distract me while he did.

"You . . . you *fiend*," I spat, my rage made up of equal parts betrayal and humiliation.

I yanked on it, testing its strength and instantly knew that it would do its job of tethering me in place.

I looked back up at him with fire in my eyes. He'd risen to his full height and backed away several steps. To his credit, he didn't look smug, only resigned.

"Why?" I choked out, hating that my anger was already starting to tip toward sorrow. I glanced away, not wanting him to read in my gaze just how deeply he'd cut me.

"I have to go meet with my men and see if they've discovered anything," he said. His voice, stoic and even. Cold. I flinched at the tone as if I'd been slapped and I heard his slight intake of breath.

"I can't—" he started, a hint of warmth in his voice.

I looked up at him when he didn't go on and saw the conflict written on his face.

"I would have stayed here if you'd asked," I said, letting him see the truth of my words in my eyes.

His brow pinched and something deeper, more raw than indecision, fell over him. It felt for a moment like he warred with himself, but then one side won.

Throwing his shoulders back, he looked down on me with a coldness that chilled me. "No. Women aren't to be trusted. I can't have you running off to betray me."

Women aren't to be trusted. Where did *that* come from?

But then my gaze tripped over the scars on Stryker's face, reminding me of a time he had put his trust in a woman, and what it had cost him.

Hatred for the woman who betrayed Stryker rose up in my heart, for she hadn't just left scars on his face, but on his heart as well. I was seeing them now.

"Your gift is too valuable to me," he went on. "I can't take the risk that you'll flee. I'll be back before first light. You can rest here."

It felt like he'd pierced my chest with an ice pick. My gift was what was valuable to him. Not me, but my gift and what I could do for him.

I'd started to truly care for this man, but all he saw when

he looked at me was a means to an end. That more than stung, it cut.

Turning away from him, I wrapped my arms around myself as I curled on my side, facing the wall. I held on tight, feeling like Stryker had just sliced me down the middle and that if I let go, I'd break apart.

"Aribella," he whispered, his voice softening. "I didn't mean—"

"Just go," I said, cutting him off. I wanted to be alone now. "I'll be here. Your captive little truth witch to use as you see fit."

Stryker didn't leave right away. He stood in the middle of the room for several more minutes, silent. I curled into a tighter ball, wishing he would go already so I could let myself fall to pieces.

Eventually, I heard him stomp toward the door and throw it open. "I'll lock the door. You'll be safe," he said and then paused for another few heartbeats.

If he was expecting a response from me, he would be waiting for eternity, for I had nothing left to say to him.

He heaved a sigh and then the door closed. A second later, I heard the telltale sound of a lock being engaged.

I counted to thirty, and then let the tears that had been clawing at the back of my eyes escape. My throat tightened as I let myself feel this betrayal and fully process it. I'd been so stupid to trust an Ethereum lord. Queen Liliana would kill me if she knew I'd been dying to kiss him.

By the time I was done crying, I was exhausted and it didn't take long to fall into a heavy sleep. My body and mind werc both wrung out from the long day. My dreams were a kaleidoscope of images. My mother and father sitting on their thrones, Stryker's stern face, the brilliant red, orange, and purple leaves of the Fall Court foliage, the dark abyss of Stryker's dungeon.

Scene after scene of my life in the Fall Court meshed with my experiences in Ethereum in a nonsensical loop. My mind was a jumbled mess so in the middle of the night when a hand clamped over my mouth, waking me from sleep, and someone warned me that if I screamed, they'd slit my throat, I was too disoriented to do what I'd been trained to and lash out at them with my magic.

By the time I became aware enough to fight back, they'd slapped a foul-smelling cloth over my mouth and nose, and darkness reached up to reclaim me.

Chapter Twelve

STRYKER

I paused for the fifth time since leaving Aribella in that room alone a few moments ago. My muscles were tense and my hand gripped the banister so tightly I expected wood shards to crack off.

The look on her face when she realized I'd chained her to the bed would forever haunt me. She tried to cover it with anger, but I'd seen the truth in her eyes. Betrayal. Sorrow. Pain. I'd hurt her, deeply.

My mind and heart warred with each other.

Aribella's large brown eyes appeared in my mind's eye, heavy with unshed tears, and I spun around. My legs took me back up the flight of stairs in jerky movements until large brown eyes morphed into crystalline blue ones.

My blood ran cold and I froze, my body locking up as a memory sucked me under . . .

Her husky laugh beckoned me. Rosaline looked over her shoulder at me with a come-hither stare. I reached out and

captured a lock of her silky, moon-colored hair in between my fingers just to have her twist out of my grasp.

"How much do you love me?" she asked, a smirk curling the corners of her mouth.

This was a game of hers. She always wanted me to tell her how much I loved her, like she was gauging my affection no matter how often I told her or how many gifts I lavished on her.

A spike of irritation ran through me, but I shoved it away, telling myself it was normal for her to want reassurances. That it wasn't because she truly doubted the strength of my love for her, but that it was her own insecurities bubbling to the surface.

Even though I was an Ethereum lord and Rosaline was a commoner from a small village within my kingdom, I didn't care a lick about our differences in station. The moment I'd laid eyes on her, I was already half in love.

But even though I didn't like it, I could understand how she might be worried I would get bored and throw her away. It was a common enough instance with nobility, but that wasn't me. My love was steadfast, and I'd spent these last months convincing her of that.

It was wildly known that I didn't love easy—I'd been let down by those closest to me and used too many times for my wealth to have a heart that readily opened—but when I did, it was deep and lasting.

Reaching for her again, she allowed me to capture her. I wrapped my arms around her waist and pulled her to me. "I love you with the strength of a thousand stars and to the depth of the deepest abyss."

She smiled at me and stroked her finger down the side of my face. "Do you love me more than you love your riches?" she taunted playfully.

"My riches are nothing next to you," I answered truthfully and her smile twisted into one of victory. Like she'd just bested an opponent and reveled in her triumph. But when my brows pulled together in confusion, the harsh twist of her lips softened, making me feel silly for reading that much into them.

Later I would look back and see the signs I missed, but as she rose and planted a sweet kiss against the corner of my mouth, the shadow of concern melted away and I fell into her and under her spell like I did every time.

I shook myself, nausea roiling in my gut at even the memory of Rosaline. Turning on a heel, I jogged down the stairs and out of the townhouse, only feeling like I could take a full breath of air once I was on the street.

No. I would not fall for a beautiful woman again only to be betrayed.

I headed toward the main street, taking a right when I reached it and looking for the tavern I was to meet my men at. I was in a foul mood as I stomped down the street and I'm sure my face showed it because fae skidded out of the way as I passed.

I shouldn't be recognized here. I was wearing plain clothes and the chance of any of my brother's subjects having met me before was low. However, blending in was never something my brothers, or I, did well. Our magic and size made it almost impossible. So it was best if I could get off the street quickly. I didn't want my prey realizing I was here, at least not until they'd fallen into my trap. Then I would relish watching their faces as they discovered I'd caught them. Seeing fear fill their eyes when they realized what horrors awaited them. I'd worked hard to build up a reputation that struck terror into the hearts of those who opposed or defied me.

Yes, that would be satisfying indeed. These thieves had been plundering my mines, and I'd wasted enough time and resources on trying to capture them. Time and resources that should have gone to my people instead of them, and for that, they had to pay.

My gaze snagged on a pair of women walking down the street arm in arm. A redhead and a blonde, and I couldn't stop my thoughts from turning exactly where I didn't want them to go: to Aribella and Rosaline.

The two women were nothing alike, at least not physically. Rosaline had been tall, even for a fae woman. In heels she'd only stood a few inches shorter than me, which was impressive since I was six-four. She radiated strength, where Aribella, in contrast, was petite, small, almost fragile, yet temptingly curved and soft in all the right places. Even now, my hands itched to pull her close and feel her body pressed up against mine.

I fisted my hands until my fingers ached, but it didn't stop my mind from comparing the two beauties. Aribella had a thick mane of loose, red curls and rich, brown eyes, where Rosaline had an ice-blue stare and straight, white-blonde hair. Rosaline was skilled in seduction, and it was clear Aribella didn't know the first thing about it, which made her all the more desirable to me.

No, they were not the same, not in looks or personality, but the feelings they both managed to stir within me were far too similar for me to overlook. And for that alone, I would never fully trust Aribella. I'd learned my lesson the first time and I'd be damned if I fell into that trap again.

I looked up and realized I'd reached my destination, *The Wily Jackal*. As I shoved into the tavern, I slammed the door on those unwanted thoughts, firmly setting my mind on one thing and one thing alone. Finding the thieves and making them pay.

After a few hours of my men divulging all of the intel they had gathered, I decided that they'd done well. They had located the hideout of the thieves. The three criminals had built a nice little empire for themselves, hauling my treasures down from the Eastern Kingdom and selling them underground here in Beggar's Hole where no one asked any questions.

It felt good to know that come morning, I'd have them in my possession. I'd already mentally picked out cells for each of the betrayers and was looking forward to breaking them. I didn't believe for a second they'd orchestrated all those heists on their own. They had to have a broader network of fae aiding them throughout my kingdom, and I intended to ferrct out every single traitor and make them pay. A task that I was sure I could accomplish with Aribella at my side.

Aribella.

Even thinking about her made my chest tighten. Day would break in a few hours and so I bid my men farewell and left the tavern. I quickened my steps as I headed back toward the guesthouse where I'd left her.

I didn't expect to be out this long and I told myself the anxious energy running through me had nothing to do with being separated from her. She was smart, crafty, and I wouldn't put it past her to find a way out of those hand-cuffs. The feeling had nothing to do with the broken look on her face before she'd turned her back on me. Or that I felt regret that I hadn't followed through and kissed her: at least that's what I told myself.

It would have been supremely stupid and shortsighted of me to have given in to my desires in that moment. And I was convinced that's all they were. Desires that needed to be squashed. I'd already learned my lesson when it came to women and determined a long time ago that I'd sooner carve my own heart from my chest than let another into it.

Despite my reflections, I still took the stairs up to the fourth floor two at a time, unable to stop myself from racing back to our shared room. I froze in front of the door, taking a beat to compose myself.

You're a powerful Ethereum lord, I said to myself. *Not some lovesick, young pup. Pull yourself together.*

Throwing my shoulders back, I pulled the key out of my

pocket and unlocked the door and then opened it, taking care to be quiet in case Aribella was still sleeping.

The room was pitch black, which gave me pause because the lamp had been set low when I left. Could the oil have just burned out, used up? It was across the room from Aribella, and since she was handcuffed to the bed, she couldn't have doused the flame.

I was used to the darkness, empowered by it myself, and so my eyes quickly adjusted to the low light even though only waning strands of moonlight filtered through the open window.

Open window?

My heart stuttered, missing at least one beat before it sped up again. I was at the bed in an instant, my eyes verifying what my gut already knew. She was gone.

The handcuffs I'd used on her were still hanging off the iron bedrail, one band sheared open. It was clear it had been cut off of her. I scanned the rest of the room and nausea roiled in my stomach. She hadn't just escaped, someone took her.

With a roar, I grabbed the wooden chair and flung it across the room, where it broke apart, splintering into a million pieces. Shadows shuttered and danced across the walls as I lost control of myself and my magic.

Fear like I'd never experienced before threatened to pull me under.

Where was she? Who took her? Were they hurting her?

A fresh wave of anger burned through my chest. I

wanted to rage, rip this room and the town apart with nothing more than my bare hands.

It took effort to pull myself back from the brink. My hands shook as I sprinted from the room, down the stairs, and into the streets of Beggar's Hole to gather my men. I didn't know where she was, but I had an idea where to start looking. I sent up a silent promise to the villains who'd taken her that when I found them, there would be nothing left of them when I was through.

The sky was just starting to lighten. There weren't many fae out at this early hour, but even so, I didn't try to hide who I was as I sprinted through the streets, shadows trailing in my wake.

Only one thing mattered, finding Aribella.

As I ran, every emotion I tried to suppress about her came rushing to the surface in an unstoppable tsunami. No matter what I'd told myself before, it all boiled down to one simple truth: Aribella was mine.

Chapter Thirteen

I came to bound to a chair with a splitting headache and some latent dizziness. It took me a second to get my bearings. The light filtering through the window told me it was at least morning. I'd been taken, that much I remembered.

I heard muffled voices and peered across the room at three fae. One male with red hair, white freckles, and two fuzzy horns protruding from his forehead. He reminded me of a fawn. Next to him was an unseelie fae who was the spitting image of Eli. His cousin, Caleb, for sure. Then, lording over the both of them, was a scary, tall seelie female who wore her black hair in a long braid at her back.

I pushed my power over all three of them, sending the emotion of fear and distress.

Immediately, something bit into my wrist and I yelped, pulling the emotions back. The three fae shared a look, and the woman stepped closer to me.

I peered down at what was causing this pain and whimpered when I saw that the previous handcuffs Stryker had put on me had been removed and now two cuffs ringed both wrists. But these were not normal cuffs: the inside was lined with metal teeth that were currently biting into my flesh.

"Nifty little contraption I picked up on the Noreum black market," the female fae purred. "If you wish any of us harm, they will tighten until your hands sever."

I bit my lip, controlling my thoughts against the three fae before me, and the cuffs loosened. A sigh of relief escaped me as the teeth retracted from my now-bleeding wrists.

"What do you want?" I breathed, trying to control my wildly beating heart.

Don't faint. Don't faint, I chanted inside my head.

The female observed me slowly and my gaze flicked to the giant diamond necklace she wore and the emerald rings and ruby bracelets on her wrists.

"I want to be left alone," she stated.

She stepped closer, tracing her finger over my throat. I wanted to bite it off, but the cuffs tightened at that thought, so I pushed it out of my mind.

"I mean you no harm. I'll do just that," I said, confused.

She rolled her eyes. "You stupid girl. I know you are here with Lord Stryker, hunting us. I have scouts all over this kingdom."

I'd found Stryker's jewel thief. Of course she wore them all over her like a sales showcase.

Chills ran the length of my entire body.

I peered at Caleb, who kept his head down and looked

uncomfortable with the turn of events. His clothing was dirty and torn and it didn't look like she was treating him very well by the looks of the bruise under his eye or his thin frame.

The woman placed a hand on either side of the chair I was tethered to and leaned into me. "Is it true you are a truth witch?"

My heart fluttered like crazy at her question. She knew more than I was comfortable with.

"Because *that* could be useful to me," she said. She smelled of metal and whiskey and nothing good.

"We . . . never talked about taking people," Caleb peeped from behind her.

The fae woman spun, throwing out her arm, and a blast of wind knocked into him, tossing him against the wall hard.

I gasped. "Don't touch him!" It was clear that there was still some good left in him and I didn't want to see him hurt.

She reached out and slapped my cheek so hard that my ears rang. "You don't tell me what to do," she snapped.

I gripped the edges of the chair handle so tightly that I thought they might break in half. I had to use every ounce of self-control I possessed not to use my power or have a negative thought against this woman. But it wasn't working very well because the cold metal teeth moved closer and closer to my already-bleeding wrists.

She grinned in my face, as if knowing that she had me. "You are going to be a good little pet truth witch, aren't you, dear?" she taunted.

I was just about to flood her with paranoia and extreme

anxiety, hoping to drive her to insanity and risk losing my hands as the cuffs bit deeper than before, when shadows began to melt down the sides of the walls.

Stryker.

Now it was my turn to grin. She cocked her head at me, confused, and then peered around the room. When she saw the shadows, she raised her hands but it was too late. Spears of darkness swept across her neck and cut her head clean off.

The cuffs at my wrist loosened and fell to the floor.

I shrieked, just as Stryker kicked the door down and burst into the room. The fawn-like fae ran for the window, and Stryker took him out next. One sweep of the shadows across his shoulders and he was removed of his head as well. Bile rose in my throat at the sight of two beheaded fae.

Stryker focused his sights on Eli's cousin next. The poor fae was shaking like a leaf. He put his hands up in surrender and kept his head down.

"Don't kill him!" I shouted at Stryker, trying to stand but unable to because my waist was chained to the seat. I was still processing the two quick deaths, but Stryker looked murderous and ready for more blood. "That's Caleb, Eli's cousin. We can get information from him."

The Ethereum lord looked at me for the first time since entering the room, and it was like a kick to the gut. There was so much emotion there. Regret, anger, need.

"Did he hurt you?" he growled, motioning to Caleb.

I shook my head. "No. It was her." I pointed to the now headless fae whose blood-coated gems littered the floor.

Stryker sent bands of shadowy ropes around Caleb's

body and then told his men, who were waiting just outside the room, to come and take him.

My heart fluttered wildly against my rib cage and I felt dizziness overwhelm me. Stryker dropped to one knee before me and used his shadows to cut the chains that held me as his men hauled Caleb from the room. When he saw my bleeding wrists, he shot the dead woman a glare that I prayed he would never send my way.

Although I was immensely grateful for his saving me, I was still emotionally battered that he'd handcuffed me to the bed after almost kissing me.

"Thanks," I muttered, keeping my gaze away from his.

"Aribella," Stryker breathed, standing up. I could feel his eyes on me.

"What?" I snarled. Now that I was going to live, anger flared to life inside of me and I stood up to face him.

We were alone in the room, except for the two dead bodies. Stryker rested his hands on my hips and yanked me forward so I was almost pressed up against him.

I gasped, looking up into his heated gaze. "I never meant for harm to come to you. Had I known . . ." His voice broke and my heart thawed a little.

I nodded. "I know. But the truth is," I held my bleeding wrists up to his face, "this pain is nothing compared to the one you left me with in that room last night."

A strangled sound left his throat and his fingers tightened on my hips. I could have pushed his hands off, but I didn't. I liked them there. They felt like they belonged there, even though I didn't want them to.

I held his gaze, daring him to do something so stupid as to kiss me. I would strangle him.

His gaze fell to my lips and I forced mine into a thin line, gritting my jaw. I'd fallen for this sick trick once before. I wouldn't again.

I turned my face away from him, giving him my cheek.

He leaned forward, pressing his lips to my temple, causing my heart to flutter and practically short-circuit. He was so tender.

"I told myself I'd never fall again," he breathed against my temple, and the breath caught in my lungs. "But I don't know how much longer I can resist you."

I felt my resolve crumble under his confession. He pulled away from me at the same time I turned to face him. I'm not sure who moved first, but the next thing I knew, his lips were on mine.

Soft, but demanding. Sensual, yet careful.

He slid an arm around my waist and hauled me against him. His free hand dove into my hair, tilting my head to deepen the kiss.

This wasn't a simple kiss, this was an awakening. Icy fire raced through my veins, making me feel more alive than I ever had been. My heart beat a furious cadence, but for once, I welcomed the chaos. Reveled in walking the thin line.

My whole world narrowed down to one thing and one thing alone in this moment: Stryker.

The way his hand pressed into the small of my back as he held me close. The way he tasted like cinnamon and cloves.

The way his stubble created a delicious friction against my smooth skin.

His mouth moved against mine again and again. Each time we broke apart and came back together was more intense than the last.

I couldn't get enough. I'd never get enough.

Something bright flashed behind my eyelids, startling me, and Stryker and I pulled apart to see we were covered in a fine, silver mist. Like ground stardust that hovered in the air for several breathless moments before disappearing as if it was never there.

Stryker's face was washed in awe. "I didn't think it could be true," he said almost to himself.

I lifted a hand, seeing it shake when I moved to press it against my chest. My heart drummed a frantic beat. A clear sign I'd pushed the limits, but it was worth it.

"What was that?" I asked in hushed tones. Some Ethereum magic I didn't know about, perhaps?

Stryker glanced down at me and I was taken aback by what I read on his face. He looked spooked, almost like he'd seen a ghost. It dampened some of the magic from the moment we just shared, but before I could question him about it, his gaze dropped to my wrists, which were still bleeding.

He growled and the spooked look melted into a mix of concern and anger. "You need a healer."

I did. It was freely bleeding and burned with the intensity of a blazing fire, but I also felt like I needed something else. Something only he could give me.

He slipped his hand under my knees and another behind my back and lifted me, cradling me to his chest.

"Stryker, I can walk," I protested, but he ignored me.

When we reached the outside, I noticed we were in a seedy part of town with dilapidated buildings. Nearly Stryker's entire entourage waited outside. Caleb was in chains fastened to the carriage.

"My Lord," one of his guards said, bowing. "We await your instructions."

Stryker lifted me onto his horse and looked at his guard. "Torture him until he tells you where the rubies are. When you get them, return home."

The guard appeared concerned. "And where will you be?"

"She needs a healer. I'm taking her to my brother's estate nearby. My messenger returned this morning to let me know Adrien was there. I'm sure his healer is with him."

"My Lord. Let us accompany you—"

Stryker's glare was enough to shut the guard up. I wanted to protest about torturing Caleb for information, that I could use my power to question him, but I was in a lot of pain. More than I'd originally realized now that the rush of adrenaline had faded. When I looked down, I could even see exposed bone in a few spots. As a royal fae I had rapid healing, but something this deep would take a long time to recover from.

"There are some clean linen strips in the saddlebags. I'm going to wrap your wrists," he said.

I nodded, and he reached very carefully into the bag to

grasp the rolled-up linen. With tender care, he cautiously bandaged my wrists. I hissed each time the cloth touched the wound and he kept muttering apologies.

The moment my wrists were covered, Stryker kicked his horse and we took off. I whimpered when the movement jarred my wrists.

"Are you all right?" He peered down at me, concerned. I was riding in front and he was draped around me like a blanket.

I nodded. "As a royal I heal quickly, you know? It will take a few days but—"

"No. You shouldn't be in pain for any longer than you have to." He was adamant, and I knew he probably felt guilty for chaining me to that bed. But the scorching kiss we'd just shared might have made up for it.

When I had finally settled on the horse, I leaned back into Stryker as his arms came around me. "You can rest if you want. It will take most of the day to reach my brother's healer."

I closed my eyes, leaning against him and letting the exhaustion take me.

As Stryker said, it took the entire day to reach his brother's country estate. I slept through most of it: my wrists had begun the accelerated healing stage and stopped bleeding, but they still bore deep gashes. Every small movement was painful, so I tried to remain still.

His brother's estate appeared to be perched on the edge of the sea, but it was getting dark by the time we reached the front gates, so I wasn't able to see much.

"Who are—" The guard began and Stryker flicked his wrist, causing the shadows to form into the wolf beast from before.

The guards fell silent and bowed their heads. "Lord Stryker."

"I need my brother's healer immediately," he barked.

The gates flew open and a messenger rode ahead of us.

"When was the last time you saw your brother?" I asked.

He sighed. "Adrien? Years."

That didn't seem right. Why would one go so long without seeing their own family? I didn't want to ask. Stryker was a complicated creature that I was unpeeling layer by layer.

We reached a magnificent castle, white stucco with palm trees that I couldn't fully admire in the fading sunlight.

A tall man with a strong build rushed outside with a woman clinging to his arm. From the loose cotton shirt blowing in the breeze, to the cutlass sheathed at his hip and the tight-fitting breeches, he looked every bit a swashbuckling pirate rather than a refined Ethereum lord. But even so, the man was easily identifiable as Stryker's brother. The streaks of honey in his shoulder-length, dark hair were different, as were the striking teal color of his eyes, but the face was so similar there was no mistaking who he was.

"Brother?" Adrien looked shocked.

I felt Stryker stiffen beside me. "Do you have a healer for my friend? She's in a lot of pain. I can pay."

Adrien looked hurt. "Of course. No payment needed."

That made Stryker coil even tighter behind me. "I will pay for services that I use," he declared, and then jumped down from the horse before pulling me down.

The woman beside Adrien was tall, with pale skin and long chestnut hair. She stroked his arm playfully and watched us with a cold expression that gave me chills.

"I'm Adrien," the man said to me. "This is my fiancée, Elisana."

The woman's chin lifted, and she looked down on me like I wasn't worth her time or regard.

Stryker's eyebrows hit his hairline. "Fiancée?"

Elisana glared at Stryker, but Adrien beamed at the woman, reaching out to stroke her hand. "Yes, recently. The wedding is in a few months. You should come."

Something felt off here, but I couldn't put my finger on it and I was in too much agony to care. The rapid healing of wounds sometimes hurt more than what I imagined the normal way did.

"The healer?" Stryker reminded his brother.

Adrien shook himself, as if refocusing, and muttered an apology before leading us all inside.

The healer was waiting, probably called by the messenger. A little bag sat at his feet. He had high-tipped ears, twice as pointed as my own, and a blue-tinged nose.

"My lady." He bowed and held his hands out for me.

"I hurt my—" I began to explain but he just shook his head.

"I know. I feel it."

I didn't have much experience with fae that had healing magic. They were rare and our palace back home didn't have one. I stopped in front of him and he lightly took my wrists in his own. A slight tingle worked up my arms from my fingertips to my elbow.

It was like balm had been wrapped around my wounds. I sighed in relief as the pain fled.

"Feel better?" Stryker asked anxiously beside me.

I nodded, sighing again. I hadn't realized how badly it hurt until the pain was taken away.

"They're not staying the night, are they?" I heard Elisana whisper to Adrien behind me.

I scoffed.

Rude!

"Well, if they want to," Adrien said.

Elisana gave a nervous laugh. "Of course if they want to, darling. I just didn't tell the maids to make up the guest bedrooms."

"No need," Stryker interrupted. "We will stay at an inn and be on our way in the morning."

Adrien said nothing.

This was so weird and not at all how I thought big families would act.

The healer released my wrists and smiled at me. "You are healed," he said plainly.

Wow. That fast?

I unwrapped the bandages and gasped when I saw a few small pink scabs but nothing more.

"You're incredible. Thank you," I told him, wanting to hug him for taking all that pain and doing such a good job mending.

He bowed deeply to me, and then Stryker held out a coin purse to him. "Payment."

The healer's gaze flicked to Adrien, who was glaring at his brother. "He's on my staff. I pay him."

Stryker kept the bag extended. "No, I know how much you need it."

Adrien's hand fisted. "That was two years ago. A small loan. And you acted as if I'd robbed you."

Elisana's hand snaked out and grabbed the bag of coins. "Thank you," she said.

I hated her. I didn't even know her, and yet I hated her.

Stryker just shook his head in disbelief. "They always want money," he said and slipped his hand into mine as he pulled me to the door.

My heart broke as I saw how damaged Stryker was. His brother asked for a small loan years ago and he cut off contact? That was crazy. That also might have been around the time his girlfriend tried to kill him and steal his wealth. I didn't blame the guy for being skeptical, but this was family.

Still, I knew better than to say anything.

"Thank you both." I curtsied lightly. I was, after all, a princess with manners.

Chapter Fourteen

W e rode in silence out of the gates and to a small town that had many cute shops I would have loved to explore if these were different circumstances. We found an inn with a tavern on the bottom floor. When we checked in at the front desk, they led us to the dining hall for dinner. It was packed with travelers, so Stryker asked for a private booth in the back.

After we ordered, I reached out to hold his hand but he quickly tucked his under the table.

Okay, not one for public displays of affection. Or did he regret that kiss? That made my heart feel like it was going to tear in half. Maybe he just needed time. He hadn't called me 'little witch' in a while, and I considered that a plus.

"I hate Elisana," I announced, and he peered up at me keenly.

"Agreed."

I wondered if he was being weird because he thought I needed his money like his ex-lover who betrayed him.

"And for what it's worth, I'm rich too and will never need money from you," I added.

His gaze flicked up to mine and amusement danced there. "Is that so?"

Just then the barmaid arrived, delivering our meal and drinks. I waited until she left before saying anything else.

"I'm just trying to show you that I don't want you for your wealth," I said as I took a spoonful of my soup.

He nodded, his expression unreadable. "I know. You haven't yet tried to steal from me."

I frowned. He was testing me? Waiting to see if I stole from him?

"Well," I said, clearing my throat. "I just thought you should know that I have my own money."

Stryker set his drink down and leaned forward, his gaze snagging my own. "To be clear," he said carefully. "I don't care if you have money or not. I have enough for several lifetimes."

"You clearly *do* care. A lot. Enough that a small loan to your brother caused you to have a falling-out." The words left my mouth before I could take them back. I watched as a wall seemed to slam down over his features.

"It wasn't really about money," he finally confessed, looking uncomfortable. "I don't truly care about money."

In the short time I'd spent with him, I'd watched him give generously, so I believed that part could be true. But I'd also seen him freak out over people stealing from him, proving that he *did* care.

"Then why did you stop talking to Adrien?"

Stryker sighed, looking like he wanted to run from the table.

"I am the eldest quadruplet brother, even if only by a few minutes, so I became a lord before any of my quad brothers," he said. "When I first arrived in Easteria as its lord, I was barely fifteen."

Fifteen. My jaw unhinged. That was so young. *And quadruplets.* His poor mother.

He continued, "Right away I uncovered three theft attempts. That's not all *my* money, it's also for my people. For new roads, for wells, for farm equipment, or schools, there is so much that a lord provides for them. When money is stolen from me, it's stolen from them, too." He growled the last part, speaking so passionately about this that my heart softened towards him.

I reached out and grasped his hand, and this time he took it into his. I knew what he was saying was true because it was the same in my court. The people paid taxes, and we certainly kept a portion, but the majority went to schools and roads and everything he said.

"So, what happened with your brother?" I stroked his palm.

He sighed. "The first assassination attempt on my life happened just after I moved in and became lord."

I gasped. "First? There have been more than one?"

I couldn't imagine having someone try to take my life at fifteen.

He nodded. "And people were stealing, and I was overwhelmed, so I put out a call to my three younger brothers for help. Begging them to help me or ask my older brothers, who were lords at the time, for reinforcements, or advice. Anything."

I held my breath, knowing this story wouldn't have a happy ending.

"They all wrote back with their apologies and said they had their own problems and could neither do, nor spare, anything," he finished through gritted teeth.

"So you felt abandoned." It was a statement, not a question, because that's how I would feel too. It all made sense now.

He nodded. "And then in the first month of Adrien's lordship, he had the audacity to ask for a loan."

It truly wasn't about the money, it was about feeling used. This poor man felt like he couldn't trust anyone.

"You were all so young," I said.

"I know what you are getting at, but they could have—" Stryker's words were cut off by someone who'd just appeared next to our table.

"Brother!" A blur of dark hair leaped into our booth and hugged Stryker.

Brother?

"Aribella," a woman's voice nearly sobbed.

I froze. I recognized that voice.

I slowly spun in my seat.

Dawn Ambrose stood before me with tears in her eyes.

"We found you," she breathed.

I peered over at Stryker, who sat woodenly in the man's embrace. It was as if by merely speaking of him, we'd conjured one of his brothers.

Considering Dawn was with him, I assumed this was Lord Roan—who Stryker had told me went by his middle name, Zander—the Ethereum lord she'd married, and Stryker's brother. From the look on Stryker's face and the set of his body, I could tell that it was taking him effort not to push Zander off. Especially considering the story he'd just told me.

At last, Zander released Stryker, climbing out of the booth again to wrap his arm around his wife.

"Adrien told us where you were," Zander said in response to the unspoken question in Stryker's eyes. "He also told us you weren't alone." His grin widened as his gaze shifted to me.

"I knew it was you the moment Adrien described Stryker's companion to us," Dawn told me excitedly.

The shock of seeing her finally wore off, and I really looked at her. Dawn had always been a serious fae. I supposed that was to be expected since the fate of Faerie had been placed on her shoulders since birth. It's not that she was ever mean or cold, but the few times we'd interacted, it was like I could almost see the weight of her responsibilities pressing into her.

But looking at her now, it was like someone had taken that weight off of her. She finally looked comfortable in her own skin and even though I detected a hint of sadness in her gaze, it was clear she was truly happy. And as Zander beamed down on her, his love for her was also clear.

That was hard for me to process, the fact that the men we were sent to kill were nothing like we were told.

Pushing those thoughts from my mind, excitement bubbled up in me and I rose and embraced my fellow Faerie princess. Well, princess no more, in Dawn's case. If what I'd been told was true, she was a Lady of Ethereum now.

"We've been all over Ethereum searching for you," Dawn said when I stepped back.

"Searching for me?" I asked, and she nodded.

"Yes, ever since the day of the fall equinox. We knew you'd be coming to Ethereum. By now, you've probably discovered that what we've been told about this place is false," she said, taking my hands in a firm grip. Her eyes begging me to understand.

"Oh, I know we've been fed a bag of lies," I told her, my gaze shifting to Stryker before bouncing back to Dawn.

I didn't miss the bemused expression on her face as she looked between us before she wiped it away.

"Here, sit," I offered and moved down the seat. Stryker sent me a scowl, but shifted down as well to allow Zander into the booth beside him.

"I'm so sorry we didn't find you sooner," she said once she and Zander were settled. "We thought you'd appear in the Western or Southern Kingdoms, which was why we started there first." She sounded a little funny when she said that and I couldn't help but wonder if rather than thinking I would turn up in the Western or Southern Kingdoms, they'd just hoped that. "We arrived from the Western Kingdom last week and have been traveling through the Southern Kingdom to find Adrien ever since then. He wasn't in Soleum like we'd expected, so we came to see him at his country house. It was just good luck that we arrived today."

"Not luck, my love," Zander said as he reached across the table and took Dawn's hand. "Fate."

She smiled warmly back at him and nodded. "Fate."

It felt like I was intruding on a private moment, but being trapped in the booth next to Dawn, there was nowhere to go to give them privacy.

Stryker cleared his throat loudly, breaking the pair apart. Dawn's cheeks turned pink as she put her hand back in her lap.

"Great. So now that you've seen I haven't killed the girl, you can be on your way," Stryker said gruffly, clearly put out that his brother was here.

Zander leaned back in his seat and assessed his brother. There was a knowing look in his eye that was clearly annoying Stryker. "So, what happened to taking your time torturing her to send a message to her descendants?"

I gasped and Stryker sent me a guilty look before glowering back at his brother. "There were . . . extenuating circumstances," he ground out.

Zander chuckled. "Oh, I'm sure there were."

"She did try to skewer me the first moment we met."

"Hey," I said defensively, and he arched a brow at me as if baiting me to refute his words. He knew I could not. One corner of his mouth twitched up ever so slightly, making him look extra roguish, so it was my turn to blush.

"Well done," Dawn said with a small smile, referring to me attacking Stryker. Seeing as she had been raised to be an assassin, I easily understood the respect in her gaze.

"If she had succeeded, I wouldn't be here right now," Stryker grumped and Dawn just shrugged and made a *meh* face as if that wouldn't have been the worst thing.

Stryker crossed his arms over his chest and shot her a glare equally as icy as the one he'd given his brother. Dawn didn't seem to care in the least bit.

I wondered what actually had happened between the two of them and made a mental note to ask Stryker later.

Zander shook his head at his brother. "Are you still mad about us not coming to help you when you first became lord?"

My gaze flicked to Stryker.

"Why would I still be mad that my own flesh and blood didn't care that I'd had an assassination attempt on my life?" Stryker asked sarcastically.

Zander groaned. "Of course we cared. We were drowning in our own problems, though. Did you think that you were the only one that had a rebellion rise up after you were crowned? I was still training under Cal and helping him fend attacks off weekly."

Stryker was silent and I wanted to urge them to patch this up, but I knew it was best not to get involved.

Turning, Stryker peered at his brother, giving him a full

view of the scar on his face. "Show me the scar that your assassin left?"

Shame crossed Zander's face and he nodded. "Fine. One of us should have come or helped get reinforcements sent or something. I'm sorry, okay. We were fifteen. Can you get over it?"

I winced at the wording, *get over it*, and so did Dawn.

She reached for her husband's hand. "I think Zander means, now that he's apologized, can you move past it?"

Zander nodded. "That's what I meant. Come on, fire dragon. Forgive me for being a young and overwhelmed jerk of a brother."

Stryker tried to fight the smile that was threatening to come up, but couldn't. fire dragon must be some inside joke and my heart warmed at seeing the brothers' relationship thaw a little.

"Fine. For now," Stryker grumbled.

Zander banged his hand on the table in triumph. "I've thawed the heart of the cruelest lord in Ethereum."

Dawn laughed at her husband's antics and I couldn't help but enjoy seeing them banter. It almost made me forget our troubles. Almost.

"My heart has thawed," Stryker agreed. "But not because of you."

He gave me a look across the table that nearly undid me, and I couldn't help the flash of heat that rushed through me. But thinking of my people back in Faerie, probably dying from the curse, made my smile slip right off my face.

Dawn turned to me with an intense look. "Don't worry, Aribella. We did it. We found a way to break the curse."

The breath froze in my lungs even as my heartbeat accelerated.

Then it was true? There was a way to save Faerie that didn't involve cold-blooded murder.

We ordered more food for Dawn and Zander and tucked into our dinner while Dawn explained everything. She mentioned some ancient group of fae who had foresight to see the future. They'd told her that rather than just satisfying the curse with an Ethereum lord's heart every hundred years, there was a way to completely destroy it. But the catch was that each princess had a task to complete before that would happen.

She also explained that the curse had started to bleed into Ethereum, starting with her and Zander's Northern Kingdom. The magical sickness that afflicted the unseelie we'd come across on the road had started thirty days after she arrived in Ethereum. Exactly when she was no longer able to use her faestone dagger to return to Faerie.

I did the math in my head and realized I'd have about two weeks before the faestone dagger would be useless in helping me get home.

"The Wise Ones?" Stryker's eyes nearly bugged out of his head.

Zander nodded.

Stryker, who was fearful of nothing, appeared concerned.

"Have you met them?" I asked him.

He scoffed. "No way. My grandfather used to tell me stories about them, though. They told one of our uncles that he would die in seven days, and he did. They always terrified me."

They what?

Zander chuckled. "They aren't that bad."

"You need to go see them," Dawn told me, and I turned to look at her.

"Visit the fae who can tell you what day you will die? No, thanks. I'd rather not know," I said.

Dawn gave me a look. "They're the ones who are helping us find another way to end the curse, Aribella. Each princess has a task and only the Wise Ones can tell you what it is. They will only answer one question per fae, so they wouldn't tell me any of the other princesses' tasks, only my own."

Silence descended over our group.

Save my people without killing the man I was falling for? Well, if it meant I had to go see some old fortune tellers, then sure.

"Okay," I said, peering across the table expectantly at Stryker. "Will you come with me?" I tried not to sound pathetic, but my voice shook. Leaving him now, after that kiss, just felt wrong.

He nodded once, but said nothing more.

"Perfect. We leave first thing in the morning." Zander

squeezed his brother's shoulder. "My wife and I have had a long day, so we're going to turn in." He then looked at Dawn and wagged his eyebrows.

Her cheeks went pink. "Zander!"

He grinned, and I couldn't help but smile at their flirting. I'd thought Dawn was insane for marrying an Ethereum lord when I first heard, but now I understood. They were perfect for each other.

She gave me a quick hug. "We'll meet you down here for breakfast. I'm so glad you are safe." She squeezed me and they both left.

After that, Stryker paid the bill and got us lodging. They only had one room left.

We walked upstairs together, my stomach in knots. Sharing a room before, when I was his prisoner, was different now that we'd shared that kiss.

He stepped inside the room and I followed him. When he walked over to the bed, which was much larger than the last few, he just stood there and stared at it. I'd overheard him telling the man he needed two rooms or at the very least two beds, but the man insisted this was the last room left.

My stomach now felt like it contained a lead ball. I'd never slept beside a man before, in the same bed, sharing the same blanket.

I stood next to him, wondering what he was thinking. Now that we'd shared that kiss, did he expect to bed me? Was he thinking about it right now? I knew he'd had a past lover, but my experience was pretty nonexistent.

After that kiss everything felt different. Days ago, I'd

slept in the same room with this man, handcuffed and in shackles, and barely thought twice about it, but now I was no longer his prisoner.

"The last time I slept beside a woman I cared about, I almost died." His voice was hollow and I was so surprised by his words that my body felt numb.

Relief bloomed in my gut that he wasn't thinking about bedding me, but instantly turned sour when I thought of him thinking about how he couldn't trust me.

I spun to him, taking him into my arms and running my fingers over the scar on his cheek. I peered into his deep, gray-blue eyes and spoke with gentleness. "I would never hurt you."

Hurt flashed across his eyes. Why hurt? That wasn't a normal reaction to those words.

"Oh how I wish I had the power to see if you were telling the truth," he said finally.

I frowned. Now it was my turn to be hurt. "You'll never know that for certain, Stryker. But can you trust me anyway?"

I didn't need a verbal response; I saw it in his eyes and the way he pulled away from me, taking his warmth with him.

"In time I hope," he said and then yawned. "I'm tired. Let's get some sleep."

My heart nearly shattered in that moment, but I had to remind myself he had some deep trauma that I knew nothing about. I'd never been tricked and almost killed by someone who was supposed to love me. I'd never even been in love.

I tried to conceal my pain, wearing a soft, fake smile when he took off his belt and peered at me.

"I'm sorry I can't give you all of me all at once," he muttered. "But please know that I want to."

This complicated man had won me over, because in those words I saw the promise of a solid future if I just waited and was patient.

"It's okay. I've been told I'm very patient. As long as you don't give up, we can work through this." This time I smiled for real.

He gave me his back as I slipped out of my dress and shoes and then was just in my chemise.

"I can take the bedroll," I offered, and he chuckled.

"The bedroll is for enemies," he said.

Stryker slipped into bed, patting the space beside him, and I smiled.

I was trying to be cautious of how he might feel sleeping next to me uncuffed, but also keep a proper distance for my own sake. Stryker was the kind of man I could lose myself in and, as much as I cared for him, I knew we weren't there yet. Sometimes, if things burned too hot too fast, they burned out. I wanted what Stryker and I had to last.

Peeling back the covers, I got into bed and faced Stryker.

We were silent for a long minute, just letting the moment settle. My eyes adjusted to the light and I realized he was watching me.

"You frighten me," he said into the dark room.

I frightened him? How? I didn't want to ask.

"You make me happy," I countered and felt his sharp intake of breath.

Reaching over, he threaded his fingers through mine.

"You make me happy too, Aribella. *That's* what frightens me." He lifted onto his elbow and pecked my nose, and then wished me goodnight.

I fell asleep with a smile on my face and hope for tomorrow.

Chapter Fifteen
STRYKER

A burning pain scored the side of my face and my eyes popped open to find Rosaline straddling my hips as she hovered over me, her moon-streaked hair curtaining her face. She held an onyx dagger with blood dripping from the tip and an expression of hatred I'd never seen on her face before.

I didn't understand what was happening. We'd fallen asleep the night before wrapped in each other's arms, whispered words of adoration lingered on our lips as we drifted off, so when she lunged for me I didn't react fast enough and her blade scraped against my face again, carving a path through my eyebrow and narrowly missing my eye.

With a shout, I shoved her off me and she fell onto the floor as I staggered from the bed. My body felt like it was walking through quicksand. Blood dripped down the side of my face so freely it half-blinded me, but through my limited

vision I saw the unmistakable green swirls of a dampener rune on my chest.

Fear gripped me and I pulled for my shadow magic to no avail. The rune was blocking it.

Stumbling to the nightstand, I grasped for something to staunch the flow of blood running into my eyes, but she came at me again with a piercing shriek. I spun just in time to grab her wrist before she could impale me with her blade. I was about to twist the weapon out of her hand when she started chanting something and the cuts on my face began to burn with the intensity of a thousand suns.

With a gasp, I released her and lurched away, my body refusing to obey me as I fell to the ground, clawing at my own face.

A husky chuckle sounded and my gut clenched. It was the same sound that had driven me wild with desire more than once.

"Magic activated poison," she said. "Without a healer, it will burn through your bloodstream, making it feel like blades are running through your veins."

That was an accurate description, for even as I tipped my face up to see her standing above me through my bloodied vision, I felt the poison moving down my neck and into my chest. The pain was so intense I couldn't move. My body spasmed as the poison continued its trek through me. And the worst part of it all. She was a healer. She could end this all now.

"Why?" I choked out, feeling the hurt of her betrayal ten times more than the poison.

"Why?" she echoed, her eyebrows shooting up. "Surely you've figured it out."

I just stared at her while twitching on the ground, and she chuckled again. The sound ran over me like razor blades.

"You've spilled all your secrets. I know everything about your riches, all your mines, and the combination to your safe. With you gone, I'll be the wealthiest fae in all of Ethereum."

Through the agony, I looked up at her, my heart shattering into a million pieces. "You've betrayed me for my riches." My traitorous voice cracked.

The look she threw me said she thought I was the most foolish fae to ever live. And maybe she was right.

"Why else would I pretend to love you?" she said matter-of-factly and then lifted the blade above her head, aiming it for my heart.

Before she could strike, I reached under my pillow and pulled out the blade I always kept there. She fell into me, and at the same time, my hidden blade sank into her shoulder.

Fighting against the dampening rune, I gathered all the strength I could muster and threw her off me with a strangled roar. She flew across the room.

In my tortured and half-blind state, I'd reacted like I would to any threat, protecting myself at all costs. Rosaline's body hit the opposite wall, but rather than sinking to the ground, she stuck there with her toes hovering above the floor.

The blade dropped from her hand, clattering to the stone floor. Her eyes were wide with shock as she slowly lowered her gaze. My own traveled from her face down her body and the blood froze in my veins.

The pointed brass end of the wall mount where I usually hung my sword protruded from her middle, just below her breasts. A bloom of red was already spreading on her white nightgown.

No.

Through the excruciating pain, I pushed myself off the ground and rushed to the wall, still wobbly and feeling like I was treading heavy water. Even though it only took a moment to reach her side, blood already saturated the front of her gown and dripped to the floor.

Ripping the sheet off the bed with shaking, agonized arms, I tried to cover the wound, to stop the blood flow, but it was no use. It was too late.

When I looked up at her, I could already see the light dimming from her eyes, but what I read in them was regret.

She tried to say something, and a trickle of blood leaked out of the corner of her mouth.

"No," I said, taking her hand. "Hold on. I'll go find a healer and we'll fix this."

I didn't know what I was saying. Even if the best healer in the world had been standing there with us, he wouldn't have been able to save her. She was a healer in her own right, and knew this was beyond something fixable.

Besides, she had just attacked me, had admitted to only wanting me for my money. Why would I want to save someone who wanted me dead?

But I knew the answer to that. Because I'd loved her. I'd loved her with a depth I didn't realize I was capable of.

Yet my heart and my head weren't synced. I knew I wasn't

thinking right. I couldn't reason correctly through the pain: physical or emotional.

She moved her mouth again and I leaned in, frantic to hear her final words. I so desperately wanted to know that this had all been a horrible mistake, that she regretted attacking me or some blood magic had made her do it, but instead, the barely audible words she spoke were, "This should have been you."

My eyes popped open and I found myself twisted in the bedsheets with a layer of sweat drenching my body. I blinked several times, trying to anchor myself in reality after reliving that nightmare.

Just a nightmare. Just a nightmare. Just a nightmare, I chanted over and over to myself as I tried to wrangle my breathing and heartbeat.

Not a nightmare, though. A memory. A flashback. Because everything about that had been real, and I feared I was falling into the same trap again.

It was impossible to calm myself completely, but when the panic dropped to a manageable level, I glanced over and spotted the slight form sleeping soundly next to me.

Even knowing it was Aribella and not Rosaline, I was flooded with terror again.

My body moved jerkily as I slipped from the bed and practically tripped to the window, flinging it open to let the fresh air in. I desperately ached for a cold slap against my overheated skin, but unfortunately the temperature never really cooled in my brother's kingdom, even at night, and so I was hit with muggy warmth instead.

As I stood at the window, I gulped the moist air in like I was starving for it. I took in lungful after lungful of it, but no matter how much I inhaled, it didn't feel like enough.

It was this room; it was stifling. I had to get out.

Trying not to make too much noise, I shoved my feet into my boots and threw my shirt on, not bothering with my coat, and stumbled from the room. I didn't want to wake Aribella, but I felt like if I didn't get outside immediately, I was going to die.

I tripped down the stairs and staggered through the dining hall we'd been in the night before. When I pushed out the exterior door, practically flinging myself out of the inn, my heart finally stopped feeling like it was going to explode.

Bending over, I braced my hands against my knees and forced myself to take in slow breaths, focusing on inhaling for five counts and exhaling for five counts.

I don't know how long I stayed like that, bent over in the middle of the street, until I was able to straighten again.

Luckily, it was well into the night, and there weren't any fae loitering around. I glanced over my shoulder, tipping my gaze up to the window of the room where Aribella still slept. The slight breeze from the open window caused the curtains to flap inward gently.

My heart sank. I couldn't do this.

I wasn't ready for a new relationship and I wasn't sure if I ever would be. Even with a woman as perfect as her.

Just thinking of Aribella made my insides simultaneously clench and rejoice.

It was like she'd been created for me alone. She knew how to handle my sharp edges and smooth them away. I'd never laid eyes on a more beautiful creature. The first time she appeared in front of me, I'd sworn my heart stopped beating. Everything about her, from her soft voice, to her kind heart, called to me.

And when we kissed . . .

She was my mate.

There was no denying it. I felt it and saw it with my own two eyes. The icy fire to my heart. The silver mist that surrounded us. But even as I'd stared in awe at the stardust particles that had hung in the air between and around us while the taste of her still lingered on my lips, dread had filled me.

And that was not the feeling that should have dominated me at that time. I was broken, and it had never been more obvious than in that moment.

Cold hard truth settled into my bones as I stood alone in the street, chilling me despite the humidity in the air.

I might never be able to trust in love again.

As much as I cared for Aribella, as much as my arms ached to hold her and something inside cried out for her when she wasn't near, I couldn't be the man she needed. The man she deserved. I was too broken. Ruined beyond repair.

My relationship with Rosaline had ended in heartbreak, scarring my body and soul.

Fate might have been pushing Aribella and me together, but I already cared too much for the redheaded beauty to risk spoiling her with my darkness. She'd fall in love with me and then I'd leave her broken, unable to commit. So I did the only thing I could to save her. To give her a chance at a life that didn't include the ghosts of my past.

I re-hardened my heart of stone, and resolved to cut her out of my soul, one bloody slice at a time.

Chapter Sixteen

I yawned, reaching my arms above my head and stretching as I opened my eyes and smiled. Turning to wish Stryker good morning, I frowned when I saw the side of his bed was made and a note lay on top.

Had I slept in? Maybe he was already eating breakfast.

Sitting up, I grabbed the note and started reading. My stomach sank further with every word.

Aribella,

I wish you had come sooner. I wish that I'd met you before her. I have invisible scars which are deeper and harder to heal than the one you see on my face. I want to give myself to you. I want to fall in love with you. But my head won't allow it. I've done that before and nearly paid for it with my *life. I'm broken and you deserve a man who can give you his whole heart, without dragging you through a minefield.*

I choked on a sob, and read the last few lines.

I'm sorry I left without saying goodbye, but this is for the best. Zander and Dawn will take care of you and if you need anything in your quest to help your people, send word and my secretary will give you whatever you ask.
Stryker

No.

He wouldn't.

A numbness spread throughout my body as I processed what had just happened. Last night things seemed okay. Maybe not perfect: he said he was afraid, but he seemed okay . . .

But he wasn't.

Would I be okay if my lover tried to kill me in my sleep? No. I wouldn't.

I had to go after him, tell him we could work on this together.

Rushing to get ready, I slipped on my dress and boots and raced down the stairs of the inn.

"Aribella!" Dawn's voice came from a nearby table as I hurried through the dining area inside the pub. I stopped and turned to find her alone and holding a note. She was frowning. "I'm so sorry," she said.

Her note was from Stryker too, it seemed. I glanced at the words, *take care of her* and *I'll pay whatever you need,* and shook my head. "I have to go after him."

I moved to leave, but Dawn reached out and gently grabbed my wrist. "Sit down," she said with compassion.

I did and blinked away tears.

"Where is Zander?" I asked her, looking around the inn.

She sighed. "We got word early this morning of a healer in the northern mountains who can temporarily freeze the effects of the curse for some of those that are more seriously affected. He's gone to get the healer and bring him to the capital to help as many people as we can."

I reached out and grasped her hand. I'd forgotten that she was having her own problems and instantly felt terrible. "I'm sorry about the curse on Zander's people. Your people. We met some on the road, and it looked painful."

She nodded. "Thank you. It's bad. One of my dear friends . . . " Her words caught in her throat and it took her a second before she could go on. "One of my dear friends, Nysa, has been in a coma-like state for months. Ever since the night of my wedding. She's growing weaker by the day and I'm so worried we're going to lose her. I truly hope this healer can help us."

I nodded, agreeing with her. It was awful that the people were suffering here as well as Faerie. It wasn't fair.

Dawn pulled her shoulders back, a determined look sliding onto her face. "Listen, Aribella," she said, and by her tone I knew she had slipped into ruler mode. "I know what it's like to want to just get lost in falling in love with your mate, but—"

"Mate?" I frowned and surprise flashed across her face before it morphed to guilt.

"Stryker didn't tell you?"

My heart fluttered wildly, causing dizziness to wash over me. "Tell me what?" I asked.

She winced. "It will only make you feel worse at this point."

"Dawn," I warned her. "Tell me what?"

She peered at me with a look that had me bracing myself.

"They have mates here," she said.

Mates?

"When you kissed," Dawn said. "Was there a magical glow?" I gasped and she gave me a sad smile. "Confirmation of the mate bond."

She was right. It made it worse. My heart felt like it had been run over by a herd of horses, and I wasn't quite sure how it was still beating.

"There will be time to go after Stryker and try to talk some sense into him, but right now our people in Faerie need you," Dawn encouraged me.

Our people. I felt so guilty for not thinking of them as often as I should have.

"Your mother is preparing Princess Isolde to come next."

Dawn's face turned flat, like she was remembering a ghost. "Did she train you?"

"For a bit, until she determined I was too weak to carry out the task. She left for the Winter Court before we finished, but then Master Duncan took over."

"Too weak?" Dawn asked.

I swallowed hard. "I have a weak heart. I faint when I grow overwhelmed. I've hidden it all my life, but she found out and left to train the next princess."

Dawn reached across the table and grasped my hand. "Sounds like my mother. I'm sorry."

"She definitely knows how to execute a task." I laughed nervously.

Dawn squirmed. "My mother knows, Aribella. She knows that the lords aren't evil. She knows they are our mates."

My mouth popped open. Queen Liliana?

"But then why would she send us here to kill them?" I asked.

"Because she will do anything for our people, so that's why we need to go now to see the Wise Ones. We're running out of time."

I wanted to run after Stryker, I really did, but I knew Dawn was right. If these Wise Ones had any information that would help our people, then we needed to go see them now. I could deal with Stryker later.

After a quick bite to eat, Dawn and I left the inn on horseback. It would take three days of almost constant traveling to make it to the mountain range in the Northern Kingdom where the Wise Ones lived. I spent the better part of that time actively trying not to think of Stryker, but failing more often than not.

Had he made it back to his kingdom? Did he regret leaving me? Did he miss me like I did him?

I was furious at him for abandoning me, but at the same time I still ached for him. I didn't know what to do with these conflicting emotions, so I did my best to stuff them to the far recesses of my heart and mind. But like anything suppressed, the thoughts kept finding ways to free themselves.

Traveling with Dawn was easy. She was the same fierce and strong Summer princess that I knew of, but also so different. She smiled more than I remembered from the few times we'd interacted and there was a glow about her that was undeniable.

Whenever we stopped for the evenings or to rest the horses, Dawn would fill me in on what had happened to her since she left Faerie. We'd laughed about how she lost focus when she stepped through the portal and ended up in a pigsty. She told me of how she believed Zander was a royal guard when they first met and had ordered him to take her to the Northern lord, and in response, he'd put magical shackles on her wrists like the ones my kidnappers had used.

Phantom spikes of pain had run through my own wrists when she'd spoken of the days she spent trying not to think about running him through with one of her blades. She'd winced when I'd admitted I had firsthand experience with those particular torture devices.

I finally learned the details of when Dawn met Stryker in person. She confessed that she'd broken into his castle with the intent to kill him because she'd realized she couldn't take Zander's life. Even knowing that she hadn't succeeded, something twisted painfully in my chest at the thought that his life had been in danger yet again.

Knowing my relationship with Stryker, Dawn was careful with her words when she spoke of him to me, but I quickly picked up that he hadn't made a good impression on her, which was easy to imagine. My first interaction with the scarred Ethereum lord hadn't gone well, either. But considering the moment I appeared in Ethereum, I'd tried to cut out his heart as well. The blame for that wasn't fully on his shoulders.

Something else Dawn shared with me was the true story of Ethereum. About how a Faerie Winter King had fallen in love with an unseelie and been banished to this world along with all the unseelie in Faerie.

I was furious to find out not only how many lies we'd been fed over the years, but also how the Ethereum lords had been branded as evil for so long. For centuries, innocent men had been brutally murdered by the princesses of Faerie. It was beyond awful, and I was determined that the legacy of lies and cruelty ended with us.

We passed from the Midlands and into the Northern Kingdom just before dawn on the third and final day of travel. Although there was no denying the cold beauty of the land, I could admit the climate was a touch more frigid than I was used to in the moderate Fall Court.

Luckily, since Dawn and Zander had set out to find me in the first place, they'd thought ahead and Dawn had given me fur-lined leathers and a cloak to wear. I was thankful for that because I would have been freezing in the cotton dress I'd worn in the Southern Kingdom.

As we traveled, I spotted more and more unseelie fae along the way that were afflicted with the same magical sickness as the family on the road had been. Dawn explained that she and Zander feared that the curse would eventually bleed into the other Ethereum kingdoms, just as it was spreading through Faerie. For Stryker's sake, I hoped that fear was unfounded.

It was well into the day when we finally reached the base of the Northern Mountains where the Wise Ones lived. After three long days of traveling, I was dirty, sweaty, and tired. I would have traded my entire court for a warm bath and a decent meal.

Freezing wind ripped at my clothes and hair as I craned my neck to look up at the sheer rock face in front of me.

"How do we get up there?" I asked Dawn with a wary glance.

"We climb," she said as she dismounted her horse.

My stomach dropped. "You can't be serious."

I looked back at the mountain, which seemed to jut straight up from the ground. I couldn't even see the top because of the thick clouds overhead. I'd never climbed more than a small fruit tree when I was a child. And even then my mother had scolded me and forbidden me from ever doing it again.

I conveyed as much to Dawn, and she went to her saddlebag and pulled out a length of rope, tying one end around her waist and then securing the other end around me.

"I'm a strong climber," she said. "If you slip, this will keep you from falling too far."

I eyed the rope connecting us skeptically.

"Trust me," she said, the look on her face nothing short of grim determination.

She was always so strong and I admired that about her. I nodded and took a deep breath.

Dawn had told me everything I needed to know about the Wise Ones. What to expect when I entered their cave, how they looked and communicated with their minds, and most importantly that I only got to ask them one, single question.

I knew visiting them to find out what I needed to do was the only way to end the curse once and for all, and also the only way to save my people without having to murder an Ethereum lord to do it.

I had to do this, so I swallowed my fear and started to climb.

～

Much to my surprise, I didn't die climbing up the vertical rock face. It took us forever because we kept having to stop whenever there was a small rock shelf so I could sit and try to slow down my heartbeats. There was one particularly frightening moment where my vision went blurry and I thought I would pass out, but I closed my eyes and breathed deeply and the spell eventually passed.

Dawn was wonderful and didn't complain about the slow pace we were taking, not even once. She only gave me words of encouragement and helped me keep my mind off the fact that we were hanging off the side of a mountain hundreds of feet in the air.

After we reached the plateau, we traversed a narrow path along the mountain's edge. It seemed like years before we stood in front of the cave that led to the Wise Ones, but I knew it must have only been a few hours by the position of the sun in the sky.

Dawn had told me I had to go alone and so after mentally fortifying myself, I plunged into darkness. Even forewarned about the voices, when the whispered hisses started in my head, I couldn't stop my heart from beating furiously.

I tried to stay strong and brave, but the darkness was so complete and the voices, each one indistinguishable from the next, grew in volume until it felt like I was going to go insane. When my heartbeats reached a furious crescendo, I swayed, knowing I was going to lose the battle to stay conscious. I welcomed the silence with open arms.

~

I awoke on my side in a candlelit room with galaxies swirling overhead instead of a ceiling. It was blessedly quiet, and for that I was grateful. My hip and shoulder ached, telling me they'd taken the brunt of my impact when I fainted, but I was just glad I hadn't struck my head.

I pushed myself up and stood on shaky feet. Feeling eyes on me, I turned to find four fae seated on rock thrones. Their skin was pearly white and each had two small horns. They looked exactly how Dawn had described them, down to their milky white eyes.

"*Another princess of Faerie,*" one of the Wise Ones said, and even though none of their mouths moved, I somehow knew it was the one who was seated directly in front of me.

"Hello, Wise Ones. Thank you for allowing me an audience," I said, and then dipped into a small curtsy. I was unsure of the correct etiquette in this type of situation, but I was first and foremost a princess of Faerie. A lifetime of manners and decorum had been bred into me, not allowing me to be anything short of polite and reverent in this type of situation.

"*Please rise,*" the fae at the far end said, and I straightened. Their faces remained the same, lips not moving, but I heard his voice in my head. "*We are very pleased to see you as well, Princess Aribella of the Fall Court, daughter of Queen Beatrice and King Leonard, child born with a weak heart, selfless protector of Easteria.*"

I gasped a little at their long-winded name for me, which

provided some very accurate details about my life, and also some confusing information.

Protector of Easteria? What did that mean?

It was just proof that these fae really did know the future like Dawn said.

"We know you seek answers," one of them said, cutting off my internal thoughts.

"So ask your question," another said, the voice infiltrating my mind.

Okay, they were getting right to it.

Dawn and I had gone over what my one question should be, so when they asked, I didn't hesitate. "What task do I need to complete to help bring an end to the curse on Faerie forever?"

We'd reasoned that since taking the heart of an Ethereum lord back to Faerie didn't end the curse, only stopped it for a hundred years, I didn't need to add that caveat to my question.

One of the Wise Ones rose, startling me. They'd been so still since I regained consciousness that to see one of them move now was a little jarring.

I held my ground as the unseelie approached me and then reached out a hand. I forced myself not to flinch away from him when he laid a palm flat against my chest, right over my heart.

"You have one question, and you don't want to know how to heal your heart?" he asked.

I blinked back at him, chills running the length of my arm.

Of course I would give anything to heal my heart. My ailment had held me back my entire life, but it hadn't even crossed my mind to ask that. My life wasn't worth more than those of my people's, and I said as much to them.

A small smile lifted the corners of the Wise One's mouth that was mirrored on the fae still seated behind him. With a nod, he stepped back and returned to his throne. I couldn't help but feel like that question was a test, but the look on his face told me I'd passed.

"*Who accompanied you here today?*" the Wise One who'd just retaken his seat asked.

"Dawn. Co-ruler of the Northern Kingdom and the Summer princess."

Two of the Wise Ones exchanged looks and then one asked, "*Not the Eastern lord?*"

They wanted to know if Stryker had come with me? Did that mean they'd expected him to?

I shook my head, a sudden ball of emotion clogging my throat. "He . . ." I was going to say he couldn't make it, but that wasn't really true, and I got the overwhelming sense that lying to these fae would be detrimental.

His mouth turned down ever so slightly. It was a micro expression, but it told me that my answer didn't please him. Why would he care if Stryker had come with me or not? But his next words surprised me so much that the question was wiped from my mind.

"*You think you are faint-hearted, but you are not,*" the Wise One said. "*You are one of the strongest fae we've ever met. Don't forget that. Especially in the days to come.*"

Tears sprung in my eyes. I'd always struggled to see myself as strong. To hear someone else say that I was, helped me believe that it was true.

"Thank you," I choked out, but then reined in my emotions. "What about my question?"

The Wise One directly in front of me nodded once and then said. *"You do, indeed, have a part to play in ending the curse that ravishes both lands."*

Both lands. To me, that was definitive confirmation that the magical sickness in the Northern Kingdom was because of the curse in Faerie.

I held my breath, waiting to find out what I needed to do. They'd told Dawn that she'd already completed her task when she bonded to Zander. I didn't think that my task would be as easy, but I secretly hoped it wouldn't involve anything to do with getting Stryker to love me because that felt impossible at this moment. He'd made it perfectly clear he didn't want me when he left.

"You need to find the Shadow Heart buried in the place that treasures are kept."

The Shadow Heart? What was that? A literal heart, or was he speaking metaphorically? If it was buried, it couldn't be a living heart, right? Either way, I had no idea how to do that.

"What's the Shadow Heart?" I asked.

"Your question has been answered. No more will be allowed. Farewell, Aribella."

That couldn't be it. I didn't understand what I was

meant to do. They couldn't just send me away without answering my question.

They all bowed and before I could contest, everything went pitch black again. My heart sank. I fumbled my way in the darkness before finally emerging from the cave to find that dusk had fallen. My final hope was that Dawn would know what I was talking about, but when I explained to her what had happened, she was just as confused as I was.

"The Shadow Heart buried where treasures are kept," Dawn mused, tapping her finger against her lip. "Someone must know what it means. We'll go back to Noreum and talk to Zander. He might know something. And even if he doesn't, we won't stop until we figure it out."

I nodded, but still felt defeated. I couldn't help but wonder if Stryker had come, if he'd have known what it was, but then I gave myself a mental shake. Going down that road wouldn't help any. Stryker wasn't here and he made it clear he didn't want to be.

Chapter Seventeen

I t was a full day's ride to Noreum if we rode fast and hard, but three hours into it, Dawn had us stop at a trader's stall and we got some fresh fruits and filled our canteens.

We walked over to a shaded rock to take a break and joined some of the seelie fae that were standing there.

"My lady." One, wearing a wide-brimmed hat, drew himself into a deep bow. His redheaded friend looked confused. "Lady of the *North*," the fae wearing the hat said pointedly, and his friend quickly dipped his head.

"Oh, I'm sorry, I missed the wedding. You are much prettier in person than people say," the redhead said.

Dawn laughed at that. "Thank you, gentlemen. It's nice to meet you."

Ever the polite princess, just as we were taught.

Dawn then turned to me. "'The Shadow Heart buried in

the place that treasures are kept', I wonder if it's in a vault or something."

The man in the hat perked up. "Does my lady like fanciful tales?"

Dawn frowned. "What do you mean?"

"The tale of the Shadow Heart," the redhead said.

"Carved of black stone, yet it glows blue with magic," the man in the hat finished.

I froze, realizing they were talking about what the Wise Ones had told me.

"Yes. I would love to hear that tale." Dawn caught on and handed them each a piece of fruit. "Would you tell it to us? I just heard it from a friend, but he didn't know the whole thing."

The men took the fruit from her and thanked her, then they sat beside us on the rocks.

"The Shadow Heart is a crystal in the shape of an anatomical heart. It's worth more than gems or gold," he said, and I could not breathe for a second.

It was real? Maybe I really could save my people.

"When the founding fathers of our realm first came here, they created the Shadow Heart to power our world. But the magic it contained was so valuable that they hid it." The man took off his hat to reveal a slightly balding head and dramatically threw his hat into the air and caught it on his head. "In the place where all of Ethereum's most valuable treasures are buried."

"Where?" Dawn and I asked at the same time.

"In the center of the Jewel Spring Mountains," he answered. "In the deepest mine within Mount Grimhorn."

"No," the redhead broke in, "I heard it was at the bottom of the southern coast. Near an island shaped like a heart."

They began to argue back and forth and I crumbled, a little defeated. I shared a look with Dawn and she frowned. It seemed like they weren't sure where it was.

The man with the hat looked me firmly in the eyes. "My great granddaddy was a treasure hunter. He said it's in Mount Grimhorn."

I swallowed hard. Stryker's kingdom. Within his precious mountain range. Could I go there without his permission? I didn't even know. Though he did say he would help me in whatever way he could.

"Well, thank you, gentlemen," Dawn told them, and we bid our farewells.

We reached our horses and I turned to Dawn. "I feel like I should go to Mount Grimhorn to look for the Shadow Heart. It's too much of a coincidence that we met these fae right after hearing from the Wise Ones. It feels like fate."

Dawn nodded. "I think you are right. I'll go with you. It's a few days' ride, which will stretch our provisions, but we can make it." We saddled our horses and were about to ride out when a woman ran after us.

"Lady Dawn," she cried.

We turned in our saddles. The woman ran at us carrying something black in her hands, but I couldn't make out what it was. As she neared, I noticed they looked like burned corn cobs.

"What is it?" Dawn asked the lady.

"The fields. They've all turned black. The crops are gone, the water too."

My stomach sank. Black water. That's how it started in Fall Court. Was it happening here, too? It was certainly what the Wise Ones hinted at.

Dawn leaped off her horse and rushed to inspect the corn. Then she looked up at me with terror in her eyes. No food and no clean water on top of a plague was a disaster for any leader.

"I need to get to Zander," she told me.

I nodded. "Of course."

Dawn grabbed a few pieces of the corn from the woman to show Zander and told her she'd be back with reinforcements in two days' time.

When we saddled back up, Dawn pointed her horse north. "Come on. We can figure out the Shadow Heart once—"

"No," I told her, pointing my horse to the east and pulling out my map. "I'm going to save our people. You need to help Zander and take care of your kingdom. But I need to find this Shadow Heart if we have any hope of ending the curse for good. We don't have time to do both. I have to go on my own."

Dawn glanced back at me with surprise. "Aribella. You don't know the land, you could be hurt, or—"

"I'm not fragile," I growled.

Dawn tilted her chin, giving me a proud look. "Okay, Aribella. Go to the Jewel Spring Mountains and look for the Shadow Heart. When you've found it, come back to Noreum and we'll figure out what to do. You'll have a home in the Northern Kingdom for as long as you need one."

I heard what she didn't say. That without my faestone dagger and the black heart of an Ethereum lord, I wouldn't be returning to Faerie anytime soon. So she was offering me what she could: a home.

I nodded, and then felt bad for snapping at her. "I'm sorry, I—"

She leaned across her horse and pulled me in for a hug. We held each other slightly awkwardly with our horses so close together.

"I believe in you," she whispered, and handed me a bag of coins and her leftover food rations.

She pointed out a village at the base of Mount Grimhorn on my map and gave me the name of an inn, saying she'd send a raven to check in on me there. Then she pulled back and rode off without another word.

I swallowed hard, slightly regretting my boldness now that I was faced with traveling in an unfamiliar land alone. This was the first time I'd been truly alone since I arrived in Ethereum. I'd been with Stryker since we'd left his castle, and then Dawn these past few days.

Stryker.

My heart pinched, but the truth was that if he hadn't left me, I wouldn't be alone right now.

After hours of riding, I stopped at a small town for the

night. As I lay down to sleep that night in an unfamiliar inn, in an unfamiliar village, in an unfamiliar land, I couldn't stop thinking about how Stryker had left me. He kissed me like I was the only woman on earth and then he slunk away in the night. My whole life I'd had a weak heart, but for the first time I could confidently say that now it was broken.

I was proud of myself. I'd gotten up, ordered breakfast, consulted my maps and compass and set off for the Jewel Spring Mountains. All alone, all without my mother's voice telling me I couldn't handle something like this.

Hah. I gave a triumphant fist pump into the air.

I was now about two hours into my journey when the sound of hooves clopping on the lonely road behind me had me perking up. I'd been getting sleepy, but someone else to talk to would be amazing.

I peered behind me to see a sweet older couple, pushing seventy and riding on mules. I smiled as they hurried to catch up with me. As far as I could tell, they were both seelie, lacking any horns or fur.

"Hello, fellow travelers." I waved.

The old woman on the smaller mule waved back and grinned, showcasing a missing tooth. I pulled on my horse's reins and let them catch up with me.

"Where you heading?" I asked.

"Oh, my husband and I are just going to the next village over." The old lady's voice cracked as she spoke.

I peered at her husband, about to ask him a question, when he pulled a polished stick from his cloak.

He pointed the stick at me and I didn't realize it was a wand until a bright green, glowing light flew out of it and slammed into my stomach, knocking me off my horse. The wind rushed out of me as my back hit the earth, and then the man leaped off his mule and hobbled toward me.

I tried to get up, but realized I was immobilized and couldn't move.

Panic rose up inside me as I noticed the rune on my stomach. My heart fluttered and I willed it not to fail on me now. If it was just an immobilizing rune, it had no bearing over my power. It would make me unable to move but not unable to affect their emotional state.

I pushed thoughts of deep regret and empathy into both him and his wife, and he faltered in his steps.

"Please remove this rune and let me go," I said calmly, and pushed sympathy and compassion into him.

"We hurt her," the woman said to her husband, looking a bit frantic.

He frowned, peering at his wand like he hadn't known why he did it. "We need the coin, Nettie," he told his wife.

"Remove the rune and let me go and I'll *give* you lots of coin," I told him, and then again pushed the feeling of compassion into him.

He stared at me for a long moment and then finally dropped to one knee and muttered an incantation as my body was released from the spell. Now free, I sat up and peered at the man in anger. But when I noticed his tattered clothes and Nettie's thin frame, I thought this might be the only way they kept themselves fed. No longer able to work in the fields or whatever they did around here.

Reaching into my purse, I gave them half of the coins Dawn had given me. Then I took all of the emotions and feelings I'd pushed into them back.

"Go on before I report this," I said.

He thanked me and they turned their mules and rode off the way they came.

With a sigh, and a bruised back, I mounted my horse.

I guess that could have been worse, but I needed to be more careful in the future. I wanted what I told Dawn about being able to take care of myself to be true. But even if I was in over my head, I had no other choice.

I reached the village at the base of Mount Grimhorn without any further issue at the end of my second day of traveling. It was one of the smaller peaks within the Jewel Spring Mountains, and a raven was waiting for me at the inn Dawn had told me to go to.

Things are bad here, but we are managing for now. Let me know when you've reached here safely.
Love,
Dawn

. . .

I penned her a quick response, telling her I had reached Mount Grimhorn safely and would send word when I found the Shadow Heart. I left out the incident with the elderly couple along the way, not wanting to worry her.

The village at the base of Mount Grimhorn, Vonryx, had seen better days. I'd caught more than one suspicious glance my way since the moment I rode into town. It was smaller than the village of Blackrock at the base of the ruby mines that I'd visited with Stryker. The Jewel Spring Mountain range was much larger than I'd thought, with many towns surrounding it and just as many mines. In Vonryx there was only one inn and a smattering of dwellings that were still occupied. There were at least a half dozen other establishments that were boarded up and abandoned.

When I'd asked the proprietor of the inn what was mined here, he said, "Nothing." I'd cocked my head in confusion, and he said that they used to mine black sapphires in Mount Grimhorn, but that the mines had all been shut down some years back, so many of the villagers had moved on. That explained the sad state of the town, but when I inquired about why the mines had shut, he wouldn't give me an answer.

That night I slept fitfully and the next morning I spent half the day hiking midway up the mountain where the entrance to the mines was. I couldn't decide if the mines not being active was a good or bad thing. I was glad I wouldn't have to try to talk my way past miners to search for the

Shadow Heart, but on the other hand, I had no direction on where to go once I reached the mines.

I was hoping I would stumble across a secret tunnel or something that led to a vault inside the mountain and that the Shadow Heart would be sitting on a silver platter waiting for me to grab it. But as much as I hoped for that, it seemed highly unlikely.

When I reached the entrance and saw that the mine was sealed, my face fell. They'd boarded it up, and then chained it shut. I hadn't considered that since the mines were shut down, they'd have sealed the entrance, but it made sense that Stryker wouldn't want fae stealing his gems. But why close down the mines to begin with? That, I couldn't figure out. Maybe it was dangerous? That thought spooked me, so I didn't allow myself to think of it further.

It took me almost a full hour to pry one of the boards loose and slip between the chains. Thank goodness I was small, or else I never would have been able to fit.

When I entered the dark tunnel, I couldn't see more than a few feet in front of me, but quickly spied a lantern hanging on the wall that still had some oil in it. Using two flint rocks I'd had in my pack, I created a spark and got it to light up and breathed a sigh of relief that I wouldn't have to blindly feel my way around the mining tunnels.

This was slightly terrifying, but I told myself it was for my people. For my mother and father, and not just the Fall fae, but Summer too. For all of Faerie.

I felt ill-prepared but determined as I started down the passageway, but as the day dragged on and I lost track of time and the number of turns I'd made, my hope started to wane. It felt like I'd been searching the mine tunnels for hours when I finally stopped for a break.

It was hotter in the passageways than I was expecting. My clothes stuck to me in uncomfortable places and sweat trickled down the side of my face.

Lifting my free arm, I wiped my brow with the sleeve of my shirt and then set the lantern down on the ground. My arm ached from holding it up in front of me for so long and my legs and feet were fatigued from traversing over the uneven ground for hours.

Not caring in the least about how dirty it was, I slid to the ground and pulled some food from my pack. All I had were a few pieces of dried meat and cheese and a small canteen with water. I couldn't stop myself from draining the canteen in seconds, and even after I'd drunk it all, my throat was still parched. My mind drifted as I chewed on the food, not really tasting it.

I hadn't wanted to admit it to myself, but I was lost. It was foolish of me to go into the mine all alone and without a plan. I should have done something to mark my path, but I was so anxious to find the Shadow Heart, and find it quickly, that I'd thrown caution to the wind and now I was paying for it. The oil in my lantern wouldn't last forever and I wasn't any closer to finding what I was looking for than the moment I squeezed between the planks and entered the mine.

What was I going to do?

As if it couldn't get any worse, my heart was beating too

fast and a wave of dizziness washed over me. I closed my eyes against it, trying to regulate the beats with slow, even breaths, but nothing seemed to help. I couldn't calm myself down because I was in deep trouble.

When I swallowed my last bite, I picked up the lantern and stood, turning back the way I came. I had to get out of here before I was plunged into darkness. I tried to make myself feel better by saying that I'd return the next day with a better plan to search, but part of my mind whispered that I wouldn't ever find my way out of this labyrinth.

My heart began to beat faster and harder, and I became short of breath. Panic seized me and I was half-running now, stumbling through the narrow tunnels as my shoulders occasionally hit against the rough stone walls.

I turned a corner and felt a jolt of relief for the first time. I was sure I'd come this way; the stone looked familiar.

A smile started to lift the corners of my mouth, but then a low rumbling echoed beneath me and I halted. Dust rained down on me from above and the ground and walls began to vibrate.

Oh no.

Run, Aribella! I screamed inside my head, but my body was paralyzed. It wasn't until right before the ground below me crumbled that I started to move, but by then it was too late.

Chapter Eighteen

My whole body ·hurt. I hadn't lost consciousness when the ground opened up and swallowed me, but at some point I'd squeezed my eyes shut, so I'd been unprepared when I landed on a pile of compacted sand and then rolled several times over some unforgiving rocks before stopping.

When I opened my eyes, the world was bathed in a blue glow and I saw a hole in the rock ceiling about ten feet above me that I must have fallen through.

How could I see? Where was that blue light coming from?

I tried to suck in a lungful of air, but immediately started choking on rock dust. When my coughs finally subsided, I sat up and looked down at myself to find I was covered in dust from head to toe. I ached all over and had some scrapes, but I didn't see any gushing wounds and was able to wiggle all my fingers and toes, which I took as a good sign that nothing had broken.

Gingerly, I pushed myself to my feet. The sand was probably the only reason that fall hadn't left me a broken and bloody mess, so I was thankful for it.

My muscles and bones protested as I straightened. Come tomorrow, I'd definitely be covered in bruises, but the truth was I was lucky to still be alive.

Turning to take stock of my surroundings, I caught my breath. I was in a cavern, lit by glowing blue stones embedded in the rock wall, ceiling, and ground. In the middle of the cavern in front of me was a large pool of crystal-clear water.

I rushed over to it and immediately cupped my hands and brought the water to my mouth to drink. It was fresh, as if it had come from a spring and tasted clean. When I'd had my fill, I splashed my face and scrubbed my hands the best I could and then stepped back to take a better look at my situation.

The cavern was breathtaking. The blue glow from the stones almost gave it an ice grotto feel, except the temperature was warm and balmy. In truth, I'd never seen anything like it. On this second look, my eye was drawn to the back wall on the other side of the pond where it looked like there was a concentrated cluster of glowing stones.

I skirted the water, taking care of where I stepped on the uneven ground, to investigate. One nasty fall for the day was enough for me.

It didn't take long to get to the spot with the cluster of

luminescent stones, which turned out to be set deep into the cave's stone wall in a circle shape that was about twice the size of my head. All of the brilliant blue stones were glowing except for the center of the circle cluster, where I realized there was some sort of deep depression. An indentation that felt suspiciously like the shape of an anatomical heart when I touched it.

Was this where the Shadow Heart had been? And if so, where was it now?

"It's not here," a deep voice said behind me and I spun, my heart hammering in my chest as if I was having an attack.

Stryker stood on the other side of the pond, staring back at me.

I blinked a few times, almost sure that I was imagining him, but as I remained frozen in shock, he moved toward me, ringing the pond like I had until he stood right in front of me.

Emotions swirled within me. Warring with each other. Part of me just wanted to jump into his arms, but the other part of me wanted to hurt him like he'd hurt me. I didn't know what to do, so I just stood there, torn.

"Are you all right?" he asked. His concerned gaze was nothing more than clinical as he looked me over from head to toe and back again, yet still made my cheeks heat.

"What are you doing here?" I asked, my voice hardly louder than a whisper.

Reaching out, Stryker tried to take my hand, but I pulled it away before he could touch me.

Hurt flashed across his face that he covered quickly. "I just wanted to make sure you are uninjured," he said.

"I'm fine," I snapped back and Stryker flinched. "How did you find me?"

"Zander contacted me and told me where you were headed," he said, surprising me. "We can mentally communicate over large distances, my brothers and I. It drains our energy, so we only do it when it's an emergency. When Dawn told him where you'd gone and what the Wise Ones had told you, he reached out to me. It's not safe here. We have to go."

It looked like Stryker was going to reach for me again, but he stopped himself this time. Wise man.

"I'm not going anywhere," I said, lifting my chin. "The Wise Ones gave me a mission, and I intend to see it through."

Turning, I started around the pond in the other direction, looking at the walls and the ground. Perhaps the Shadow Heart had fallen on the ground? Maybe the tremor had caused it to fall from its spot in the wall?

"Aribella, what are you doing?" Stryker asked from behind me. I knew he was following me, but I didn't give him the satisfaction of glancing back at him.

"Looking for the Shadow Heart."

He sighed loudly, which just made my annoyance spike. "I already told you it's not here."

"How would you know?" I shot back.

"Because I'm the one that moved it."

Finally stopping, I spun around to look at him.

"You moved it?"

He nodded.

"Why? Where is it? We have to get it right now."

"Slow down," he said.

"Explain," I ordered.

Stryker pressed his mouth into a straight line, but nodded. "The legends always said that the Shadow Heart was buried deep within Mount Grimhorn. From the time the first lords were banished to Ethereum it was only a myth, a legend, until three years ago when one of my miners broke through to this chamber," he said with a wave of his hand, indicating the blue-drenched cavern.

"At first I left the Shadow Heart here and ordered the entrance to this cavern sealed, and kept the mine open, but word quickly spread and looters and treasure hunters kept trying to break into the mines to steal it. Eventually I decided to move it somewhere safer, but after I moved the Shadow Heart, something happened and the mines became unstable. Something about moving it and removing its magic from this mountain caused cave-ins and gas leaks and a plethora of other issues these mines had never had. More than one miner lost their life."

"So you closed the mines," I said, filling in the blank.

He nodded. "The sapphires weren't worth people's lives," he said, and my heart tweaked. It was more proof that Stryker cared for far more than just his riches like so many people believed.

"I tried to relocate the workers to my other mines," he

went on. "But as you probably noticed, the village never truly recovered."

I nodded. It all made sense now. "Where did you move it?"

"An island towards the south, just past my eastern shore," Stryker said. "We can go retrieve it. Together."

Together. Part of me balked at the idea of doing anything with him after he'd abandoned me, but the other part of me felt like it was right. That it was something we were supposed to do together. No matter how I felt about it, I couldn't get it without him.

"Fine. We should go," I said, mirroring his earlier words. "Do you know an easy way to get out of here?"

He nodded and indicated I should follow him, but he paused at the spot where I'd fallen into the cavern, noticing the hole in the ceiling. "Did you fall through here?" he asked.

"Yes." I rubbed my sore hip. "I'm glad you know of a less painful way out of here."

Stryker tensed and then went stock-still.

"What's wrong?" I asked when he didn't start moving again.

"Aribella, I need you to come here," he said carefully.

Before I could answer, I felt something gently rub up against my back and looked over my shoulder to see Stryker's shadows nudging me toward him. "Stryker, stop—"

Stryker closed his eyes and a shudder wracked his large frame. "Please," he said, not bothering to hide the pleading tone in his voice.

It was that tone, full of anguish, that had me surrendering and going to him on my own. I stopped in front of him and he opened his eyes. There was a wildness in them I hadn't seen before. Like he was trying very hard to control himself, and losing.

"I just need to check for myself that you're okay. I know you don't owe me anything, but will you please let me do that?"

That's what had him so upset? Because he'd just realized that I'd fallen and thought I might be hurt? What did he care?

I thought about denying him, but Stryker looked about two seconds away from losing it, so regardless of my better judgment, I nodded.

When Stryker reached out and started running both hands over my body, checking for injuries, I had to smother a gasp. His touch was butterfly light. I knew he wasn't trying to take advantage, but it still affected me.

He started at my head as he gently prodded my skull, watching my face carefully for any winces and twitches. Then he moved to my neck and then down one arm and then the other before slowing checking the rest of my body, being respectful of my physical boundaries.

I was red-faced and a step away from full-out panting when he finally finished. He was kneeling before me, but when he stood, I immediately noticed the wildness had left his gaze.

"I'm glad you're okay," he said, relief heavy in his voice and I half wondered what he would have done if I'd had an injury.

I'd ask him what that was all about, but I already knew. He couldn't calm down until he knew for himself that I was unharmed. I tried not to let it affect me, but it did. Despite the ways that Stryker tried to push me away from him, tried to push me out of his heart, this was evidence of how important I was to him.

A week ago it would have made my own heart soar, but a lot had changed since then. Now it just felt like he was poking at an unhealed wound, making it bleed all over again.

Without saying anything, I turned from him and started walking in the direction he'd indicated the exit was. Right now I wanted nothing more than to get out of this mountain, to retrieve the Shadow Heart, and then go somewhere and try to heal my own.

Chapter Nineteen

We climbed out of the mountain and all the way back down to the inn in silence. Once there, I went right to my room and told Stryker I would meet him in the dining hall below in the morning. I wanted a bath and a good night's sleep.

The next morning we ate a quick breakfast in relative silence, only asking small questions when needed, and then rode on horseback to the very eastern ends of his lands where the boat docks and seashore were. My arms were covered in bruises from my fall that Stryker kept looking at but said nothing about.

When we got to the boat docks, Stryker seemed to know the men there, and rented us a boat with a small cabin that had a single bed. I hoped we wouldn't be on the water long enough to use it because I'd rather sleep in the water and drown than next to him.

After we'd been out on the water for about an hour,

245

Stryker turned to me, regret heavy in his gaze. "I'm sorry I left you like that." It was as if he was reading my mind.

My eyes filled with tears, but I blinked them back, forcing a strong face. "I don't want to talk about it," I snapped, facing the beautiful ocean and allowing the wind to bite at my skin as I tried to calm my frantic heart.

"Aribella, I—"

"I *don't* want to talk about it," I shouted, and his nostrils flared, but he remained quiet.

What good would speaking about the past do? What would telling him that he'd been the first man in my entire life to kiss me like that accomplish? Telling him that I fantasized about kissing him again daily or that I couldn't stop thinking about him.

"You know what? Let's talk about it." I spun around and stormed across the wooden deck until I was right in his face. He gripped the wheel and met my gaze. "I'm not *her*, Stryker. I'm sorry that you've been hurt in the past, but we all have our baggage. I grew up my whole life hiding a weak heart from an entire kingdom. You're just a coward," I spat, hating that my cheeks were wet with tears. "And worst of all, you knew I was your mate."

His mouth popped open in shock, like I'd struck him, and I shook my head, giving him my back and walking away.

I had intended to step down into the little cabin beneath the boat when a wall of shadows rose up before me, barring my way. I turned, and Stryker was right behind me, chest heaving and eyes glittering with a mixture of rage and passion. My gaze flicked to the wheel to see that a rope of shadows was steering the boat, and then I peered into his eyes.

"What, Stryker? Say your piece and let's just move on from this." I crossed my arms defensively.

"I'm falling in love with you, and it frightens the life out of me." His voice was so broken and vulnerable that my walls began to crumble. His words knocked the breath out of me.

I dropped my arms and he stepped closer.

"I know you're not her," he said. He reached for my fingers and then brought them to the scar on his cheek. "But no matter how hard I try to forget the nightmare that she engraved on my face and my heart, sometimes it's hard."

I stroked the knotted skin, tracing my fingers along the scar and tried to imagine what it would be like to have someone I loved try to kill me in my sleep.

"I was already halfway to Noreum to look for you, to win you back, when Zander contacted me. Can you forgive me? Can you give me another chance to treat you how you deserve to be treated?" His voice was husky and it made my entire body melt. "I'm sorry, Aribella, I made a mistake. I see that now."

I'd tried to resist him, but I felt that resistance crumble and I couldn't find it within myself to be sorry about that.

I whimpered, leaning closer to press my lips against his. His arms came around me and my mouth opened to deepen the kiss.

Was I so rigid and unforgiving that I couldn't allow him a second chance after that heartfelt confession? No. I was not. We all made mistakes and it was how we moved forward that mattered.

Even though it had only been a few days, it felt like it had been years since I'd tasted him, and I found I couldn't get enough. I pressed closer, falling into him, and cherished the feel of his mouth against mine, of the hard lines of his body up against my softness. I had to grasp onto him to keep standing because the longer we kissed, the weaker I became.

My feet might have been on the boat deck, but my head was in the clouds high above.

Nothing felt this good. Nothing felt this right. I could have stayed like this in his arms forever, and when we finally stopped kissing, it didn't feel nearly long enough.

I was tempted to pull Stryker back down to me again when I saw the same silver sparkles hovering in the air around us, exactly as they had the first and only other time we kissed. The proof of our mate bond as I understood it from Dawn. And just like before, they stayed suspended in the air for a few moments before disappearing.

I looked up at Stryker and smiled. He peered down at me with relief, his lips slightly swollen from our kiss, and I had to stop myself from going back for more.

"I feared I'd have to go forever without ever kissing you again," he confessed.

"That would be a crime," I agreed with a smile, feeling lighter than I had in days.

Something behind him caught my eye, and the smile was instantly wiped from my face.

Stryker spun and we both stared at the small island

coming into view ahead, with a tall, black smoke cloud hovering above it.

"Is that supposed to be there?" I asked.

"No," he growled.

"Is that where we're going?"

"Yes," he said. "But when I left the Shadow Heart there three years ago, the island wasn't on fire."

Great. Just when I thought things were getting easy.

It took another half hour of sailing before we actually reached the shore. When we did, Stryker tied up the boat to a wooden post sticking out of the sand and then carried me to shore so my feet wouldn't get wet, since there was no proper dock.

"You're really trying to win me back, aren't you?" I asked him and he chuckled, sliding me down his body slowly before setting me down onto the sand. "I thought I already had," he answered playfully.

I smiled, and then a deep growl emanated from the woods. The smell of smoke hit my nose and I winced. Stryker held his finger to his lips, indicating I needed to be quiet, and then took my hand, leading me into the woods. We stepped over fallen logs and scorched earth until we reached a meadow and Stryker stopped. Peering through the trees, I noticed a rocky outcrop and a yawning cave.

Lying in front of the cave opening was a giant, winged beast. He was sleeping and around him piles of wood burned. The deep growl I'd heard moments ago was actually the creature snoring. His hulking body was made of black scales and his head bore two knobby horns with a tail of serrated spikes.

Stryker went rigid, backing away slowly, turning and not stopping until we were back where we'd tied up the boat. The sun was setting, and I was shocked to find fear in Stryker's eyes when I peered up at him.

"What is that thing?" I asked.

"It's a shadow dragon," he breathed, looking at the boat like he wanted to flee. "They're attracted to objects of great power and will defend them to the death. It must have found the Shadow Heart."

My stomach dropped. "Okay . . . so now it's protecting it?"

He nodded. "Did the Wise Ones say there was another way?"

Whoa. If he was asking that, it meant that this shadow dragon was more dangerous than I'd thought.

"I can't leave here without it, Stryker. It's the only way to stop the curse and save my people. To save Ethereum too."

He nodded and then removed his boots and shirt and pulled a sword from his belt.

My eyebrows shot up.

Stryker's broad shoulders tapered into a narrow waist. He was steel covered in flesh. Everything about him radiated strength and as the warm rays of the dying sun danced over the dips and valleys of his muscular chest, I became jealous of the light.

"What are you doing?"

He peered at me with a gloomy expression. "Preparing for the fight of my life. Shadow dragons wake at sunset and they feed on . . . shadows. My power will be useless against him."

Oh stars. That was possibly the worst thing he could have said.

"Feed on shadows?" I wanted to make sure I understood that correctly.

He nodded. "They only make them stronger. So get ready, darling, because getting the Shadow Heart back will cost me."

I faltered. "Well, maybe we should think about this. I don't want you getting hurt."

He glanced up at the setting sun. "We're out of time and options. You need it and I'm going to get it for you. Stay here." He gave me a chaste kiss and then ran into the forest.

Aww, he thought I was going to stay behind like a damsel in distress. That was cute.

I waited a minute and then ran after him, staying about twenty paces behind so he wouldn't hear me and put up a fight. I could see now why he had taken his boots off. He was silent as his bare feet hit the mossy floor and I stopped to do the same, losing sight of him as I ditched my boots and padded barefoot in the direction he'd gone. There was no way I was letting Stryker fight my battles for me. This curse plagued both our lands; it wasn't his responsibility to bear alone.

When I reached the clearing, I peeked into the fading light to see Stryker walking on his tiptoes before the beast, trying to skirt him and sneak into the cave while he slept. I froze, holding my breath as Stryker held his blade aloft and disappeared into the darkness.

A wave of dizziness washed over me with the anticipation of waiting for Stryker to return, and I realized my heart was beating so fast that my hands shook.

Relax, Aribella. The worst time in your life to faint would be right now.

Just as I saw Stryker reappear in the cave opening, the sun sank below the horizon and the shadow dragon's eyes burst open.

Stars help us.

The creature's nostrils flared and he whipped his head in Stryker's direction. I leaped out from the protection of the thick trees and waved my arms to draw his attention. "Hey!" I yelled and the beast snapped his head toward me, standing on all fours.

Stryker slipped out from the cave and into the woods, and I watched in horror as the shadow dragon began to suck the darkness from around him. It filtered in threads, absorbing into his skin, and I gasped as suddenly he grew to nearly triple his previous size.

I heard a noise behind me but didn't dare take my eyes off the beast, who was now forty feet high and peering down at me like I was a snack.

The noise turned out to be Stryker, who appeared beside me covered in soot and holding a black crystal the size of a fist. The Shadow Heart. "Take it and get on the boat, float into the water and wait for me a mile offshore. I'll swim."

He was just saying that. If I left him alone, he'd die. He said himself that his powers didn't work on this beast.

I shook my head. "Let's both go. We still have time to—"

"No. I have to kill it or the beast will give chase and we'll both be doomed."

He deposited the cold, heavy crystal into my hands and a powerful buzz ran up my arms when my skin touched it.

Leaning forward, he placed a kiss on my lips. "Forgive me," he breathed against my mouth.

I didn't even have time to wonder what he was talking about when shadow bands wrapped around me and began dragging me backward towards the boat.

"Stryker, no," I screamed as he used his power to ferry me to safety. "Don't do this. I can help."

He turned his back to me and held his sword up just as the shadow dragon breathed a wall of fire right at him.

I struggled against the shadow ropes that held me, screaming and tearing at them with my hands to no avail. My toes dragged along the forest floor as Stryker used his power to carry me across the sandy beach and directly into the boat. The bands set me gently down onto the boat deck and then they gripped the boat itself, shoving it into the ocean and away from the shore. The post we'd been tied to snapped and I screamed in desperation as the shadow ropes disappeared into nothing.

I stood, heart pounding, tears welling in my eyes. How could he do this?

No. He would die fighting that beast. Unable to use his shadow power, with only a sword against a fire-breathing shadow monster that seemed to grow bigger as the night drew darker. I couldn't let that happen.

I peered at the dark, deep water, almost black now that the sun had set. My childhood fear that some ravenous creature swam in its murky depths and would eat me alive rose up inside me, causing my heart to flutter wildly.

Stryker's bellow cut through the night. It was deep and filled with pain, and I didn't even think before dropping the crystal on the deck and then diving into the cool water.

I was always a good swimmer. The one thing my mother would let me do as she was told it helped strengthen my heart without stressing it too much. Of course that only applied as long as I didn't swim too fast or too long. I was doing both right now, but I barely felt the icy bite of the frigid liquid as I raced for the shoreline, trying to think of a plan.

No shadow powers. Fire-breathing monster.

There was only one option. I had to try to use my magic on the beast. Something I'd never attempted before. I wasn't even sure it would work on a non-fae being, but I had to try.

I reached the sandy beach in no time, hurrying out of the water so fast that I fell over. My soaked clothing felt like it weighed four times as much as before, but I didn't care.

I tore across the sand and into the forest at double speed, pulling on my powers as I went. I thought about sleepiness and the emotions and feelings that went into making someone fall asleep. The heavy feeling that settled over your body making your eyelids droop, the relaxed way your mind went fuzzy before you eventually succumbed to the darkness.

When I hit the clearing, which was half on fire, I took stock of the scene before me.

Stryker stood in the center of the meadow with his sword brandished as the creature lunged for him.

I didn't hesitate. I hit the beast with the biggest blast of drowsiness I could muster just as his spiked tail came crashing into Stryker's chest, tossing him twenty feet into the air.

My heart seized at the sight of Stryker being impaled, but my magic had worked because the second it hit the beast, his eyelids drooped and his feet stumbled.

Come on, you bastard. Go down.

Keeping an eye on the drowsy, but still very much awake, shadow dragon, I ran for Stryker, who lay motionless on the ground all the way at the other side of the meadow. I couldn't see all of him, so I wasn't sure how injured he was, but the fact that he wasn't getting to his feet scared me.

Fall asleep. I encouraged the monster and he stumbled again. I pushed even more magic into him, feeling my legs go a little weak with the effort and his body finally crashed to the rocky ground, shaking the earth around me.

Ignoring the fallen beast, I ran faster and leaped over a log, stopping as I took in the sight of Stryker lying in a pool of black blood, unconscious.

No. Shock ripped through me at the sight of the blood, of his unconscious form, and it caused a wave of dizziness to wash over me as I begged my heart not to do this to me, just as I blacked out.

Chapter Twenty

I came to and immediately sat up, panic spiking through me as I peered down at Stryker lying face up on the ground next to me. His chest was still rising and falling, but there were open gashes on his stomach that were leaking blood. Black blood. And a lot of it.

A quick check over my shoulder confirmed that the beast was still asleep, so I must have only been out for a few minutes.

"Don't do that to me again," I beat a fist against my chest, scolding my heart for causing me to faint at such a time as this.

At the sound of my voice, Stryker's eyelids fluttered open.

"Stryker, can you walk?" I asked, trying to press my hands onto his wounds to staunch the bleeding.

He attempted to sit up but fell backward, moaning.

"No. You're too heavy. I *need* you to walk. We have to get out of here."

I lifted one of his arms, sticking my head under it, and then with a grunt I stood, feeling the strain on my back as I pulled him to a standing position. Stryker groaned in pain and I winced, but I didn't have time to be gentle with him. The shadow dragon was asleep, but since I'd never pushed my magic on an animal before, I wasn't sure how long the effects would last. It could awaken at any moment, and then we'd be easy prey.

I'd just gotten Stryker back. I wasn't about to lose him a second time.

We got a few paces and then Stryker's legs gave out, which made me topple sideways. I barely kept us standing, and by some miracle, managed to drag us forward. I was physically exhausted from swimming from the boat to the shore and then the mad dash to the clearing, and mentally drained from the amount of magic I'd forced into the beast. Every step we took felt like it could be our last, but I forced us to keep going.

It took forever to get Stryker to the shoreline. His eyelids fluttered open and shut and blood flowed out of him like a broken ink pen. His hold on consciousness was tenuous, at best.

I was not equipped for this kind of thing. I had no idea what to do. And even if I did know how to suture and dress his wounds, I had no medical kit. My only hope was that there was something on the boat I could use to save his life.

Laying him on the shore, I swam out to the boat, which

had mercifully drifted only a little with the tide. After climbing onboard, I tried adjusting the sails and turning the wheel to navigate it closer to shore and then dropped the anchor.

I knew next to nothing about sailing, but used my basic knowledge to try to get through this. My mind was a frantic, jumbled mess. I just needed to get Stryker on the boat and get those wounds closed somehow.

After getting back on shore, with little help from him as he went in and out of consciousness, I heaved him onto my back. I nearly buckled under his weight as I waded out into the water and rolled us both sideways onto the boat deck. Stryker hit the hardwood with a heavy thud and then I spurred into action to try to save his life. My legs shook with fatigue, but I pushed myself to the limits.

Running into the little cabin under the boat a mere three feet high, I cracked my head as I tore through storage cabinets until I found some medical supplies. Relief flooded my body at the sight, and I rushed back onto the deck. Small droplets of rain began to fall around us and I cursed the sky with shaking hands as I started to wipe away the blood. A sob ripped free from my chest as I saw at least seven deep puncture wounds an inch or more wide.

"No. You can't leave me," I whimpered as I began to shove gauze into the holes and then pulled out the needle and stitching thread. I was an expert seamstress. It couldn't really be that different, could it?

It was. Piercing the skin of a man you'd fallen in love with was horrifying and I forced myself to do it over and over, pulling the gauze out of one hole to stich it up and then moving to the next.

But there was so much blood. As it mixed with the rain, it made the entire boat deck so black that it felt like we were floating in ink. Even in the shallow waters, the boat began to thrash as lightning ripped across the sky and thunder shook the air.

Once I had the wounds closed to the best of my ability, I hoisted the anchor, setting us adrift. I knew it wasn't safe to send our boat out in the storm, but it was more dangerous to stay moored near the island, and therefore the shadow dragon. I believed Stryker when he told me the beast would give chase and knew we had to get away from here.

After setting the boat free, I spotted the discarded crystal heart sitting on the slick deck beside me. The flashes of lightning reflecting across the gem's smooth surface almost made it look otherworldly. Even though we'd come all this way for the magical jewel, I'd give it back to the shadow beast in a heartbeat if it would take away Stryker's injuries.

The truth of that thought rocked me to my core because it revealed the depth of my feelings for the Ethereum lord. I might not have known him for very long, but in a short time, he'd become more important to me than anything else. More than my own wellbeing and perhaps even more than my kingdom. And that scared me. But I didn't have the luxury of examining those feelings right now, so I snatched the heart and shoved it into my discarded pack and slung it over my shoulder.

Using all my strength, I grabbed Stryker under the arms

and dragged him out of the rain and onto the little bed in the cabin below. I was exhausted, huffing and puffing as I collapsed beside him.

"You can't die," I whispered into his ear. "I'm in love with you."

Even though I was wet and cold and filled with terror, somehow, in the darkest hours of the night, sleep took me.

"Ahoy!" someone shouted, and I sat up so fast my head cracked against the ceiling with a loud thud.

I rubbed at the sore spot as I peered over at Stryker beside me; the memories of last night all coming back to me at once. I was dismayed to see that he was as pale as a ghost, his skin waxy looking. But his chest still rose and fell, so that at least was a good sign.

"Stryker." I shook him, but his head only flopped back and forth. "Stryker." I tried again.

"Ahoy! Anyone there?" the voice called again.

I made sure the crystal heart was still shoved in my pack and crawled outside into the blinding sun to see a large boat at least four times the size of ours had pulled up alongside us. Over a dozen men stared down at me. I assumed the one wearing a tricorn hat to be the captain.

I was scared, hungry, tired, and not in the mood to be overtaken by pirates.

"If you're pirates, I will have you know that I carry magic that can make a man go mad and I will use it," I yelled.

All of the men balked, and the captain removed his hat, showcasing a balding head with a small tuft of remaining hair clinging on. "Ma'am, we are humble southern fishermen just seeing if you needed help as your mast seems to have broken in the storm."

He pointed to the top of our boat and I followed his gaze to see that he was right. One of the masts had snapped.

Well, in that case.

"I need urgent help getting my injured friend to Easteria," I told the men, knowing instinctively that I shouldn't tell them who Stryker was. If word got out that a lord was hurt, it could end badly for his kingdom. "If you help us, I can assure that you will be handsomely compensated."

The captain nodded. "I was going to offer to tug you to shore for free, but compensation is appreciated if you can afford it."

It only took a few hours as their boat was large and moved much faster, even towing us. When we got to the small marina, I paid them with all the coins left in my pouch.

After thanking the fishermen, they sailed off back to the south. The boat dock attendant tied up and anchored our boat, and I approached him.

"Do you want a hundred gold coins?" I asked him in a low voice.

His eyebrows hit his hairline. "Of course, but what would I have to do to earn them?"

I told him I was the truth witch, able to ferret out lies if he double-crossed me and asked him if he'd heard of me.

He shook his head with wide, fearful eyes. I then told

him that I had an injured Lord Stryker on board and that I needed him to help me get him back to the castle. I also asked him to send a raven for me to Dawn, and told him that if he breathed a word of this to anyone, I could afflict him with madness.

He looked both horrified and intrigued when I finished laying out what was needed of him and the consequences if he double-crossed us, but he quickly obliged. By the end of the day, we were back at the castle with a whole host of healers and physicians tending to Stryker, and the boat attendant was paid his one hundred gold coins by Stryker's castle treasurer without question.

Stryker had remained unconscious throughout the entire journey, which left my stomach in knots. I left his side only once for a few minutes to lock the Shadow Heart away in the same room he'd given me before. When I returned to his side, they still hadn't been able to rouse him.

"Why isn't he healing?" I asked the room of nurses, physicians, and healers.

Shantel, the nurse who had tended to me before, peered at me in sadness. "A power to heal is in an Ethereum lord's blood. He's lost too much. It will take time. He's in Fate's hands now."

I don't know what Stryker had conveyed to his staff in the short time we'd been apart, but they treated me as the lady of the castle from the moment I stepped foot back in Easteria. I hardly left Stryker's side, but when I did, they came to me with questions and updates on the kingdom. It was overwhelming, but also . . . familiar. No matter my current circumstances, I was still the Fall princess and had been raised to rule, so I stepped up to the challenge and did my best to keep Stryker's kingdom stable while he recovered.

I quickly learned to be thankful for the distraction because I became more anxious each day that slipped by when Stryker didn't wake. They tried to hide it, but I caught the healers' and physicians' somber looks when they tended to him. They repeatedly told me to give it time, that their lord was strong and just needed rest to heal, but I knew from their expressions that they were losing hope. He should have woken by now. The thought that he might never wake, or worse, finally succumb to his injuries, was terrifying.

He was my mate. My true love. I wanted more than the few stolen moments we'd had with each other. Now that I'd found him, I wanted, no I demanded, a lifetime with him.

It was the morning of the third day after we'd returned to Easteria when a messenger found me poring over an ancient text in the castle's library. Clearing his throat to get my attention, he waited until I looked up to tell me Lord Roan and his wife, Lady Dawn, had arrived.

I blinked back at him in surprise. It took me a second to remember that Stryker had told me Zander had also went by the name Roan. Dawn and Zander. They came.

I'd sent word to Dawn about what had happened to Stryker and finding the Shadow Heart, but hadn't requested any aid. What could they do for us that Stryker's healers and physicians weren't doing already? They had their own kingdom to worry about, but it was sweet of them to drop everything and come.

The messenger nodded, and I quickly shut the book I was reading and rushed out of the library. I'd taken it upon myself to do research on the Shadow Heart. Stryker's library was vast, and when I wasn't sitting vigil at his bedside, I was usually deep inside the ancient texts, trying to figure out what we were supposed to do with it to stop the curse.

So far, I'd come up empty, but I was trying not to let that be another thing that discouraged me. Right now it was a problem for another day. Or possibly another princess. It was not lost on me that the Wise Ones had only told me to find the Shadow Heart, not to use it.

The castle guards had led Dawn and Zander into the throne room, which was customarily where royalty greeted each other and where I waited for them now. I'm sure more than one eyebrow rose when I ran forward and flung myself in Dawn's arms. Ethereum wasn't so different from Faerie, so the castle staff probably weren't used to their leaders being informal, but I couldn't care less. I was scared and needed a friend.

Dawn's strong arms came up around me instantly and she squeezed me back just as hard.

"I can't believe you battled a shadow dragon," she said when we finally broke apart, concern shining from her eyes even though I was no longer in danger from the vicious beast.

I gave a wobbly half-laugh. "It's an experience I hope to never repeat. And Stryker did most of the battling."

"How's my brother?" Zander asked from behind Dawn.

She shifted to the side and he stepped up beside her, wrapping an arm around her waist to draw her near. I didn't even think he realized he was doing it, but I could tell that his concern for his brother was making him anxious and he needed her physically close.

Seeing them interact and how they leaned on one another made something twist in my chest. I could easily picture Stryker and me being each other's rocks and safe places, but what if we never got the opportunity to have what they did?

I mentally shook myself, knowing that wallowing in fear would get me nowhere. Besides, that's not what Stryker needed from me right now. He needed my strength, not my weakness.

"The same, I'm afraid," I told him. "He still hasn't woken. The healers and physicians think he just needs more time, but . . ."

I let the sentence trail off, not knowing what else to say. The grimness in Zander's face told me he understood what I left unsaid. That he should have woken by now.

"Come," I said, turning and gesturing that they should follow me. "You must have come to see him for yourself. I'll take you to him."

When I glanced over my shoulder to see if they were following, I caught them exchanging a look that made my stomach plummet to my toes. That's not why they were here. At least not the only reason.

"What is it?" I asked bluntly, turning back to them.

Zander sighed. "I do want to see my brother, but before that, can we go somewhere to talk?" He cast a glance around the throne room, his eyes catching on the few guards stationed around us. "Somewhere private?" he added, and a feeling of foreboding settled in my chest.

Stealing myself, I took Dawn and Zander back to the library and then instructed the guards that followed us to wait outside. I shut the double doors behind us and turned to face them. "What's going on?"

"We think there's a rogue group planning a coup against Stryker," Zander said plainly.

My heart pounded wildly in my chest. "Why would you think that?"

"You may or may not know that my kingdom was taken over by rebels led by a creature from darkness called the rondak. They killed my brother and then seized the kingdom from me. It wasn't until Dawn arrived," he said, shooting his wife an affectionate smile that she returned, "that I was able to reclaim what was mine."

I nodded because Dawn had filled me in on what happened during our time together, so I knew exactly what he was talking about.

"Ever since that happened, I fortified my spy network," Zander continued. "I never want to be caught unawares if something like that starts brewing again. I have several trusted spies embedded in what's left of that rebel faction.

Two days ago I received word from them that news of Stryker's condition has reached the rebel leaders, and that they are planning on trying to take this kingdom while my brother is unable to do anything about it."

I gasped and pressed a hand to my stomach. Stryker was literally fighting for his life right now, and this group was planning on taking advantage of his weakness? To take everything that meant anything to him away from him.

Anger rose up on the heels of fear and disbelief. I wouldn't let that happen. This was Stryker's kingdom, his land. I wouldn't let him lose it.

I started back toward the doors, already forming a plan in my mind.

"What are you doing?" Dawn called to me before I reached them.

"Getting ready to defend my mate's legacy," I said with conviction.

Respect flared in Zander's eyes and a small smile lifted the corner of Dawn's mouth.

"Although I admire the initiative," Zander said, "can we talk before you sound the alarm? We have an idea."

Chapter Twenty-One

D awn, Zander, and I stayed in the library throughout the afternoon, planning. I left three times to check on Stryker, but his condition was the same. Even though it killed me to be away from him, I knew my time was better spent strategizing with his brother and Dawn about how to save his kingdom.

Thankfully, Dawn and Zander had come prepared. They'd left half of their army in their lands on high alert. The last thing they wanted was for the rebels to try to take over while they were off helping Stryker and the Eastern Kingdom. But they'd quietly sent the other half into the Eastern Kingdom the same day they themselves departed. Their troops were now camping south of the Jewel Spring Mountains, awaiting their command only a little less than a day's ride from us, but hidden so that the rebels didn't know they were close.

We decided it was best to make the rebels believe that we

were unaware of their plans, and therefore unprepared. We hoped that would make them sloppy when they finally made their move. We also decided to send coded messages to Stryker's brothers, Zane and Adrien, asking for help. Zander wasn't sure if they'd be able to send any troops, both brothers had their own inter-kingdom issues to deal with, but if Stryker ever needed his brothers, it was now.

Eventually, we did call in Stryker's captains and explain what we knew. We kept the knowledge to a small group of people, though, concerned that our plans would make it back to the rebels and ruin everything. I had ensured there were no traitors in Stryker's army with my truth-telling power, but Zander explained how devious and tricky the rebels could be and cautioned me to only reveal knowledge to the most trusted of Stryker's men. It was a warning I was going to heed, so before we let anyone know what was going on, I used my magic to ferret out if they were still trustworthy or had been recently bribed to turn on Stryker in his weakened state.

At the end of the very long day, Zander asked if he could see Stryker before he and Dawn turned in. I led both of them to Stryker's room and saw real anguish in Zander's eyes when he spotted his brother, lying defenseless and unconscious in bed. He immediately went to Stryker, clasped his hand, and began talking to him.

I didn't know if Stryker could hear and understand what we said to him in his current condition, but I hoped he could. Zander told his brother he was sorry for not helping him in the past and asked for forgiveness. He told Stryker he loved him, and that he was so glad that Stryker had found his mate. My eyes welled up a little at that point, and I left the room to give Zander privacy.

I was shaken awake by Dawn. I sat up, bleary-eyed with my heart pounding in my chest.

"There has been an attack at the front gates. Zander is locking down the castle," she said.

Those words had me jumping from my bed and throwing on my boots and a thick dressing gown. "Was anyone hurt?"

Dawn nodded sadly. "It appears that one of the rebels got inside the castle. Zander took care of him, but not before he killed two guards. We think he was going to bring word back about the defenses of the fortress and the number of guards. Things like that."

"Which means the rebels are close by?" I asked her.

"We think so," Dawn confirmed. "Sunup is in an hour. Let's have an early breakfast and adjust the plan. War is at our doorstep."

Ten minutes later, I was pacing the dining room as Zander and Dawn ate.

"You need to keep up your strength, Aribella," Zander said. "For if a battle breaks out. I don't know the next time we'll be able to eat."

I waved him off. "I don't care about food. I want these bastards out of Stryker's kingdom," I growled.

Dawn grinned. "Princess of the Fall Court, I always thought you were the shy and meek one. I'm glad to be proved wrong."

I sent her a half smile, but my mind was racing. "What if we sent out scouts to try to find their camp and report back how many troops they have?" I asked.

"Already done." Zander smiled.

"We should send a new raven to Zane and Adrien, ask for them to send troops."

Zander's face fell a little. "I did, but they still haven't responded to the first raven, and Stryker has not been the kindest to them over the years."

"He's their brother," I shouted.

Zander just nodded. "And it's complicated. If this battle wasn't as imminent, I'd risk contacting them telepathically. But it could put me down for an entire day, and we can't afford that right now."

I groaned, feeling flustered that there wasn't more I could do. "How big is Stryker's army? Is everyone ready? Should we call for volunteers?"

Zander placed his fork down and stood, walking over to stand before me. "You are doing a great job, Aribella. But we've done all we can. I've sent word for my men to move closer in the event of an attack. Stryker's army is stationed and ready to fight. All we can do is wait."

I deflated, sinking in on myself. Wait until we were attacked? It was a horrible option, but seemed like the only one. "What if we went out to meet them, fought before they even got here?"

Zander nodded. "Once my spy gets back with numbers and their location, we will consider that option."

He was right. We'd done and tried everything, and I needed to just sit here and wait for more information.

I picked at my food and anxiously cast glances out the window for the next few hours until two men entered the dining room. A man dressed in all black, but covered in dirt, with a black gauze scarf wrapped over most of his face, entered with a guard. The man unwrapped the scarf from his face and puffs of dust flew into the air around him.

"Samuel. What have you learned?" Zander asked. This must be his spy.

I stood as well as Dawn and we waited on bated breath for him to speak.

Samuel bowed slightly to all of us and then fixed Zander with a troublesome gaze. "My lord, it's worse than we thought. They have over ten thousand men. An uncountable amount."

Dizziness washed over me. Ten thousand? Did he say ten thousand?

Zander didn't say anything back, so I looked over at him to find that he was utterly speechless.

"How many men do we have here in Easteria?" I asked.

Zander swallowed hard. "Two thousand."

"And how many did you bring that are waiting to help?" I hoped it was another two thousand.

Zander appeared ashamed. "Five hundred. I took heavy losses with the sickness ravaging my land. And we're still replenishing the troops after reclaiming my kingdom."

No.

"If ten thousand fae attack this city, what will happen?" I asked frankly.

Zander peered at Dawn and then me. "We will be defeated. They will scale the walls and take the city and the castle. I will be killed and you two will be . . ." He drifted off, and I used my imagination.

"How did they get ten thousand?" Dawn spoke for the first time. She looked at her husband. "There weren't that many when you drove them out of our kingdom."

"A lot of them looked like Midlanders," the spy said.

Zander nodded. "They've long been in need of a ruler. Thank you, Samuel. Stay nearby in case I need you again."

Samuel inclined his head in obedience, and then he and the guard left.

"We aren't going to let this happen, right?" I asked Zander.

His gaze flicked to his wife and then to her belly for half a second. "You should take Aribella and flee to the north."

Dawn shook her head. "I have powerful magic. I can help."

"Me too," I interjected.

Again, Zander looked at her belly. "Dawn," he pressed. "I think it's best for your *health*," he emphasized the word. "And safety, if you flee."

I gasped, my gaze snapping to Dawn. "You're pregnant!"

She gave me a sheepish grin. "Barely. I just missed my monthly bleed a few weeks ago. It's too early to—"

I crashed into her, hugging her tightly. "I'm so happy for

you. Amidst all this craziness, this is wonderful news." When I pulled back, Zander was beaming; they both were.

"We don't want to seem too happy about things while our people are suffering, so please keep this private," Dawn asked, and Zander stepped over and rubbed her stomach.

"Of course," I told her. "And I agree, you should flee to the north. Both of you. There is no reason to stay if this war cannot be fought."

Zander frowned. "And if we did . . . what about you?"

"I will stay with Stryker."

"You could both come," Zander offered. "I can still have my men fight to give the castle a chance."

I shook my head. "Stryker would never leave his people. And I won't leave him."

Dawn pursed her lips. "We're not going. We can at least try to fight."

"Ten thousand, Dawn. That's a lot of soldiers. You need to go. I'll give you the Shadow Heart, and you can figure out a way to get word to Isolde so she knows not to kill Adrien or Zane."

Dawn shook her head, but Zander pleaded with her. "You have our child in your belly. Would you really risk its life for something that's futile?"

Dawn, strong unflappable Dawn, began to softly weep then. It was a horrible choice, to feel like she was leaving me and all of these people to die, but I knew she had to think of her future and that of her unborn child.

"Go. Our people still need you," I told her, thinking of Faerie.

How much time had passed? I'd lost track while Stryker had been ill. Had it been a month already? If it had, I'd already lost my ability to return home. Not that I cared; I'd never have been able to do what it took to create a portal back to my world. To carve out Stryker or any of his brothers' hearts from their body with my faestone dagger. That hadn't been an option for weeks now. I was staying here, so best not to dwell on that any longer.

"Okay," Dawn whimpered. "Okay." This time, she was resigned.

It was decided Dawn and Zander would flee to the north and send another round of ravens to their brothers for help. Dawn would try to find a way to speak to Isolde so we could save Adrien or Zane from being harmed by her.

I went to my room and got the Shadow Heart, giving it to Dawn. Zander helped her get into a carriage and I pulled him aside. "Can I evacuate the people?"

He shook his head. "Mass movement like that would tip off the rebels and if they attacked you out in the open, it would be a bloodbath. Their quarrel is not with the people. They will likely let them live. They need slaves and taxpayers." A grim assessment with a sliver of light.

"Thank you." I reached out and grasped his forearms. "For everything."

He nodded. "I would stay if it were up to me, but Dawn would never allow it," he said.

I smiled, thinking of their love for each other and not wanting to be parted. "As she shouldn't. You belong together."

He frowned. "Last chance to come with. I can bring Stryker and my healers will tend to him around the clock."

I shook my head. "I don't know your brother as well as you do, but I know he would never leave his people without a leader."

Zander smiled, but it didn't reach his eyes. "You're right. He would go down with the ship."

And that's what I would do. Stryker and I would do it together.

Dawn peeked her head eagerly out of the carriage and I stepped over to her.

"It doesn't feel right to leave," she said.

I nodded. "It never will. But you must." I gave her a hug and she held me for longer than would be considered normal.

"Tell me you won't hate me for this. Tell me you forgive me for being selfish," she whispered in my ear.

I laughed. "Oh Dawn, there is nothing to forgive. This isn't selfish. You have to think of your unborn child and the people of Faerie."

She nodded, determined.

Zander slipped into the carriage and then they left before sunup. They needed to leave before the castle doors were locked and reinforced. Dawn said they would take a path that was lesser known and avoid the giant army, bypassing them completely.

Once I lost sight of their carriage, I sighed in relief. Knowing that she had the Shadow Heart and would try to somehow speak with the Winter princess brought me some peace. I'd done all I could for my people, and now it was again up to the Summer champion to help them.

I informed the household staff that a ten-thousand-troop army was coming to attack the city and then relieved them to go home and be with their families. I told them not to fear, that the men taking over the city were not likely to hurt them but that it would be unsafe to flee as they could be found on the road.

I then called in the heads of Stryker's army. All through the night, we formulated our defensive plans and then sent them out to get the troops in position. It was going to be morning soon and the men finally left, so I made some tea. I wouldn't be sleeping at all, not even a wink. After drinking a cup, I poured a second and slipped into Stryker's room. The healers and physicians had been dismissed to be with their families as well, so it was just us. I set the tea down on the windowsill near the bed and slipped into the covers next to him, resting my head on his shoulder. The soft thumping of his heart against my cheek brought me comfort.

"I dreamed up my future husband when I was seven years old," I told him, praying he could hear me. "He'd have blonde hair, be super nice, and know how to make chocolate cake." I laughed at the seven-year-old's version of my Prince Charming. "But instead I got you."

I propped up on my elbow and stared at his strikingly handsome features. I ran a finger down his cheek scar, and then over his lips. "The darker version of my handsome dream man. I wonder if you know how to make chocolate cake?" I asked him.

But his silence was heartbreaking.

"Answer me," I begged, trying to keep the tears from welling in my eyes.

"Wake up, Stryker." I shook him a little, feeling desperate. But the rise and fall of his chest did not change, nor did his eyes open.

There was a knock at the doorway. I glanced up to see one of Stryker's captains.

"The rebel soldiers' lanterns can be seen on the horizon. We think they mean to attack at first light. It's time," he said.

I nodded, wiping my eyes and then planting a chaste kiss on Stryker's cheek. "I will do you proud, my love," I told him and then stood from the bed.

My tea had cooled and so I chugged it and then followed the captain to war.

If Stryker could not lead his people, then I would. If nothing else, then as a penance of not being able to save my own. My blood would run in rivers down these streets before I let one rebel soldier cross this threshold.

Chapter Twenty-Two

The city of Easteria was surrounded on all sides by an imposing city wall. The wall offered protection to the capital city and castle, but was in no way unscalable. As I climbed the rampart steps, I quickly realized Zander was correct. As soon as the army arrived, they'd have the numbers to overwhelm our forces and breach the first line of defense.

The first enemy troops were spotted coming from the west, from the direction of the Midlands, so the captains and I diverted the majority of the army to the western-facing rampart. But since the city could be attacked from any side, we still assigned guards along the northern, eastern, and southern walls as well.

I would be the first to say that I didn't have any battle experience, but I was well read. I'd spent countless hours back in Faerie reading of different wars and battles throughout our history and I knew that attacking us head on could possibly be a diversion. I didn't know the opposing rebel army, but I wasn't about to leave parts of the city exposed. These rebels might be trying to distract us with a battle in one area only to slip in the back when we weren't looking.

When I reached the top of the city wall, more than one set of eyebrows rose. I was decked out in full armor, just like all of the other troops. Dawn had left me her armor, but I was shorter and more petite than her, so not everything fit perfectly. I used which pieces I could, and then some of the guards helped me find the rest. I think that they dug out some children's training armor, which perhaps wasn't the best, but I would make do.

One of the captains named Thierry rushed up to me, concern heavy in his gaze. "Milady, you shouldn't be here. Please go back to the castle where it's safe. This is not a place for a lady."

He tried to shoo me back down the stairs, but I held my ground, tilting my chin up to look down my nose at him, even though he was at least a foot taller than me.

"If Lord Stryker was well, would he be cowering in the castle at such a time as this?" I asked, putting steel into my voice.

Captain Thierry stopped trying to get me to move. He looked at me with a hint of weary respect. "No, milady. He'd be right here with the rest of his men."

"Exactly," I said. "So this is where I will remain." I moved past the captain and through the troops until I reached the ledge and could look out over what would soon become the battleground.

The sky was only starting to lighten. The rebel troops had been spotted late last night, the light from their lanterns dotting the horizon line, but they'd stopped and now remained in the distance, just out of our archers' range.

Our best guess was that they were waiting for the early morning hours to attack when the light would show them their target. The anticipation of knowing the battle was coming with nothing left to do but wait, turned my stomach to knots.

I was careful not to let my anxiety show on my face as I strained my eyes to see the line of rebels in the distance. I was determined to be strong for our troops, just like I knew Stryker would be if he were here. In the face of almost certain failure, these brave men deserved that much, at least. To see me facing the same fate as they did. To look death straight in the eye and dare it to come for us.

I don't know when exactly I'd started to consider Stryker's people my own. But it happened, and here I was, willing to die for them.

An eerie sort of silence fell over our troops as we waited. I sensed someone come up beside me and looked over to see Stryker's head captain, an unseelie named Greylocke. Greylocke had tawny skin and yellow eyes. A pair of leathery wings sprouted from his back and his feet were hooved. He said he'd been part of the Eastern Army for more than three decades, serving under previous lords before Stryker. The layers of scars on one side of his face and neck, as well as his exposed hands, said that this would not be the first battle he'd seen. I was thankful for his experience at a moment such as this.

"It won't be long now," he said, his gaze fastened on the rebels.

"Have any other troops been spotted from the other walls?" I asked.

He pressed his lips into a hard line, but shook his head. The look on his face didn't lighten, though, and I knew he was as concerned as I was about fighting this battle on multiple fronts. We didn't have the troops to hold all four walls. But for now, we could only hope our fears wouldn't come to fruition.

It was just as the first ray of sun crested the hill that a battle cry rose in the distance, piercing the silence. As if moving as one, a line of rebel soldiers started marching forward. The footfalls of so many striking the ground sent a small vibration through the rampart wall. I could practically feel the fear of the soldiers around me as they saw what we were up against.

"This is suicide," someone yelled and I craned my neck to the side to see who had spoken. A middle-aged seelie fae had broken ranks and was backing away from his position. "There are too many! We'll all be killed!" he screamed frantically, stirring up the already frightened troops.

"Silence," Captain Greylocke growled at the fae. "Get back in line. Your family is depending on it."

"We should concede now before it's too late," someone

else cried, and I looked to see another one of our men turn and try to run for the steps.

To the left and right of me, the troops' faces showed their fear. A few more started to back up as the rebels' battle cry grew louder. If I didn't do something, this was going to spiral out of control. Already, soldiers had started to drop their weapons and break ranks.

I'd never tried to stretch my powers over so many, but digging deep, I reached inside and gathered my magic, and then sent it out over our troops, pushing calm and peace into as many as possible. I specifically targeted the two that had started yelling and trying to flee. Immediately, their bodies sagged in relief and they grew silent.

The murmurs that had begun to circulate throughout the rest of the troops also ceased. Soldiers picked up their discarded weapons and fell back into line.

With the troops calmed, I slowly pulled my influence from them. It wouldn't be fair to let them go into battle with a false sense of peace and security. They needed to be sharp, and sometimes fear is what gave that to them. I wouldn't take their autonomy away from them at a time such as this. I wanted them to fight with me. Needed them to. But I wouldn't force them.

When I'd pulled all of my magic back, there was still a heightened sense of alarm hanging in the air, but no one was bolting.

"You can do this. We must stand as one," I yelled, raising my voice as loud as possible so that it would carry far. "For your lord, and for your kingdom!"

"For lord and kingdom," someone shouted and then the rest of the troops started banging their shields and stomping their feet until the enemies' battle cry was drowned out.

The rebel army was almost within striking range. The plan was to take out as many as we could with arrows. We didn't have the numbers, but we had the high ground, and that counted for something.

Captain Greylocke pulled his blade and then raised it into the air. Our troops stilled.

He looked down at me and said, "On your mark."

Shock froze my tongue. In fae battles, the ruler always led his or her troops into battle. If Stryker had been here, Captain Greylocke would have deferred to him, but since the Eastern lord wasn't here, he was letting me take the lead.

This wasn't a small thing. This act showed the entire army that I was in charge.

A ball of barbed wire formed in my gut.

Who was I to lead an Ethereum army? I was just a princess of Faerie. A stranger in a foreign land. But the way Captain Greylocke looked down at me gave me the confidence I needed.

If the last several weeks proved anything, it was that I wasn't *just* a princess. I was a survivor. I was a champion. I was a warrior, and it was about time I acted like it.

Stryker was counting on me. I wouldn't let him down.

Nodding once to Captain Greylocke, I faced west, cupped my hands around my mouth and shouted, "Archers, ready your bows!"

To my left and right, arrows nocked and bows tilted up.

"Aim for under their arms and their necks," I said, reminding them of their opponents' weak points. "If they are flying, shoot through their wings."

I watched the approaching army. The ground shook beneath their feet as they pounded toward us. I lifted an arm, signaling that they were nearing the mark. For every second that passed, my heart beat stronger than the next, but I knew I needed to wait until just the right moment. We had to take out as many of the rebels as we could in this initial round. And we wouldn't get a second chance.

The rebels were now close enough that I could make out some of their features. It was clear that unseelie outnumbered seelie in their army at least three to one. The only reason that made me nervous was because I wasn't versed in all the magic of the unseelie, and also that could mean they had a good number of troops who could fly. The flyers would have the easiest time breaching our walls.

The first fae finally crossed the marker in the field in front of us, which told me they were in our archers' range. I counted a couple more seconds to make sure a good number of them were in range, and then screamed, "Fire!" At the same time, I dropped my arm.

A spray of arrows shot into the sky, muting the sun's rays for a few seconds as they soared through the air before plummeting back down to the ground. Death cries rang out as our arrows found purchase in the enemies' flesh.

The battle had begun.

The first three rows of rebels fell dead, which caused a

clog of five rows back to stumble over them. Relief rushed through me that we had bought time to reload.

"Reload!" I screamed.

By the time the rebels had crawled over and trampled the dead, our archers were ready for another round.

"Fire at will," I announced.

Another onslaught of arrows loosed, some of them dipped in oil and lit on fire, and I grinned as they hit their mark.

"They're splitting. I'm going to the north wall," Captain Greylocke said, running along the top of the wall, leaping over the crouched legs of our bowmen.

He was right. The rebels splintered off and created a V formation as they moved to our front north wall.

No. This was what I feared. Fighting on all sides.

The bow men rained another set of arrows and that's when I saw something blurry in the sky coming for us.

"Take cover!" I shouted and ducked behind the stone barricade.

An iron ball that had been shot from a catapult soared over our heads and crashed into the center of town, taking out a thatched home.

When I popped back up, dizziness washed over me. They were on us. Already crawling on the shoulders of the men in front of them and climbing the wall.

No way. We were not going out like that. Not that quickly. We'd barely just begun fighting.

"Pour the fire," I commanded.

Buckets of oil, alcohol, and anything flammable we had

were poured on the men, and then they were ignited with a fiery arrow. It was a horrible way to die but I told myself it was just what happened in war.

Two flying unseelie tried to breech the wall, but our archers took them down quickly.

I breathed a sigh of relief. We were holding our own. I heard shouts of command from the two walls to my left and right and prayed they were holding up as well.

"Low on arrows," one archer said. "Low on arrows," another called back until one by one I was informed that we were running out of supplies to keep up the fight.

We'd been at this for maybe thirty minutes. Was that all the history books would say about Stryker's kingdom? Easteria fought in the great battle of the rebels for a whole half hour before they succumbed.

No. Not on my watch.

"I'm out," an archer yelled after loosing his last arrow. "Out, out, out," rang across the northern wall.

"We should surrender," someone screamed.

"Hold your positions," I shouted to the men. "I'm going to use my power."

I wanted to warn them because if I pulled this off, what they were about to see would be very disturbing without context.

Taking in a deep breath, I felt for my magic. It was like a river, a current that ran right through me and I changed the shape and contents of the water depending on the emotion or thoughts I wanted to use to influence the person or people. The fae coming at me had every intention of killing me and Stryker, so I broke my own rule . . .

I needed the rebels to come unhinged, to drive them to insanity so that they would be easy to defeat. Gathering my magic, I pushed paranoia and extreme anxiety out into the throngs of people rushing up the wall. You could see the moment it hit them. Their faces contorted and they began to peer over their shoulders with wide eyes. Then a few of them dropped to the ground, grabbing their faces. They screamed, scratching at their own skin and running away from the castle.

I flicked my gaze to Captain Thierry, who now stood beside me. He appeared to be a mixture of horrified and proud. I was slightly alarmed myself, but this was war and I wasn't about to allow the innocent people of Easteria to die.

I ran to the front north wall where Captain Greylocke slashed out at a rebel fae attempting to climb up over the wall, and I did the same thing. I pushed pure paranoia, laced with anxiety and fear, into the first few rows of soldiers. It was like a ball of the worst emotions a person could experience, and even though I was doing this to help our people, my heart ached with regret.

A strong hand came over my shoulder. "You're saving countless lives. Don't feel shame about that," Captain Greylocke said. He must have read my expression.

"East wall needs help," one of the soldiers near me called.

I ran that way, stumbling over legs of the men crouched and reached the wall just as the first line of men came over.

My chest heaved with all the running, but I shoved my own discomfort aside.

I pushed my power into the rebels, this time focusing just on fear, which I hoped would cause them to flee.

It worked.

The men screamed, running away and scrambling down the wall as if they'd seen a ghost.

"Lady Aribella!" someone yelled from beside me. "The north wall needs you again."

I sprinted to reach them, my lungs burning and heart feeling like it was going to burst from my chest. This was a large city and sprinting across the tops of walls during a battle was not ideal. As I appeared, a new set of men had reached the top.

I used my power on them, fear and paranoia sending them fleeing in droves.

And so this went for hours, until the sun was low in the sky, resting just above the horizon. I ran from wall to wall, blanketing the rebels with my power, never taking it back. I ignored the frantic beat of my heart, the burning in my limbs, the sweat dripping from my face and chest from running wall to wall, and the pounding in my head. None of that mattered because we were holding our own against a ten-thousand-strong army, sending hundreds of men fleeing in all directions.

It was nothing short of a miracle that I didn't pass out.

"Lady Aribella," Captain Greylocke grasped my shoulders and forced me to look at him.

Why did he look so horrified?

Some wetness trickled from my nose and I reached up to touch it, only to come back with blood.

"My lady, you have fought with honor. But you need to rest. You can't do this all day and night."

I yanked my shoulders from his grasp. "I can and I will," I snapped, tripping over my own feet and catching myself at the last second by gripping the wall.

"At least have some water, some dried fruits." He handed me a canteen.

"North wall needs help!" a soldier cried, and I ran to them, plugging my nose and keeping my head tilted back in an effort to stop the bleeding.

I'd always wondered if there was a limit to my power. I guessed today I would find out.

I reached for my magic and whimpered when I didn't feel it there. The river had run dry and now I grasped at nothing.

My magic seemed to work in such a way that I sent it out, but eventually I pulled it back or it came back to me over time. Since it was still on the enemy troops that had fled, I found that I didn't have any more power to pour over the rebels that were still advancing. So I reached out and started to pull back the magic I'd sent out, and I felt the river fill within me until it was roaring.

I sucked in a cleansing breath, ready to take down more rebels, when another iron ball sailed over my head and towards the castle Stryker currently lay in. I could only pray it didn't harm him as I pressed on with a battle cry.

Chapter Twenty-Three
STRYKER

My hearing returned first. Screams of agony and battle cries broke through the fog that held me captive. I still wasn't fully aware of my body, so when the first piercing noises broke through the haze, I thought I was dreaming.

But it wasn't a dream, it was a nightmare.

I tried to come back into myself, to force the arms and legs that I couldn't feel to move, but my body wasn't my own.

Bits and pieces of some faraway slaughter filtered through to me in audible chunks that would tear apart my ear drums one second, and then go silent the next.

Inch by inch, I dragged myself back into consciousness. Driven by the desperate instinct that I was needed, that I was about to lose something precious, I clawed against the dark abyss that threatened to pull me back under.

After what felt like an eternity, I finally forced my eyes

open. My limbs were heavy as lead and my mouth was as dry as the Southern deserts.

Through blurred vision and the low light of a dying day, I made out that I was in my chamber, back in my castle in Easteria.

How did I get here? What's happening?

Just as I formulated the questions, an explosion ripped through the outer wall of my room, punching a hole and causing rocks and mortar to rain down on me.

Forcing my body to move, I rolled out of bed just before part of the ceiling caved in and the bed collapsed.

If I had still been lying there, I would have been crushed.

I shoved to my feet and quickly stumbled to the door. When I looked through the giant new hole in the room, I gasped.

From my vantage point high in the castle, I could see the chaos on top of and beyond the city walls. Throngs of rebel forces pressed in on all sides.

We were under attack. And from the looks of it, losing.

Fear grabbed my heart and squeezed, stealing my breath. *Aribella.*

Where was she? Was she safe?

It was all coming back to me. Going to the island with Aribella to look for the Shadow Heart and finding the shadow dragon instead. Using my magic to force her onto our boat and away from danger.

The last thing I remembered was seeing Aribella's sweet face across the burning clearing before getting swatted by the dragon's spiked tail.

I didn't remember the impact, but when I looked down at my chest and abdomen, I could see the freshly healed scars.

But what had happened between then and now?

I was here and alive, which meant Aribella must have battled the dragon and won.

My brave girl.

She must have also figured out a way to get me back to my castle, which couldn't have been an easy feat with me unconscious and gravely injured.

Pride rose up in my chest for my little truth witch. She was as strong in spirit as she was beautiful.

But the warm feeling chilled as I glanced back through the hole in my wall at the devastation that was being wrought on my beloved capital city.

There were multiple fires speckled throughout the districts. Pillars of smoke rose up from other areas. And the sounds of anguish and agony as well as weapons clashing filled the air.

I prayed Aribella was far from Easteria. That she'd left me here and traveled safely back to Dawn and my brother.

The thought of being separated from her tore me in two, but I'd rather see her safely away from me than be caught up in this mess. I may not understand why my kingdom was under attack, but I saw enough to comprehend one thing: today was most likely my last.

Springing into motion, I had enough sense to grab a sword and pull on some boots before leaving my half-destroyed chamber. The hallways were completely empty as I ran down them toward the front entrance.

When I finally stumbled out of the castle, I was dropped into chaos.

My people ran this way and that, trying to put out fires and triage the wounded. I grabbed the arm of a dark-skinned fae as he rushed by me, halting him.

"My lord?" he said, his eyes wide as saucers.

"What's happened here?" I asked, having to yell to be heard over the ruckus around us.

"A rebel army of Midlanders attacked the city at dawn. They say it's close to ten thousand strong."

Ten thousand rebels.

I did some quick calculations in my head. Not all my troops were in Easteria at the moment, but even if they were, that still wouldn't be enough to face an army that large.

"Why did they attack?" I asked.

The man cast a look over his shoulder, anxiety rolling off him in waves. He obviously needed to be somewhere, but I couldn't let him leave before he answered me.

"Because, my lord, they heard you were ill. Near death. They knew we were vulnerable without you. They saw an opportunity to take your kingdom and riches, and took it."

Of course. It was a lesson I'd already learned and the reason I worked so hard to keep up a fierce reputation. The moment your enemy smelled weakness, they would be on you, ready to shove a blade in your back and take what was yours.

"Aeon!" someone yelled, and the man in front of me went tense. A woman ran toward us, her eyes wide with fear.

"That's my wife, my lord," the man said and held up some bandages. "My daughter was injured and I was getting—"

"Go," I said, dismissing him.

He turned and ran to the woman, and together they disappeared down a side street.

Anger stoked in my gut and I reached for my magic.

I may not have the men to match this rebel army, but I was a force to be reckoned with. I would crush the insurgents with my darkness. They wouldn't be able to see who they were fighting, giving my troops the opportunity to pick them off, one at a time.

But as I tried to gather my magic, I found the well dry. I couldn't do more than create a few small puffs of darkness.

The blood chilled in my veins.

The shadow dragon.

I'd been stabbed with the tail spikes. No wonder it had taken me so long to regain consciousness. I must have lost a ton of blood, for the magic that regenerated and healed me was carried in my blood. For all intents and purposes, I'd been as weak as a magicless fae, and forced to recover as slowly as one. Even now, my muscles felt feebler than they should and waves of dizziness hit me, telling me I wasn't fully recovered.

I didn't fear that I'd lost my magic. I knew it would return along with my strength, but it would take time.

Time that I didn't have right now.

I looked up at the city wall nearest me. It hadn't been breached yet, so the bulk of my army was still up on the ramparts, keeping the rebels from overrunning the city.

Since the castle staff were all missing, I needed to find one of my captains. Immediately. My top priority should have been protecting Easteria, but the truth was I needed to know that Aribella was safe. One of my captains would surely be able to tell me where she was. I hoped they'd sent her away to the safety of Noreum before this attack.

After I'd come back to Easteria and realized the mistake I'd made by leaving her, I'd given my captains strict instructions that if she were ever to return to the castle, she was to be afforded every privilege as the lady of the house. It was clear they hadn't understood my reasoning at the time, but I trusted that they'd followed my orders. Once I knew she was safe, I could focus on saving my kingdom.

Taking off for the closest city wall, I spotted one of my captains shouting orders at the base of the west wall.

Shock showed on his face when I reached him, but it quickly morphed to relief. "My lord, you're well again. We're saved!"

Not quite.

"Aribella, where is she?" I asked, hoping against every hope that he said somewhere far from here. But to my dismay, he lifted a hand and pointed in the direction of the north wall.

"Last I saw of her, she was up on the wall, fighting beside the rest of the army."

No.

Dread tore through me, and without another word, I raced to the north wall. Every step I took felt like I was running underwater. I couldn't get there fast enough.

The wall and my soldiers upon it finally came into view. I started to search frantically for Aribella, when out of the corner of my eye I spotted a splash of red hair. Turning my head, my heart skipped a beat.

There she was.

I couldn't see her face because she was looking out over the battle beyond the walls, but I'd know her anywhere. Her deep red hair hung in tussled waves down to the middle of her back. Mismatched armor hugged her petite frame as she shouted commands to my men that they rushed to obey.

She was magnificent.

I started for the nearest stairs, my gaze fixed on her, when a rebel crawled over the wall in front of her.

Terror like I'd never experienced before slammed into me like a raging bull.

"Aribella!" I shouted, my hand outstretched to send a wave of shadows to take down her attacker before he could strike, but nothing happened.

As he lifted the blade in his hand and angled it at her, I was powerless to do anything but watch.

Chapter Twenty-Four

A rebel popped up in front of me, a dagger in his hand, but I punched out with my fist, connecting with the side of his head and sending him backward.

Using my power, I pushed fear and paranoia into the new crowd of rebels and they fell back.

"My lady, they are breeching the door," a soldier called, pointing further down the wall.

In that moment my brain was fuzzy. I could have sworn I'd just heard Stryker call my name.

I ran, my foot catching on a loose brick. I tumbled forward, cracking my chin on the stone floor. Pain shot across my jaw as blackness danced at the edge of my vision.

I shook my head, standing and walking more slowly to the wall's edge. I peered out at the mass of rebel soldiers. They had cannons aimed right at us.

I pushed a wave of terror into the men manning the cannons and they ran away screaming.

"My lady," someone called to my right.

"Help us," to my left.

Tears lined my eyes as I pushed a mass of my power outward, trying to encompass as many rebels as I could.

A slice of sharp pain ripped through my head then and I inhaled sharply, grasping the side of my face. The dizziness won over in that moment and I staggered backward, but managed to stay conscious.

Captain Greylocke caught me, and I looked up at him. "I'm tired," I said weakly.

He peered down at me with pride. "You did well. You gave Easteria everything you could."

Why was there resignation in his voice?

"No. We must keep fighting." I grabbed the sword from my belt and tried to hold it up, but my fingers were weak and it clattered to the ground.

"Take a carriage out of the south wall and flee with Lord Stryker. I can hold them off to give you time," Captain Greylocke said.

Tears flowed down my cheeks, but I shook my head. "I won't leave you."

Stryker's people had become my people. I was in this battle to the end.

He sighed, helping me up into a sitting position and then put a small dagger into my fingers. "I wish my lord could have seen you battle today. It was a sight to behold."

He held a fist over his chest and bowed to me as I rested my back against the stone wall.

I peered out over the sea of rebels and sighed. We'd barely made a dent.

And where were Zander's five hundred men that had been waiting nearby? They'd likely fled. I didn't blame them.

"I wish I could have seen that too." Stryker's husky voice came from my right, and I spun in shock.

He stood shirtless, his messy hair splayed out atop his head as he loosely held a sword and peered at me with concern.

"Are you injured?" He dropped to one knee before me, swiping at the blood on my upper lip.

"She's been using her magic on the advancing army for hours," Captain Greylocke said.

It was nothing short of a miracle I'd stayed conscious this entire time.

Stryker pressed his lips to my forehead. "Why didn't you flee?"

I peered up at him. "Because you wouldn't have."

A rebel flew over the wall and I cried out. Stryker spun, lashing out with his sword and shearing off the man's wing, which caused him to drop.

"My powers are still weak. I cannot fight with shadows," he told Captain Greylocke, and I panicked. He held out his hand and a tiny puff of shadow formed before fading away.

Stryker pulled me into a standing position, and the general faced us both. "It was a pleasure to serve you, my lord." He saluted Stryker and my stomach clenched.

This was it. After all that, Stryker would wake, only to see his men be slaughtered.

"And you. Go be with your family," Stryker said. Then he turned to every man on the wall. "Retreat. Go be with your families in these final moments," he announced.

It was like a punch to the gut. He was giving up?

But even as he said it, I peered down to see thousands of rebels climbing the walls, about to breach the city.

We were done. This was the end.

"Did you send ravens to my brothers?" Stryker asked me. I just nodded. "They did not respond. I'm sorry."

The hurt in his face gutted me.

He pulled me into his arms then and held me. When I peered back at him, he looked devastated. "I wanted so much more time to love you, Aribella. I didn't get enough time."

I nodded, blinking back tears, and then our lips met in a frantic kiss.

This was the end. The end of my mission to save my people, the end of this battle, the end of my time with Stryker, the end of it all. In minutes I would be wiped from this realm and sucked into blackness forever.

I was so glad I gave the Shadow Heart to Dawn for safe-keeping. I could only hope Isolde, the Winter princess, would succeed where I failed. For Faerie *and* for Ethereum. The curse had gone on for too long. Seelie and unseelie in both realms deserved to live free from it.

The wall we stood on shook as Stryker held onto me tightly and the sounds of screaming men filled my ears. They were ravenous, absolutely deafening in their cries of war. I tried to push more of my magic outward to them, but was overwhelmed with a wave of dizziness. There were just too many of them now.

"Defend Easteria!" The cry reached our ears, and both Stryker and I snapped our heads to the battlefield.

Oh my stars.

They came.

Fanned out across the entire horizon were three sets of new troops, each holding a flag that represented the Northern, Southern, and Western Kingdoms. Thousands upon thousands of these new men and women chanted, beat at their breastplates, and pushed the rebels toward the castle so that they had to make a choice. Flee east into the sea, west back to the Midlands, or try to enter our city only to be dead within minutes when this new regiment arrived.

A wall of black shadows ripped through the crowd, throwing soldiers left and right, and I smiled when I recognized Adrien sitting atop a white mare and controlling them all.

My gaze scanned further, and I noticed Zander among the warriors holding the Northern flag. It wasn't hard, then, to pick out who must be the final brother. Zane was a tall man with broad shoulders who was currently cutting down rebels with a sword in each hand. He was the spitting image of Stryker, but with lighter hair that was short on the sides and not quite as long as his on top. And of course, his face was free of any scars.

"They came." Stryker staggered beside me, clearly in shock, and I couldn't help but grin.

I slipped my hand into his and squeezed. It felt like some deep wound had been created years ago when these brothers did not come to his aid and I was watching now as that wound healed.

"They did," I agreed.

We just stood there, watching the glory unfold as Stryker's brothers crushed the rebel army, pushing a quarter of them to their deaths into the sea and sending the rest fleeing to the Midlands. Our door to the city, as well as our walls, still stood strong.

We survived and not only that, we'd won.

Chants of joy went up as the men cheered and hoisted their fists and weapons into the air.

I glanced over at Stryker and I smiled when I saw Captain Greylocke walk over and bow to his knee before him.

"My lady. You have won this battle and my allegiance."

My lady?

Stryker stepped to the side and I realized that the captain was bowing to *me*. One by one, every single man on the wall took to one knee and bowed their head.

"Why are they doing that?" I whispered to Stryker.

He peered at me with an unreadable expression. "Because I told them before I left to find you at Mount Grimhorn that you were the lady of the house, and now that you've led them in battle, they are your men to command as well. If you want them to be."

I swallowed hard. Did he just? Lady of the house meant . . .

"Stryker, are you asking me to marry you?"

He grinned. "Only if you're going to say yes."

I laughed, feeling butterflies take flight in my stomach. Proposing on top of a city wall, at the end of a bloody battle among hundreds of dead bodies was exactly what I would expect of this man.

"Yes. A thousand times, yes."

I leaped into his open arms and he pulled them around me, holding me tightly as he crushed me to his chest. The men on the wall began to cheer and everyone stood.

"Hey," someone called from down below. "You going to invite us in for a meal, or are you still mad?"

I smiled as Stryker pulled me back and we peered down at Zander, who now sat atop his horse with Adrien and Zane beside him.

Stryker crossed his arms. "I'll think about it."

I smacked his chest. "Open the gates!" I cried and the soldiers below did my bidding.

Stryker gave me a playful glare, but I shrugged.

"You said they were my men to command as well," I reminded him.

That got a belly laugh out of him. "I have a feeling you're going to keep me on my toes."

With a grin, I grabbed his hand and took the steps one at a time, slowly. I was a mess, still slightly dizzy and crusted with blood, but I wasn't going to let the opportunity to patch things up with Stryker's brothers go by.

An hour later, after both Stryker and I had cleaned up, Dawn arrived. Apparently, she and Zander never really left. They'd decided to head south to seek Adrien's help, but he was already on his way with his entire army. Then they met Zane and his men on the way, and the rest was history.

Dawn had hidden out in a carriage nearby until Zander sent one of his men to give her the all clear. Since we'd released the household staff for the day, I offered to make dinner.

"Have you ever cooked?" Dawn looked at the raw chicken in disgust.

I laughed. "Of course. My mother taught me how."

She looked sad for a second. "You and I have very different mothers."

I matched her wan smile. "We do. But mine isn't perfect, and yours means well . . ."

I think.

"She does. But she has a very one-track mind. She will not stop until one of Zander's brothers' hearts is carved from their chest."

It was a dark truth that we needed to remember.

I rubbed some spices into the meat. "So what are we going to do about it?" I asked as I lit the gas stove.

She chewed on her lip. "I may or may not have learned some information recently that could help us."

I raised an eyebrow. "That's coy."

When the oil was hot, I threw as many chicken breasts as I could find into the frying pan and a satisfying sizzle filled the space.

"Well," Dawn went on, "as we were traveling with these thousands of soldiers I overheard one talking about . . . a blood witch."

I stilled with my hand over the chicken. "Okay . . . I'm listening."

Dawn began to pace the kitchen. "Apparently she can . . . project your soul anyplace in the realm. In *any* realm. She normally communicates with the dead—"

"The dead," I shrieked. "Whoa, that sounds dark. What are you suggesting?" I tossed some diced potatoes and leeks into a pot of boiling water and then started ripping some rosemary to add as well.

"I'm suggesting she project our spirits or whatever to Isolde. So we can warn her not to listen to my mother. Not to kill Adrien or Zane or whoever she's going to be sent to assassinate."

It was a good idea. But a blood witch? I didn't know much about them—we didn't have them in Faerie. They were a special kind of unseelie that had great and terrifying magic. More terrifying from what I'd heard.

But if there was a chance we could talk to Isolde and prepare her, it was a risk worth taking. If she came to Ethereum set on killing one of its lords, someone could get hurt. It would be a game changer if we could get her on our side quickly.

A bubble of hope rose in my chest. Perhaps whatever Isolde could learn from the Wise Ones would bring us closer to ending the curse for both of our realms.

"Let's do it. After dinner," I said resolutely, and Dawn nodded her agreement.

It was decided. After Stryker mended things with his brothers, we would find this blood witch and try to reach Isolde.

When we finally entered the dining room with a few giant platters of food, the men were laughing.

"I was six years old," Zane protested. "Everyone wets the bed that young."

Dawn and I shared a look and burst into laughter with the rest of the brothers.

"Let us help you." The men suddenly realized we were there and all four stood, rushing forward to grab the hot trays of food for us.

"Thank you for cooking," Zander told me.

Dawn scoffed. "How do you know *I* didn't cook?"

Zander gave her an *oh please* look and she grinned.

It wasn't until we were all seated again that I realized Adrien's fiancée Elisana was here. She was so quiet, sitting there eyeing the kitchen door.

"Can I make some tea?" she asked.

"Of course, I can boil some—"

"No, you enjoy the hot meal. I've got it." She slipped away into the kitchen and we all served our plates.

"It's good to see you, brother." Zane kept sneaking

glances at Stryker, at his scar. You could tell he hadn't seen his brother in a long time.

"It's good to be looking on the bright side of life again," Stryker admitted as he held my hand.

When he took his first bite of chicken, he moaned and then looked at me. "I'm firing my chef."

I smiled, and caught Zane and Adrien eyeing me and then Dawn.

"So what's with this?" Zane pointed at Stryker and me and Zander and Dawn. "Two mates happen to be from Faerie?"

Zander and Stryker shared a look and Stryker cleared his throat. "Like Ethereum has four territories with four lords, Faerie has four courts with four princesses."

Zane nodded.

"And we think that each princess is the mate of one of ours," Zander finished, and both Adrien and Zane froze with a fork full of food to their mouth.

This was so weird. We had suspicions that each princess of Faerie was the mate of an Ethereum lord, but that meant Adrien was currently engaged to the wrong person. Talk about awkward.

"What did you just say?" Adrien said, just as his fiancée stepped back into the room with two cups of tea.

"Here you are. Your special tea." She placed a cup before him and he smiled up at her. "Thank you, darling."

Then he looked at all of us. "I was having a horrible time sleeping and Elisana made me a custom tea. It's really helped. I don't even dream anymore."

I frowned, sharing a glance with Stryker, but said nothing. That was kind of weird, right? Not to dream?

"I fancy myself as an herbalist. In another life I would have studied and became a physician," she said and sat back next to Adrien, watching him keenly.

He picked up the tea and took a long sip, and she relaxed a little. I didn't like her, but it wasn't my place to say anything about it, and she was being nicer this time than the last, so maybe she'd grow on me.

We ate the rest of the meal in relative silence. Anytime someone tried to speak to Elisana, she gave one-word answers, and had something of a weird vibe. This was a family dinner and although they were engaged, no one really knew her and she was kind of standoffish, so it had created an awkward aura around what should have been a wonderful meal.

Stryker cleared his throat, patting his belly. "Thank you for the lovely dinner, Aribella."

Everyone chorused his kind words, and then Stryker glanced over at Elisana.

"I don't mean to be rude, Elisana, but I need to speak with my brothers privately about matters of state."

Elisana bristled, peering at me as if wondering why I got to stay, but I looked away and then she stood. "Of course," she snipped.

Adrien stiffened, looking slightly uncomfortable as she left the room.

"Sorry, brother, but I don't know her," Stryker said flatly.

Adrien frowned. "She's the woman I am to marry."

Stryker swallowed hard. "And I'm happy for you, if you're happy, but until you are married, I would like to keep what we are about to tell you private. For the sake of our realm as well as Faerie."

Adrien looked at the door Elisana had gone out of one more time and then nodded.

Dawn reached under the table and pulled out a bag. She hefted it on top and opened it to reveal the Shadow Heart.

"I had to go and see the Wise Ones—"

"The Wise Ones?" Adrien gasped.

Dawn and I then went into a ten-minute explanation about both of our experiences with them and how the Wise Ones had given us each a clue on how to hopefully destroy the curse and fix both of our lands. Without killing one of them. Then we told them that we wanted to contact a blood witch to see if she could help us get a message to the Winter Court princess to not kill anyone.

"You want to bring a blood witch here?" Stryker growled.

"We are running out of options and time," Dawn reminded him.

The dining hall door opened and one of the guards stumbled in looking ashen. Stryker stood so fast, his chair nearly fell over. "What's wrong? Are the rebels back?"

"No, my lord . . . but the plague that has infected the Northern Kingdom is now here," he said.

It wasn't a plague; it was a curse, and now it was here. My heart sank.

Zander leaped to his feet as well, and we all ran outside.

The streets had turned to celebration after we'd won the battle, but something was wrong. People were laying prone on the floor and others were trying to tend to them.

"Oh no. It's spreading," Dawn whimpered and then looked at me. "How long have you been in Ethereum?"

How long *had* I been here? I'd stopped keeping track of the days weeks ago. It felt like I'd both been here forever and also just arrived.

I took a moment to try to gather the days and weeks and realized with a start that it must have been exactly one moon's cycle to the day.

I hadn't thought of my faestone dagger in so long, but I realized my window to return to Faerie had passed. I wasn't sure how I felt about that. Obviously I wanted to save my people, but I didn't want to leave Stryker.

When I told Dawn and the others how long it had been, Dawn and Zander exchanged a weighted look.

"Exactly when the sickness broke out in our kingdom as well," Dawn said.

"It's the curse, isn't it?" I asked, and she nodded solemnly.

Looking around, my eyes welled with tears when I took in all the affected fae. Fae whom I now considered my own people.

I followed Stryker to the fallen unseelie fae nearest us and gasped when I saw that there were black veins shooting out from their eyes and running down their neck.

Stryker looked at Zander. "What do I do?"

Zander sighed. "We need the blood witch, brother. The faster we can get these princesses to see the Wise Ones and complete their task, the sooner we can destroy the curse and restore our land."

Chapter Twenty-Five

We spent the rest of the night helping the people of Easteria who'd been hit by the curse which everyone kept referring to as the plague. We delivered hot meals to families that were affected in the city, helped carry unseelie who were too sick to walk on their own back to their homes, and brought those who were completely unconscious to the medical ward in the castle. Just like in the Northern Kingdom, it seemed like the unseelie with the strongest magic were hit the hardest.

By the time five a.m. rolled around, we finally headed back to the castle and passed out. We went back to my old room, and Stryker slept next to me because his sleeping quarters now had a giant hole in the wall. Yes, there were many other vacant rooms in the castle he could have taken, but neither one of us felt comfortable being separated right now. When I awoke, there was a note on my pillow.

Meet me in the kitchen.
-S

The kitchen? Was the staff out sick and he needed me to cook again?

I got up to brush my teeth and put on a light blue sundress. Stepping out into the hall, I passed through the dining room hoping to see Dawn and any of the others, but it was empty. It was later in the morning since we all got in at such a late hour so they were probably still sleeping.

I pushed the door to the kitchen open and paused when I saw Stryker in an apron with flour up to his elbows and chocolate on his chin.

The counter was strewn with various baking supplies, including dirty plates, eggshells, a bottle of oil, and about thirty small plates, each one holding a weird, lumpy chocolate dessert.

I burst into laughter and Stryker spun.

"What are you doing? If you were hungry, you should have woken me. I would have made you something," I told him.

There was a seriousness in his gaze that wiped the smile off my face.

"Hey," he said nervously.

"Hey?" I called back with a smile and stepped forward to wipe the chocolate off his chin and plant a kiss on his lips. "What are you doing?"

He cleared his throat. "I know how much you like chocolate cake."

I smiled. "You do?"

He nodded. "You ordered my staff to bring you chocolate cake instead of mush, and then I heard how you literally licked the plate clean when I had the cook's chocolate fudge cake delivered to you."

I coughed out an embarrassed half laugh and ducked my head. I had licked the plate clean. So unprincess-like.

Reaching forward, Stryker placed two fingers under my chin and lifted my face so he could look into my eyes. What I saw in his gaze took my breath away. Love. Shining so brightly from his gaze that it was unmistakable. "I wanted to make you something you'd enjoy," he finished.

My heart exploded with adoration at that moment. "And so you wanted to learn?"

He nodded, grabbing something on the counter behind him that he'd been concealing. It was a small, four-inch, round chocolate cake. It looked to be two tiers with the uppermost tier kind of sliding off and the icing was hastily done, but when my gaze landed on the giant decoration on top, I gasped.

"It only took nine tries, but this one tastes good. On try number five, I replaced the sugar with salt on accident."

I was speechless, staring at the gigantic red ruby ring lying atop the cake. The gem alone was almost the size of a walnut.

"You hate it," he said, lowering the plate.

I grasped his hands, taking the plate from him. "I love it. But Stryker . . . is this ring for me?"

He nodded. "Of course. We can't get married without a ring."

I laughed, pulling the huge ruby ring from the cake and licking the frosting off the band. "It's beautiful and so sweet, but I'll be robbed the second I step outside with this thing on."

Stryker grinned. "I'll have to get you your own security detail then."

Laughter poured out of me. "No way. It's too expensive. I can't."

He frowned. "I'm the richest man in all of Ethereum, Aribella. This is the ring I want to give you. And you deserve ten more. One in every color."

He took the band from my hand, slipping it onto my ring finger, and my heart couldn't take it anymore.

"I love it," I told him, looking down at the ridiculous thing. Was it way too big to be appropriate? Yes. But it was a testament that his love for me was greater than his love of money, and I liked that very much. Stryker had turned out to be a very generous soul.

"Maybe we can get one that's a little bit smaller for everyday wear?" I asked.

He rolled his eyes. "Fine. But with a matching necklace and earrings."

"Deal." I grinned, and then Stryker reached out and picked up something else from the counter. This was wrapped in a muslin cloth.

He looked nervously at me. "I feel it is only fair to tell you that the day I threw you in my dungeon, I had your dagger melted down."

I gasped, but then shook my head with a smile. He wasn't a stupid man, and keeping a weapon around that could kill him and send me home would have been stupid.

"But the stone survived. Both in your dagger and in Dawn's," he said and unfolded the cloth, revealing two lumpy hunks of metal. One had Dawn's sunstone in the center, and the other held my carnelian. "I thought maybe the stone was of value to you and wanted to return it." He set it on the counter beside me.

I reached up and cupped his cheek in my free hand, stroking his scar with my thumb. "You have a good heart, Stryker Warrick."

"Shhh, don't tell anyone that." He pressed a kiss to my lips and I laughed. When he pulled back, I grabbed one of the forks littering the counter.

I cut a small bite of the cake and slipped it into my mouth. Dark chocolaty goodness exploded across my tongue, and I moaned. It was the perfect amount of sweet. Three bites in, I hit an eggshell, but said nothing.

"It's perfect."

Stryker laughed. "I heard that eggshell crunch from here. But I love you for saying that."

Now it was my turn to laugh, and Stryker set the plate down and pulled me into his arms, peering down at me. "Listen, I know that life with me will not be easy. We have this curse attacking the people, I'm constantly being robbed, and there are attempts on my life all the time. You still have your part to play trying to help Faerie, but—"

I put a finger to his lips. "We will handle it all together."

He nodded, the lightness in his gaze dimming. "You deserve the biggest wedding Ethereum has ever seen, but I can't give that to you right now. Please know that I want to marry you more than I've ever wanted anything, but with the curse having just descended on the kingdom, I can't be selfish right now. We'll have to wait until the people are healed to have a large celebration or it would look bad."

The expression on Stryker's face told me waiting was the last thing he wanted to do, but I knew exactly what he was saying and agreed. Now wasn't the time to pull our resources or attention from his people. It would be selfish to have a big wedding at such a time as this. Once upon a time, a big wedding might have been something I desired, but right now, I just wanted to be with Stryker, as his wife, as Lady of the Eastern Kingdom.

"Who says it needs to be big? I'll marry you right now in this kitchen. Just fetch me a priest," I joked.

His eyes went half lidded. "Don't toy with me. Are you serious?"

I gestured to the messy kitchen. "I was half serious. I wouldn't mind the reception hall, though. With Dawn as my maid of honor and your brothers present."

He stood erect. "Go round up Dawn and my brothers. I'll be back in an hour with the priest."

He sidestepped me to move for the door and I laughed. "Wait, Stryker, are *you* serious?"

He peered back at me. "Do you want to marry now or in several months' time when the land is healed? I will do whatever you want, but if my vote matters, I would not live another day without you as my wife."

I couldn't believe how much we'd changed over the past month. From being a tortured slave in his basement to his wife.

"I'll meet you in the reception hall in an hour." I grinned.

He matched my smirk and went in search of a priest as I ran screaming in excitement towards Dawn's room.

An hour later I stood in a pale pink, silk gown with little white flowers Dawn had tied in my hair. Dawn was at my side, tears rolling down her face as she clutched wild flowers from the garden. Zander, Adrien, and Zane all stood next to Stryker as Elisana and the castle staff that were still on duty sat in chairs in front of us.

For a fleeting moment, I missed my mother and father, wishing they could have been here, that he could have walked me down the aisle. But I had hope that we would see each other again. Life couldn't be that cruel.

The ceremony was quick but perfect, and Stryker's and my vows were simple but powerful. We pledged our lives to each other, and as I looked into Stryker's eyes, I knew that there was no one else in this realm or any other that would love me as much as this man.

When the priest finally declared us man and wife, Stryker leaned forward and slipped his arms around me, dipping me backward like you would while dancing. Stryker's brothers, Dawn, and the small crowd seated before us erupted into cheers and then he placed his lips on mine.

"I've never been a big fan of Fate. But now I want to meet her one day and thank her for sending me you," he whispered against my mouth.

I smiled and then we pulled away and the priest raised his arms.

"May I present Lady Aribella Warrick and Lord Stryker Warrick."

Stryker scooped me up into his arms and I peeled out in laughter. Dawn was basically sobbing at this point and I wondered if it was the pregnancy hormones. I'd never known her to have a reputation for crying easily.

A small area off to the side had been set up with candles and flower petals and a violinist.

I smiled.

"All I could get on short notice," Stryker told me.

As the violinist began to play a soft melody, Stryker spun me around on the dance floor and indicated that his brothers should join us.

Zander clung to Dawn as Adrien pulled a delighted Elisana up to dance, and Zane just sat there with his arms crossed. "This isn't awkward or anything," he grumbled.

"Care to take an old lady out for a spin?" the head housemaid asked him.

Lettie was in her seventies, and still as smart as a whip. Zane took her hand and led her in a beautiful waltz as Stryker smiled down at me. "I never thought in a million years that I would ever love again. True love," he told me and then peered around at his brothers.

Zander burst into laughter when Dawn did a funny dance and Stryker's smile grew. "Or that this house would be filled with joy, with family." He then peered at me. "And that's all because of you."

I beamed at him, my heart full. Perhaps too full considering it felt like the world was falling down all around us. We'd lost so many good souls in the rebel battle, and the curse was growing daily both here in Ethereum and back in Faerie. Fae were suffering, and it wasn't fair.

I hadn't forgotten any of those things. I now carried the weight of two kingdoms on my shoulders, but for this one, perfect afternoon, I pushed it all aside.

I didn't know what the future had in store for Stryker and me, and we may only have today. Perhaps some would accuse us of being selfish, but I believed we deserved to have this moment of happiness. To look into each other's eyes and focus on one another without letting the rest of the world in. To celebrate the fact that through everything we'd endured, we still found each other. That we still found love.

Leaning in, I captured his mouth in a kiss. "What can I say? I'm a sucker for a man that can make chocolate cake after eleven tries."

His deep laughter shook his whole body against me. "Nine."

"I love you," I breathed against his ear, stroking my fingers against his neck. The shadows in the room moved a little, and it startled me until I realized it was Stryker. His eyes were half lidded as he gazed at me.

"Thank you all for coming," Stryker said loudly and suddenly. The violinist stopped playing, and everyone looked over at us just as Stryker scooped me into his arms. "Aribella's reallllly tired so we're going to go to bed, but carry on and have fun."

Zane grinned. "It's noon."

I fake yawned, and Dawn smiled too. "Good *night*, lovebirds."

I was red-faced by the time we reached my room, which was now *our* room.

"Listen," Stryker said as he cupped my face in his hands. "Just because we are married now doesn't mean we have to rush anything. If you aren't comfortable with—"

I reached up and tore his shirt open, the fabric ripping in my hands like it did in the romance novels I'd read.

Stryker's eyes went wide. "Or we could do that."

I burst into laughter and he tossed me onto the bed like I was made of feathers. Boxing me in with his arms on either side of me, he leaned forward and peppered my collarbone with kisses. "Lady Aribella Warrick."

"Yes?" I panted.

"I promise to love you forever and to kiss every inch of your body any night you will let me."

I smiled, and then he made love to me while shadows danced on the ceiling and I cried out his name.

Chapter Twenty-Six

I t proved harder to find a blood witch to help us reach out to the Winter princess than I thought it would. Apparently, blood witches had been banned from all four of the Ethereum kingdoms for decades, their magic having been considered too dark. The ones that remained were either in hiding or lived in the Midlands.

It took the combined effort of all four Ethereum lords' spies to finally track one down who had been living in a remote village on the southern border of the Eastern Kingdom. After a couple of days, we received word that they were bringing her back. But the message also told us that when they approached her about returning to Easteria with them, she tried to flee, fearful Stryker would put her in his dungeon.

Four men had been seriously injured before they could subdue her, telling me she was powerful.

I didn't know much about blood witches. They were

relegated to myths and fairytales to us back in Faerie. The only thing I knew for sure, because Stryker confirmed for me, was that they were seelie fae who used blood to enhance their magic. In our stories, they were always portrayed as soulless creatures, power hungry enough to taint their natural abilities with dark magic to gain power.

I didn't know how much of what I knew about them from Faerie was true, but it was clear that the fae in Ethereum were wary, if borderline scared, of them. And that said something. When I heard about how difficult it was to bring one in, I understood why.

When we got word that the men had returned with the blood witch, we all congregated in Stryker's library and waited for her to arrive. I fidgeted, wringing my hands, and chewed on my bottom lip. I startled when Stryker reached up and lightly brushed his thumb over my bottom lip and then tugged it free.

"That lip is too pretty to abuse," he said, his gaze both soft yet filled with desire, and I felt myself blush.

I looked into Stryker's gray-blue eyes and then glanced at his mouth, remembering how it tasted and felt brushing against my own. My face heated even more, and a low growl rumbled in Stryker's chest as he read the look in my eyes.

I almost forgot we were in a room with all three of his brothers until someone cleared their throat. I peered up and saw Zane smirking at us from across the table.

"Do you need the rest of us to give you two some time alone?" he asked, his smile growing.

Stryker glared at his brother and Zane broke out in a full-on laugh.

"What's going on?" Adrien asked, walking over to our table from his spot across the room. Thank the stars that Elisana wasn't with him. I got the impression we had hurt her feelings by not including her very much and now she was keeping her distance.

Zane opened his mouth to say something, but with a flick of Stryker's wrist, a shadow shot from his palm and slapped over Zane's mouth, muffling him. Zane clawed at the shadow to no avail before finally lifting his hand in front of his face. A bolt of black lightning shot from his palm and zapped the shadow, which disintegrated into thin air.

Adrien doubled over in laughter, and even Dawn and Zander looked amused from their place by one of the floor-to-ceiling bookshelves.

Zane frowned at Stryker. "Not funny."

The corner of Stryker's mouth twitched, which for him was almost equivalent to a full smile. "He seems to think so," Stryker said, pointing at Adrien.

"You know I'm going to get you back for that . . . eventually," Zane promised.

Stryker leaned back, slinging his arm over my shoulders. "You can try."

Zane, whom I considered the most lighthearted of the brothers, couldn't keep his sour face for long and finally smirked. "It's on."

My heart warmed seeing Stryker so relaxed and happy around his brothers. He was still the surly and dark lord I fell in love with, but over the last several days I'd seen more sides of him appear. He was wise and strong with his people, soft and gentle with me, and lighthearted and even a touch mischievous with his brothers. I treasured each new facet of him as much as any of the others.

I would have taken Stryker just as he was and loved him for the rest of my life, but it was obvious to me he was starting to heal. When I looked at my new husband, I no longer saw a fractured man, broken and scarred. Even in the midst of turmoil and uncertainty, he was finally beginning to learn what it was like to accept love and be happy. The pieces of himself he thought he'd lost forever were coming back, reforming him into something beautiful.

Our worlds were quite literally falling apart. Even after exhaustive research we still couldn't figure out what we were supposed to do with the Shadow Heart, and at any moment the curse might strike out in a new way, causing even more devastation. But even with all of that, I still felt like the luckiest fae in the world to have him by my side through it all.

The brothers had started in on another ribbing session, good-naturedly calling each other out on their childhood antics when the thick library doors swung open. The conversation stopped as we all came to our feet.

In walked four, heavily armed men surrounding one, petite woman. The woman had flowing, lavender hair down to her waist that shimmered in the torchlight, and matching large, purple eyes. She was beautiful, but in an unconventional, otherworldly way.

Her small nose, rounded cheeks, and pointed chin made

her appear elf-like and innocent. She looked to be about in her early forties, but then I remembered Stryker telling me that the blood witches were rumored to use blood sacrifices to keep themselves looking young, and my stomach soured.

Is that what this one had done, or did her features represent her true age?

Part of me didn't want to know because intuition said I wouldn't like the answer.

One of the men stepped forward and even with a scarf covering part of his face, I recognized him as Samuel, Zander's spy. "My lord," he said, dipping his head in reverence to Zander. "The blood witch you asked us to track down and bring back for you." He gestured toward the woman who had crossed her arms and was glaring back at him.

"Thank you, Samuel," Zander said as he stepped forward. "You and the others may leave her here with us."

"My lord," Samuel said in surprise. "I don't think that's wise. She is very powerful and—"

Just then, Stryker produced a shadow beast like the one I'd seen before. It was just as vicious and intimidating as I remembered, yet this time I wasn't scared of it as I had been before. Perhaps because I was no longer scared of the lord himself.

Zander's mouth twitched. "I appreciate your concern for us, Samuel, but I believe the point my elder brother is trying to make is that the most powerful beings in all of Ethereum are in this room." He made a point of grabbing Dawn's hand and drawing her closer, letting her know he wasn't just talking about him and his brothers. "We can take it from here."

"Of course, my lord," Samuel said, and with another quick bow, he and the other men left the room, closing the door behind them.

Uncrossing her arms the purple-haired blood witch flicked her hair back and lifted her chin to look down at the rest of us. Her suspicious gaze traveled over the group. And I'd be lying if I said that a chill hadn't run through me when it landed on me before moving to the next.

I usually tried to reserve my judgment of people, but I was starting to understand why the citizens of Ethereum were cautious of blood witches. There was just something about her that seemed off. Wrong. Perhaps evil was too strong of a word, but her vibe was unnerving to say the least.

"Thank you for coming," Stryker started, but the blood witch scoffed.

"You say that as if I had a choice in the matter."

I frowned. This already wasn't going well.

"What's your name?" Stryker asked, ignoring her last comment.

Her chin lifted even higher and she paused, as if answering to an Ethereum lord was beneath her. "Rowena," she finally said.

Stryker nodded in acknowledgment and then quickly introduced the rest of us. I could tell she was wholly unimpressed to be in the presence of all four Ethereum lords, and didn't seem very concerned with me either, but a spark of interest showed in her eyes when she looked at Dawn.

Her gaze dropped to Dawn's belly and I read the alarm in my friend's eyes. Zander quickly sidestepped to shield his wife from Rowena's view. His hand twitched and I swear I saw a black shard begin to protrude from his palm before disappearing into nothing.

A sly smile lifted the corners of Rowena's mouth that caused a queasy knot to form in my gut. I knew we needed her, but I now wished we'd looked harder for another way to reach Isolde.

"You have me here, *my lord*," she said, making Stryker's title sound like a sneer. "Since you went to so much trouble, I'd love to know why."

"Do you know of the land called Faerie?" he asked.

She raised one eyebrow. "I do."

He nodded. "We need to reach someone in Faerie," Stryker said. "We require you to project our consciousnesses to her."

Her eyebrows shot up. Whatever she assumed we would ask of her, this wasn't it.

"I usually only communicate with the dead," she said.

"Can you do it or not?" Stryker asked.

"How many of you?" she peered around the room at our large group.

"All of us," Stryker said.

She tilted her head in consideration, but I didn't miss the gleam of calculation in her eyes. "I can, but it will cost you."

Stryker nodded. We'd all already discussed this and assumed she'd demand a steep price for her help. "As payment, I'll send you on your way with as many jewels and gold as you can carry on your person." Stryker crossed his arms over his chest. "*And* you'll have my word you won't be imprisoned in my dungeon."

I didn't miss the threat in that statement and from the narrowing of her gaze, I could tell she didn't either.

"Gold and jewels are nice, but I require more than riches," she said with a grin.

"What is it you want?" Stryker asked, and I could practically hear his molars grinding against each other.

Her lips curled in a sly smile. "Oh, I believe you are well aware of what I want."

"No," Stryker said with a definitive shake of his head.

I noticed the muscles in his shoulders tighten as well, and then I felt something nudging me. I looked down to see some of Stryker's shadows trying to push me behind him.

Part of me appreciated the gesture. I knew he was just trying to protect me. But I wasn't pregnant like Dawn with an innocent life inside of me to shield. I would stand right where I belonged, next to my mate, not behind him.

I stepped forward, coming in line with Stryker rather than dipping behind him like he wanted. A muscle jumped in his jaw, but when he glanced down at me, his gaze was a mixture of pride and frustration. I smiled up at him and took his hand and he just shook his head and refocused on our lavender-haired visitor.

"No one here will be giving you a blood payment," Stryker said and I had to stifle a gasp.

Blood payment?

That's what she wanted? I didn't like the sound of that

one bit, and from Dawn and the other lords' grim looks, neither did they.

"Well then," Rowena said with a flip of her hair. "I'll bid you farewell and let you get on with your day." She turned and started toward the door, but before she could get there, a rush of shadows slammed into it, barring her exit.

The look on Stryker's face was nothing short of murderous, but Rowena turned back and faced him down without a hint of fear.

"It wasn't a request you are free to deny," he ground out.

"Yet here we are," she said haughtily. "And if you think that a *blood* witch can send your consciousness to Faerie without a drop of each of your blood, you are stupider than I thought."

A drop of each of our blood?

Stryker took a menacing step toward her. "Fine, a single drop for the spell. But *none* for the blood payment."

She shrugged. "No deal."

"Perhaps a night or two in my dungeon will change your mind?" Stryker threatened.

Anger flashed across her face. "If you even try to—"

"I'll make the blood payment," Zane said, rolling up one sleeve as he stepped forward.

"Yeah, that's not happening." Zander stepped in front of his brother. "You have no idea what these witches are capable of."

Zane looked down at his brother. "I'm a big boy. I can handle myself, and we don't have two days to torture her in

Stryker's dungeon to get her to agree. We need to warn Isolde now."

Zander shook his head and moved like he was going to grab Zane, ready to physically restrain his brother if he had to, but Zane shot him a look that stopped him in his tracks. "Isolde could be my mate," he said, his voice filled with emotion, and for the first time I realized that he must be lonely.

There was a sadness in his eyes I hadn't seen before. He was willing to risk it all on the chance that Isolde might be his mate. It was extremely romantic, though not smart by the greedy look in Rowena's eye. Before anyone else had much of a chance to stop him, Zane pulled a dagger from the sheath on his belt and cut across his forearm. Zander stepped back, sighing as he conceded.

"Nice to see one of the lords is levelheaded," Rowena said smugly. Walking over to Zane's arm, she slowly dragged her finger across the thick, black blood that dripped down it, gathering a large amount on her fingertip. She then put it in her mouth and sucked.

She closed her eyes and I gagged as I watched her face in semi-horror. It looked like she was savoring the taste like she might a fine wine. It made me nauseous.

When her eyes popped back open, there was almost a feverish look to them. Like she was drunk or high on poppies. And I was shocked to see that she looked five or ten years younger.

I wanted this blood-licking freak to do her thing and leave. She had officially given me the creeps.

"Let's get on with it," Stryker barked, and I knew he wasn't any happier about Zane having just given her his blood than I was.

Rowena pulled a small box from under her cloak and opened it carefully. I couldn't see the contents from where I was standing, but I saw the long, sharp needle she pulled out.

"What are you doing now?" Stryker asked, his tone accusing.

"This is the one little drop for the spell we spoke about, *my lord*," she said, annoyed.

"I'm not letting you take even a single drop of my wife's blood," Zander said, his hand covering Dawn's belly.

Rowena shrugged. "Fine. Then I can't project her consciousness. This isn't a price I require for payment. This is the price the spell requires. Whoever doesn't want to pay it can't participate."

Dawn laid a hand on Zander's shoulder. "I have to do this. Isolde needs to see me and Aribella."

His nostrils flared and he flicked his gaze to the witch. "If you put our blood in your mouth, I'll puncture you with a hundred shards of glass and then have my wife light your body on fire." He held out his hand and a black, pointed shard of glass formed in the center of his palm.

Rowena nodded. "The blood goes on the cloth, my lord." She held up a square piece of red linen and gave him her most innocent look.

"It's just a drop, my love," Dawn said, placing a hand on the side of Zander's face. "I'll be fine."

Pressing his lips together in a hard line, Zander nodded once, but the look he shot Rowena was cold enough to send a chill through the air.

Seemingly unfazed, Rowena positioned us all in a circle around her. One by one, she went to each of us and pricked our finger with a needle, pulling out a fresh one for each of us and tossing the dirty ones back in her box. When a bead of blood formed, she blotted it with the square of red cloth.

Once we'd all shed our drops, she walked to the center of our circle and Zander snatched the box that held the needles she'd used to poke us with. "I'll be keeping this, thank you very much," he told her. "And when the spell is over, I'll be taking that cloth too."

Rowena growled at that, but then rolled her eyes. Whatever trick she'd been planning to pull with our blood afterward, Zander wasn't having it and I was grateful he was looking out for us.

"Who knows this Isolde person best?" Rowena asked.

Dawn raised her hand and Rowena held out her palm. "Take my hand and hold her in your mind. It will guide me."

Dawn exchanged an intense look with Zander but took the witch's hand.

Rowena held the red cloth in her other hand and then started to chant under her breath. I didn't know what to expect, but it was only a few moments before the cloth caught fire and started to burn, but the flames were green.

Stryker grabbed my hand and squeezed. But when I looked over at him, his intense gaze was fixed on Rowena and a phantom wind that started to whip her hair and cloak around her.

Her chanting sped up and now she was practically screaming the unfamiliar words. My heart started to flutter in my chest, and I gripped Stryker's hand tighter, looking for an anchor to help me calm down. I didn't know what would happen if I fainted in the middle of this spell.

All of a sudden Rowena stopped chanting. Her hair and cloak settled back around her and the fire extinguished, but I gasped when I looked at her face. Her eyes had gone completely black. The creepiest part was the small smile on her face right before she threw her arms out, unleashing her magic on all of us.

Her magic slammed into me and it felt like someone was sucking the soul from my body. I fought against it, but it was too powerful, and with a final gasp I was separated from myself and tossed into a different realm.

I just hoped Isolde would listen, because the future of both of our kingdoms now rested squarely on her shoulders. The Winter princess's mind was not known for being easily swayed.

Epilogue

ISOLDE

I drummed my long, black-painted fingernails on the windowsill, looking out at the clumps of snow as they fell from the sky. What a wild past several weeks it had been. My body was covered in fading bruises and defined muscles from the constant training Queen Liliana and her staff of tutors had been giving me. I had heard rumors that Dawn had failed her task and never returned—news that had gutted me. Dawn and I had been very close, making sure to connect every year during our famous Winter Festival that drew revelers from all four courts. And I'd gone to see her during the Summer Court's Honey Bee Fair.

I peered wistfully at the dried flower crown of daisies I'd bought just last year with Dawn while visiting the Summer Court. I'd wanted to believe the rumors were untrue until Queen Liliana and the Summer Court refugees flooded across our borders and then asked me to take over where

349

Dawn had failed. She put no stock in sweet Aribella and knew that this task would end with me.

I gripped the hilt of the blue kyanite dagger my mother had given to me when I was twelve. Winter princesses never expected to be called as champions: we were third in line to travel to Ethereum, but my mother was a prudent woman who left nothing to chance. I and my six younger sisters all started training when we reached womanhood. I was ready for this, maybe not quite to Queen Liliana's reckoning, but I wasn't going to hesitate to do my duty for my people. I would make sure that the curse never touched our land.

I would complete what Dawn had set out to do. I just wished I'd been able to say goodbye to her first . . .

"Isolde!" a familiar voice shouted behind me and with my heart in my throat, I spun around, expecting to see a ghost.

What I saw instead was a spectral form of not only Dawn but Aribella as well and four handsome men with them. I screamed, staggering backward against the wall.

Was she visiting me from the afterlife? Summoned by my thoughts of her? Or was there something more nefarious at work here?

I gripped the blue kyanite blade in my hand and pointed it at all of them.

"You're not Dawn," I said, certain I was hallucinating. But even as I shook my head, I stared at her familiar face and the braided plait of long, blonde hair that hung over one shoulder. Everything about her was as I remembered. Would my mind even be able to conjure such a perfect likeness of my beloved friend?

She stepped closer to me, ghosting straight through my bed, and I yelped.

"Izzy, it's me. Dawnie," she pleaded, using our childhood nicknames. "And we have so much to tell you, but I'm not sure how much time we have. These are the Ethereum lords. All four of them." She pointed around the room and I scanned the handsome men, my gaze falling on one in particular.

He had chin-length, dark hair with streaks of gold running through it. He peered at me with a bit of an aloof expression, but even so, it stirred something within me. Something I pushed down because this was insane.

"You're not real. If you were, one of their hearts would be on the tip of your knife." I knew Dawn too well for this ruse. She was the strongest of us all, lethal, brutal, and there was no way she would have just grabbed that guy's hand and held it. The Ethereum lords were our enemies.

"Izzy," Dawn pleaded with me, pulling the dark-haired man beside her forward. "Zander, the Ethereum Northern lord, is my husband. We're married." She held up her hand and smiled softly. "And I'm pregnant," she whispered, but not quietly enough because everyone else heard her.

The other men's faces showed shock right before they broke into cheers of excitement.

I shook my head. "Lies. Go. Leave me, ghosts."

I could feel the tears brimming in my eyes, but I pushed them down.

"I'll prove it," Dawn said. "You have a birthmark in the shape of a triangle on the back of your left thigh." I froze at her words. "Your first crush was Tanner Larson, Sir Henrick's squire. You used to steal sweets from the kitchen and bring them to bed when we had sleepovers at the Winter Festival."

I stared at the apparition in disbelief. How did she know those things unless . . .

"Izzy, it's me. I know this is hard to believe but . . . I need you to try."

Her words practically ripped my soul from my body. It must be her. How else would she know all those details?

I fell to my knees, hands shaking as the dagger dropped onto the carpet of my bedroom.

"How?" I asked, trying and failing not to hyperventilate. She married an evil Ethereum lord? And now she was pregnant? That meant she didn't come back on purpose. She wasn't dead . . . she just gave up on us.

Dawn's apparition stepped closer, kneeling down before me. "Isolde. They're our mates. We've been lied to and all these years they've been preparing us to kill our mates."

I gasped, looking up at the men present again.

Mates? I could guess at what that meant, but it wasn't something we believed in here in Faerie. Mates were as much of a fairytale as any other I'd heard, but as I scanned the room, I saw that Aribella was now in the arms of one of the dark lords. The scariest-looking one. His longer hair hung loosely over his face, but even so I saw the scar on his cheek.

"It's true," Aribella confirmed, her mouth curving into a soft smile as she glanced up at the man next to her.

The man I'd been glancing at before, the one who looked like he'd spent too much time in the sun, cleared his throat. "Technically, I'm engaged, but Zane could be your mate."

He gestured to the tall lord next to him, who waved awkwardly and looked at me hopefully. He was undoubtedly handsome. I grudgingly admitted they all were, yet I didn't feel a thing when I looked into his unusual eyes. They were dark blue with a smudge of brown in one of them.

I glanced back at the lord who'd spoken about being engaged and something uncomfortable flipped in my chest. Leave it to me to think the one unavailable guy was the hottest.

"This is a lot." I finally stood, taking in a shaky breath. I peered back at Dawn, lowering my voice. "What do you mean we were lied to? Your mother has been training me for the past several weeks to kill one of those guys."

"Please don't do that," Dawn said with her hands out in a gesture to calm me. "My mother . . . means well, but Isolde, you have to be careful around her. She knows we are sent here to kill our mates. That's why they tell us to never let them speak, to kill them quickly. I think they are afraid of what would happen if we actually got to know them."

"You'd fall in love," Aribella said wistfully, and I frowned.

Mates? Love? These were things that horrified me. After

my own parents' ugly divorce, I wanted nothing to do with so-called love.

"Listen, Dawn, that all sounds nice for you both, but your lands are dying. Your people are refugees. It's going to keep coming, and I can't just forget that for a chance at *love*." It was ridiculous.

Dawn nodded, shame covering her features. "Aribella and I did not make our choices lightly. But these men, they have people too, and families and feelings. They aren't monsters, Izzy. And we found another way to end the curse, not just put it off for another hundred years. Once you get here—"

"Isolde," Queen Liliana's voice called from behind the, door and my eyes flew wide at the same time Dawn's did. She looked longingly at the door, but then it started to open and Dawn ran back to the others.

"Bring us back!" she cried, to someone I couldn't see.

Then they were gone, nothing more than air.

Queen Liliana strode into the room, scanning the space with wide eyes. "Who were you talking to?" she asked.

My gut tightened as I replayed Dawn's words. *They send us here to kill our mates.* The four men I had seen didn't look like evil monsters. They looked . . . normal.

"Oh." I laughed nervously, pointing to a romance novel on my bedside table. "I was reenacting a part from my favorite book."

Queen Liliana frowned. "Well, that's silly. You need to grow up now, Isolde. We're all counting on you."

I swallowed hard. "Yes, Queen Liliana."

"I came to tell you that your poison class has been moved up, so I need you to come now." She moved her hand in an irritated gesture.

What was I supposed to do with this new knowledge? Was it even true, or was Dawn lying to me? But I couldn't think of a single reason why she would.

I peered at my room, wanting to see Dawn again, but knowing somehow that it wouldn't be possible.

"Okay." Sure, go learn poison making so that I could kill my best friend's new husband. Great idea.

As I followed her down the hall, my mind spun out in a hundred directions. Dawn insinuated that her mother couldn't be trusted. That she knew the Ethereum lords weren't evil.

"Queen Liliana?" I asked.

She peered at me. "Hmm?"

"I've always wondered, why don't we allow the Ethereum lords to even speak?"

She stopped walking, her face taught. "Because they lie, dear," she said.

I shrugged. "So we can't hear a lie?"

She raised one eyebrow. "Why are you suddenly asking this? Do you have any idea what is at stake, Isolde? If you fail me, I have to go to the Spring Court and we all know that Lorelei is soft. Softer than even Aribella had been. You are our best hope, so all of these questions need to stop. I need you to be a killing machine by winter solstice, and questioning why we do things isn't how you're going to get there," she snapped.

Whoa. That was quite the response to such a simple question.

My stomach sank at that moment. Dawn was right. Queen Liliana knew, and she didn't want me poking around in things.

I inclined my head in indifference, but fear seized me in that moment. Dawn had said there was another way to possibly help our people, but she disappeared before she could explain more. So what was I supposed to do? And why couldn't I stop thinking about the tanned guy with the blonde streaks in his hair? The engaged one.

Oh Dawn, what have you gotten me into?

Suddenly, traveling to Ethereum and cutting out the heart of an Ethereum lord had become much more complicated. The fate of our people rested on me, and I had no idea what I was going to do.

Please Write a Review

Reviews are the lifeblood of authors and your opinion will help others decide to read our books.

If you want to see more co-written books from Leia and Julie, please leave a review on Amazon.

Please Write a Review:
http://Review.FaintHeartedBook.com

CURSED FAE BOOK THREE

BROKEN HEARTED

USA TODAY BESTSELLING AUTHORS
LEIA STONE & JULIE HALL

Broken Hearted Preview

CURSED FAE BOOK 3

It was the night of the Winter Solstice. The portal was going to open, and I was about to either betray my people or my best friend. I was in an impossible position.

My mother smoothed down my long, dark hair, which mirrored her own. "You should have no fear. You've trained for this, and we always knew it would be a possibility, even if a small one."

She was right. As the Winter princess, I was third in line to go to Ethereum. This had never happened before, as the Summer princess had never failed, but the possibility was always there.

I peered down at my bag, packed with maps and rations. I was as ready as I'd ever be.

I'd been surprisingly calm after Dawn's ghostly apparition, along with Princess Aribella and the Ethereum lords, had come to see me. I knew Dawn at her core. She was not a woman easily fooled, and she would never give up on her people, so I had to believe that she had a plan to save us. I trusted her, which meant I could no longer trust Queen Lilliana.

It had been hard to keep my questions buried deep inside over the past few months of training with the Summer queen. But I did. I trained with her, and I said *yes ma'am* when she told me that I was Faerie's only hope and ordered me to cut out the heart of the first Ethereum lord I saw.

I told my mother I would do the same. I had been living a lie and it was eating at me.

Negative thoughts crept in my mind. What if Dawn was wrong? What if it hadn't been Dawn that visited me at all? What if it was someone pretending to be her in order to trick me?

But she knew about my birth mark and my first crush. Of course it was Dawnie.

I took a moment to really look at my mother. She was strong, emotionally and physically. She'd led our people well with my father by her side for twenty years. Until they ripped the illusion of a perfect marriage away from me and my sisters when I was fifteen, by telling us they were divorcing.

Unhappy. Affair. I hate you. How could you. I'd heard my mother scream all of those things at my father one night when I was supposed to be sleeping. She wouldn't stand for the betrayal, and I didn't blame her. But I also still loved my father. It was a hard place to be. Stuck between two people you loved. Now I felt that way again. Nineteen years old and I was torn again.

Between Dawn and all of Faerie.

"Your sisters want to say goodbye." My mother gestured to the door.

I turned to her. "If I don't make it back—"

"Nonsense," she dismissed.

"Mother, if I don't make it back in two days' time, take everyone to the Spring Court," I told her sternly.

She appeared a little shaken then, but the truth of the matter was that Dawn and Aribella had both been in my position and hadn't returned. The same could happen to me, especially if Dawn's plan to save Faerie was not immediate. In that case, I wouldn't be returning right away.

"I will get the heart immediately, or something has gone wrong," I lied. I had no intention of killing one of those men. Not after Dawn claimed one was my mate.

Mate. That word was foreign to me, and I wanted nothing to do with it, but I recognized that I might have been lied to my entire life. That there was a chance the Ethereum lords weren't evil like we'd been told, but rather that they were just men with families and people who depended on them.

She nodded once and we both left the room.

Seraphina, Elowen, Aria, Freya, Thalia, and Amara were waiting outside the door to my dressing room with stiff backs and hands at their sides. I knew they were trying to be brave, but their misty eyes and quivering lips betrayed how they really felt.

After me, Seraphina was the eldest at seventeen years old, and the one I was closest with. The rest of my sisters were spaced apart by two years. My mother planned her heirs perfectly, as she did everything else in her court.

I looked Seraphina in the eyes and grasped her shoulders. "Be strong."

For weeks I'd agonized about whether or not to tell her about Dawn and what she'd said, but in the end, I decided it might endanger her life and my plan. So instead, I sent a letter to Lorelei telling her about Dawn and the Ethereum lords who had appeared in my bedroom. If I failed in my task of breaking the curse, she needed to know there might be another way to save our worlds that didn't involve carving a heart from someone's chest. Lorelei was the gentlest and most kind-hearted fae I'd ever met. Her gifts were rooted in bringing forth life, not ending it. Even with Queen Liliana's training, she wouldn't be able to kill an Ethereum lord. Of that, I was certain.

"Come back to us," Seraphina growled, and I grinned. There was the sassy sister I knew.

I pulled her in for a hug and then all the rest of my sisters pressed in around me, holding onto me and pushing me into the center of a giant sister hug.

Emotions clogged my throat, but I kept it together for them. When everyone pulled away, I was looking down at little seven-year-old Amara. She was missing one of her front teeth, and her hair had some streaks of red like my father. She was the sensitive one of us who had yet to fully control her power, which was evidenced by the snow now falling on my head even thought we were still inside.

Reaching out, I brushed my fingertip along the falling tear on her cheek and froze it. She smiled and it fell to the ground as a tiny shard of ice. Amara constantly asked me to freeze things. Fruit. Flowers. The annoying birds that chirped early Sunday morning. I, of course, ignored that last request but she loved to see my power on display.

"You be good for mother and father, okay?" I told her.

She nodded and I gave her one final hug.

I had to leave before I lost my nerve.

I nodded that I was ready to mother, who was waiting patiently for me to say goodbye to my sisters, and we continued down the hall to the throne room, stopping at the closed doors. My father stood there in his finest black velvet suit and gave my mother a nervous glance.

"Can I say goodbye?" he asked timidly.

Even after four years, he wasn't sure where things stood with her. She was queen and he was no longer the king consort now that they'd divorced. She'd allowed him residence on palace grounds in a guest house for the sake of my sisters and me, but it was a constant strain on our family when they were both in the same room.

"Of course. I'm not a monster, Leif," my mother said defensively.

"I never said you were," he added.

"Can we not?" I asked.

Always fighting. I'd vowed to never marry, just to avoid such a thing.

My father pulled me in for a hug. "Do what you have to in order to survive and come home," he whispered to me.

If only he knew. In order to do that, I'd have to massacre Dawn's husband or one of the other handsome and seemingly kind men that had been present that night.

They weren't monsters. They were our mates, whatever that really meant.

It was a good thing the only one I'd truly been attracted to was already engaged. That would make all of this easier.

I hoped.

After my father released me, I took his hand and squeezed it. "I love you," I told him, and pled with my eyes for him to get along with my mother while I was gone.

He must have learned to read minds because he nodded and said, "We'll be fine."

With a relieved sigh, I dropped his hand. My mother stepped up next to me, chin held high.

"Ready?" she asked.

I traced my fingers over the blue kyanite faestone dagger at my thigh and nodded.

Would I even use the weapon?

For a wild second I had a dark thought. What was the heart of one man to save an entire kingdom? Even if he wasn't a monster, even if he was my mate, if he could save my people, maybe the sacrifice was worth it.

I'm pregnant. Dawn's words filtered back to me, and my heart pinched.

The princesses of Faerie were marrying the Lords of Ethereum. Having children with them. I couldn't just take one of their lives, not when there appeared to be another way. A way that wouldn't just delay the curse for a hundred years, but actually destroy it once and for all.

I strengthened my resolve. I'd already made my choice. And that was to trust Dawn.

The doors opened and the cavernous throne room broke into applause as I smiled and waved, and followed my mother to the dais. Everyone who was anyone in the Winter Court was here.

My mother's most cherished advisors and courtiers stood around us, dressed in their finest attire. I nodded to the Honeyworths and then Mr. Thorpe before making my way past the Larkins. I'd grown up around these families, played with their children, and had dinner parties with them. It warmed my heart that they'd all come to wish me well.

We were Winter, we were resilient, we survived above all odds. This would not bring us down.

Suddenly, one of my mother's messengers ran forward, breaking through the crowd, alarm evident on his face. He was holding a scroll between his fingers.

A messenger would never interrupt my mother during a big event like this, it must be urgent. She took the scroll with a smile as if she'd expected the document and waved him off. Then she clutched it in her hand as we moved quickly around the room thanking people for coming and accepting their well wishes.

Once we got to the stage, we stepped back into the small

private alcove behind which was the ancient mirror portal. It was covered in dust yesterday, but now it shone.

Queen Liliana was there and greeted me as I gave her a small bow. My mother ripped the seal from the paper and scanned the message, her lips pursed as fear crossed over her face.

"What is it?" I asked.

She folded it and stuffed it into her pocket. "Nothing we can't handle. Let's get you off to the mirror world so that this entire nightmare can end."

Chills rose on my arms. I was a Winter fae, so that was saying something. "Mother, what does it say?"

I'd been preparing to take over for her for the past few years, she shared all matters of state with me.

She shared a look with Queen Liliana and cleared her throat. "The curse has started at the western edge of our lands. A deep freeze hit in the night and killed a dozen people. They are frozen solid, and it comes this way."

I gasped. It was eerily similar to my power. Okay, it *was* my power, but without any intention behind it. It was just moving forward, killing everything in its path. It took a lot to freeze a Winter fae solid.

"It doesn't matter," Queen Liliana said. "You are about five minutes from ending this entire curse and brining harmony back to all of Faerie."

Right.

Crap.

I gave her a small smile, but I didn't like the way she

scanned my face as if trying to ferret out something I was hiding. Her gaze went to the dagger at my thigh, and I grabbed it, gripping it tightly like she taught me.

She relaxed a little then. "Remember, dear. Don't even let them speak. Get the heart, get home, and this is all over."

I nodded, my mind a whirlwind of anxious thoughts. What if that whole thing with Dawn was a trick? What if she lied to me? What if—

The mirror began to swirl in front of me.

"Okay, clear your mind. Just focus on the heart. The black heart of an Ethereum lord," she said.

I closed my eyes, taking in a deep breath and did as she said.

Black heart.

Black heart.

Tan skin with dark hair with honey-blonde highlights and bright teal eyes.

No. Don't think of the engaged guy, you idiot.

Black heart.

Before I lost my nerve, I opened my eyes and looked over at my mother.

"I love you. Forgive me," I said, and then jumped through the swirling portal before Queen Liliana could stop me, but the echoes of her furious screams followed me.

There was a tug at my navel as dizziness washed over, and then my boots landed on white sand. I was temporarily blinded from the bright sun, something we barely saw in the Winter Court. My eyes adjusted and I gasped when I came face to face with a shirtless man. Beads of sweat rolled down his neck and onto his abs, cascading over each knot one by one.

Bless the stars.

I glanced up at his face and swallowed hard. It was him. Long hair. Honey-colored highlights. Engaged.

It was him.

We were on a sandy beach right in front of a giant castle, as waves rolled in and out on the shore behind him. He had a basket full of fresh crabs at his feet.

For a moment he looked as stunned as I felt, but then his eyes flared as they raked over me from head to toe and back up again. I reacted to that look like a physical touch and flushed under his inspection, but then his gaze caught on the blue faestone dagger clenched in my hand and he seemed to come back to himself.

Taking a step backward he held up his hands in defense. "Don't kill me, Isolde. Remember me? We've already met."

My heart did a summersault at the way he said my name. It was like there was music in his voice for a split second. Hearing and seeing him in real life was so much more potent than the ghost-like version of him that appeared in my room, and for a moment it overwhelmed me. But then his gaze dropped to the faestone dagger again, reminding me of who he was and why I was here. And for a wild minute I considered just killing him and going home, saving everyone. It was the easiest solution, even if perhaps not the moral one.

"Dawn said you might come. She sent a letter. It's inside," he said as he pointed to something behind me.

At the mention of Dawn, my murderous thoughts

dissolved. She'd begged me not to hurt the Ethereum lords, and even though I didn't know this man's true character, I trusted Dawn. I couldn't kill this man. He was someone's family.

I sheathed the dagger, my hand slightly shaking with defeat. I was sweating gumdrops in my fur cloak, and I was pretty sure I would already get a sunburn from this mild exposure.

I peered over my shoulder at a giant white stone castle and then looked back at him.

"I'm Adrien," he said a little breathlessly and held out his hand. "This must be really weird for you."

I relaxed a little, realizing I hadn't spoken yet and probably seemed like a spooked animal. Or a rabid one, considering I'd just held a blade for half of our conversation.

"I'm Isolde," I said, even though he already knew that. When our fingers touched, a slight tingle went through my palm, and his brows drew together in confusion. His gaze then snaked slowly down my body and my stomach heated.

"Adrien," a woman shrilled behind us. "Who's that?"

He yanked his hand away from me like he'd been burned.

"Elisana, darling," he laughed nervously. "Isolde has arrived just like Dawn told us she might. We should give her Dawn's letter."

I spun and came face to face with a tall woman with long chestnut hair who did not look very pleased to see me. The fiancé. It had to be.

"Oh... interesting," she said, but her gaze was calculating. "Darling, why don't you put a shirt on and have your afternoon tea. I'll give her Dawn's letter."

"Yes, my love," Adrien said, and stepped away from me, lugging the fresh crab basket into the castle as I stepped onto the back veranda and shook sand off my boots.

"Sorry about the intrusion." I gave a nervous laugh, expecting Elisana to tell me that it was no trouble, but instead she just stared at me with cold, unforgiving eyes.

I wanted to give Adrien's fiancé the benefit of the doubt. I didn't know her after all, but after only a few moments in her presence, I already greatly disliked her. Perhaps she was an acquired taste and would grow on me.

"This way," she said, leading me through the same door Adrien disappeared into moments before.

Despite everything, I found myself looking for him as soon as I crossed the threshold, but with a shake of my head, I forced my gaze forward as I followed Elisana through an open sitting room, down a hallway and into what looked to be a kitchen.

The basket of crabs that Adrien carried inside was sitting on a counter next to a portly woman who looked up from where she was filleting a large fish as we passed. Her eyes grew a little wide when she saw us, and she dipped her head and murmured a quiet, "my lady," to Elisana, who breezed right by without acknowledging her at all. The chef's gaze shifted to me, and I gave her a warm smile that she returned before returning to her task.

We exited the kitchen and passed a food storage room, before popping out into a large open foyer and taking a winding staircase up, up, and up. I tried to shrug off my heavy cloak, but Elisana wouldn't slow her steps as we ascended, and I didn't want to fall behind.

By the time we reached our destination, a small library on one of the upper floors, I was huffing and puffing and coated in sweat. I'm sure my face was red, and after finally freeing myself of my cloak, I wiped the wetness off my brow with my sleeve. Unfortunately, taking off my cloak only offered a small measure of comfort, because my pants and long-sleeved tunic were both fur-lined. This served me well in the Winter Court, but here, which I assumed was the Southern Kingdom based on the map and journals that had been given to me, I was struggling with my wardrobe.

Without explaining herself, Elisana went over to a desk and pulled a key out of her pocket. Then she unlocked a drawer and pulled something out.

I was parched and swayed a little on my feet. I needed to get out of these clothes and into something lighter, if for no other reason than to be able to think straight again.

"Do you have anything more appropriate to the climate that I could wear?" I asked, feeling like I was standing inside a furnace.

Elisana turned, looking down her nose at me even though we were both around the same height. "No, my clothes would be too *far* too small on you."

My mouth dropped open. Yes, Elisana was a slender

woman, but from the disgusted look on her face, it was clear she was insinuating that I was twice her size, which I was not. I may have a few more curves that she did, but if she had a loose-fitting dress, I was certain it would fit me.

I was about to give her a piece of my mind when Adrien swept into the room, fully clothed this time. He'd pulled his shoulder-length hair back, and the sleeves on his shirt were rolled up to reveal strong forearms that I hadn't noticed before.

Much to my disappointment—or perhaps secret delight —covering up his chest did little to dampen his attractiveness. I was used to the pale complexions of the Winter fae in our realm, but I found Adrien's bronzed skin particularly appealing, and had trouble tearing my gaze from him.

"You look like you are melting," Adrien said, snapping me out of my trance. "If you like, Elisana can get you something else to wear."

I shot him a look as I self-consciously pushed back the black hairs sticking to my forehead. Did he know his fiancé at all?

Elisana sauntered over to Adrien and slipped her arm through his. "I already informed her that there was no way any of my clothes would be large enough for her," she said as she stroked his arm, a small smirk on her mouth.

"Oh, well, I don't think that..." Adrien glanced back and forth between his fiancé and me, and even more warmth infused my already overheated cheeks.

It was one thing to insinuate I was large in private, but in front of someone else was a whole other matter. I didn't care that I'd only known her for less than an hour, I hated the woman and was already convinced that would never change.

Adrien cleared his throat. "I'll instruct my lead house-maid to find you something more comfortable to wear, Isolde. The Southern Kingdom's climate isn't for everyone, and coming from the Winter Court, I know this heat must be particularly uncomfortable."

The smirk quickly dropped off of Elisana's face, and the sour look that replaced it brought a smile to my own.

"That would be greatly appreciated," I said sweetly, purposefully batting my lashes at Adrien to further infuriate his dreadful fiancé.

A look came upon Adrien's face as he stared at me, almost as if he was seeing me for the first time. It made me feel a little lightheaded, but maybe it was just the heat playing tricks on me.

"Darling," Elisana's shrill voice cut through the air as she tugged on his arm. "Have you had your tea yet?"

He shook his head, his gaze shifting to the woman at his side. "Oh, no, I was just about to do that, but wanted to make sure Isolde had seen the letter."

"I have it right here," she said, holding up a piece of folded paper in her other hand that I hadn't noticed before. "Why don't you have your tea and I promise I'll get this *issue* sorted out."

Issue? I was an issue now that needed to be sorted?

I brushed my fingers over my faestone dagger, imagining

burying it in her instead of Adrien. The mental image was oddly comforting.

"And there is no need to alert Fiona, my love. I'll make sure to find Isolde something to wear," she went on. The evil smile on her face should have worried me, but at that point, I'd happily don a potato sack if it meant getting out of these sweaty clothes.

Adrien smiled down at the wench. "Thank you, my love."

My love? Please. I rolled my eyes as they stared at each other. How did he like this woman, let alone love her?

I couldn't fathom what he saw in her, but reminded myself that I didn't care who this Ethereum lord bound himself to. He could engage himself to a broom stick as far as I was concerned. I was here for one reason, and one reason alone.

To end the curse and then go home.

Elisana finally released her grip on the lord when Adrien started to leave, but right before he left the room, he turned back. "Isolde, I'm glad you made it here safely. Dawn has been quite worried. I'll see you for dinner tonight?"

"Oh no, darling," Elisana started. "I'm sure the princess would much rather eat alone in—"

"I'm looking forward to dinner with you *very* much," I said, cutting her off, which earned me a glare that gave me nothing but pleasure.

When Adrien was finally gone, Elisana thrust the folded letter at me, slamming it to my chest. I met her glare with one of my own and had to take several deep breaths to keep my cool. I peered down at the letter. Even though my name was scrawled across the front, the seal had already been broken. I ground my teeth at the invasion of privacy, but pushed it from my mind when I saw Dawn's handwriting.

My dearest Izzy,

I'm so sorry that I can't be there to welcome you to Ethereum. I've missed you terribly, but the curse that plagues Faerie has also spilled into our land in the northern section of Ethereum, and Zander and I are doing all we can to keep it from destroying the people and the land.

If you are reading this message, it means two things. First, that you have arrived in the Southern Kingdom rather than the Western Kingdom. For that I am truly sorry, because I surmise that you won't get as warm of a welcome as you would have if you'd arrived in Zane's kingdom.

I glanced up at Elisana, who was impatiently watching me with her arms crossed over her chest and a frown pulling down her features. Dawn wasn't wrong about that. There's not much about my arrival that I'd call welcoming so far. Except for maybe Adrien.

As if to punctuate the point, a drop of sweat rolled off

my forehead and landed on the page, smudging my name. I swiped the sweat away and continued to read.

Secondly, it means that you have chosen to trust me and haven't tried to kill Adrien. For that, I will be forever grateful. I want to assure you that I believe with my whole heart that we are doing the right thing, and that we will succeed in destroying this curse on our lands once and for all.

In the letter, Dawn went on to describe a crystal called the Shadow Heart that Princess Aribella and her new husband, Stryker, the Ethereum lord of the Eastern Kingdom, found. They all believed this Shadow Heart would play a part in destroying the curse, yet they didn't know how. She wrote that I needed to collect the Shadow Heart, which they'd given to Zane in the hopes that I'd arrive in his kingdom instead of here. Then I had to travel to see some sort of prophetic unseelie fae called the Wise Ones, who lived in the Northern Mountains near where Dawn now lived. She assured me they would set me on the right path toward ending the curse. The letter ended with...

As soon as we have things stabilized here in the Northern Kingdom, I will come to where you are. My thoughts are with you, but I know how strong you are and that you will be able to overcome anything in your path.

Your friend,
Dawnie

Refolding the note, I stored it in my bag. Elisana didn't bother pretending not to know what it said. We both knew she'd opened the letter and read it already.

"We had hoped you'd appear in the Western Kingdom. Terrible timing that you are here as Adrien and my wedding is in only three weeks. We don't need the intrusion."

She paused, as if waiting for a reaction from me. But I didn't have one to give her. Besides the rudeness of the comment, what did I care that they were getting married? Better them than me.

"But I suppose there's nothing to be done about it now," she went on when it was clear I wasn't going to respond however she expected. "The important thing is to get you out of our kingdom as soon as possible. We'll send word to Lord Zane to let him know you are here, and then you can be off the moment he arrives to collect you."

"I'll *gladly* leave the second he gets here," I said, meaning it. I didn't want to spend any more time in this woman's presence than I had to. I was already regretting agreeing to dinner.

"Then we agree," she said, her smile looking sickeningly sweet.

"In this, we do."

"Well then, I'll show you where you can stay until I retrieve you for dinner."

And with that, I followed the wench out of the room, trying not to second guess all of my decisions up to this moment. Killing the handsome lord Adrien would have been easier.

Continue the story!
https://mybook.to/brokenheartedbook

About Leia Stone

Leia Stone is the USA Today bestselling author of multiple bestselling series including Matefinder and Wolf Girl. She's sold over three million books and her Fallen Academy series has been optioned for film. Her novels have been translated into five languages and she even dabbles in script writing.

Leia writes urban fantasy and paranormal romance with sassy kick-butt heroines and irresistible love interests. She lives in Spokane, WA with her husband and two children.

www.LeiaStone.com

About Julie Hall

Julie Hall is a *USA Today* bestselling, multiple award-winning author. Before diving into the world of publishing, she was publicist and marketer for Sony, Summit Entertainment, Paramount, The Weinstein Company, and the National Geographic Channel.

Now, she crafts addictive action-packed fantasy stories that leave readers with epic book hangovers. Julie's books have been translated to four languages and won or were finalists in over 20 national and international awards.

Julie currently lives in Colorado with her four favorite people–her husband, daughter, and two fur babies.

www.JulieHallAuthor.com

Join the Fan Clubs

Get involved, make some friends, and get exclusive sneak peeks before anyone else.

 *Leia & Julie*

Acknowledgments

A big thank you to my amazing co-author and best friend Julie for being my ride or die and sending me gluten free cookies. You deserve a pet otter. A huge thank you to my agents Flavia and Meire at Bookcase Literary for all they do and a special thanks to our readers for supporting us all these years.

~ Leia

My first thanks goes to Leia for putting up with all my quirks and keeping our co-writing ship moving forward. It's such a pleasure to get to work with such a talented co-author and amazing friend. I couldn't be more excited to be writing this series with you! Thank you to my husband, Lucas, for being both the shoulder I cry on and my biggest cheerleader. You're my fun buddy for life and I adore you. And finally, thanks to all our amazing readers. You're the reason we get to do what we love!

~ Julie

Books by Leia Stone
LEIASTONE.COM/BOOKS

FANTASY

Vampire Hunter Society

Shifter Island Series

Wolf Girl Series

Daughter of Light Series

The Titan's Saga

Supernatural Bounty Hunter Series

Dream Wars Series

Fallen Academy Series

Dragons & Druids Series

Matefinder Series

Matefinder: Next Generation

Hive Trilogy

NYC Mecca Series

Night War Saga

Water Realm Series

The Kings of Avalier Series

Gilded City Series

ALL TITLES

LeiaStone.com/books

Books by Julie Hall

JULIEHALLAUTHOR.COM/BOOKS

CREATURES OF CHAOS SERIES

Creatures of Chaos

FALLEN LEGACIES SERIES

Stealing Embers

Forging Darkness

Unleashing Fire

Supernova

LIFE AFTER SERIES

Huntress

Warfare

Dominion

Logan

SHADOW ANGEL SERIES

Shadow Angel Book One

Shadow Angel Book Two

Shadow Angel Book Three

Julie's books have won or were finalists in over 20 awards.

Made in the USA
Las Vegas, NV
03 January 2025